DEATH IS BURIED

A fourth case for Commissario Beppe Stancato

Richard Walmsley

Other titles by this author

The Puglia series

Dancing to the Pizzica *(2012)*

The Demise of Judge Grassi *(2103)*

Leonardo's Trouble with Molecules *(2014)*

+

Long Shorts

(A collection of unusual and humorous short stories)

+

The Commissario Beppe Stancato novels set in Abruzzo

The Case of the Sleeping Beauty *(2015)*

A Close Encounter with Mushrooms *(2016)*

The Vanishing Physicist *(2017)*

+

Puglia with the Gloves Off – Part One, Salento

(A travelogue – 2019)

+

The Curse of Collemaga *(2019)*

(A story of modern-day sorcery set in Italy – based very loosely on real events)

© Copyright 2020

Richard Walmsley

Cover design by Natalia Dalkiewicz
natalia.dalkiewicz@gmail.com

Published by nonno-riccardo-publications

Email: author@richardwalmsley.com

Web: www.richardwalmsley.com

Author's Introduction

This is the fourth novel in the Abruzzo series featuring Commissario Beppe Stancato. He is faced with two very different problems when he is summoned back to duty after his three month 'suspension' from duty. (See 'The Vanishing Physicist')

Firstly, he arrives at Via Pesaro police headquarters only to discover that he has a new 'boss' – who is a woman. He is also confronted with a serious crime involving two young children who have been hospitalised as a result of their contact with dumped toxic waste. For Beppe, the crime has all the hallmarks of illegal mafia activities.

My approach to the storyline in this novel has been influenced by a number of notable Italian TV dramas that have captivated my imagination over the years. Notably, two drama series: one called 'Sorelle' (Sisters) and the other, the unforgettable story by Elena Ferrante called 'L'amica geniale' (My Brilliant Friend).

Both dramas involve children, who play pivotal roles as the stories unfold. Like it or not, children, in a family context, cannot help but become part of the plot – as in real life.

Throughout 'Sorelle', we are treated to the subtle presence of the supernatural, providing a chilling substratum to the very human events in the story. The element of the paranormal is implied and always ambiguous – leaving the viewer to interpret events in whatever light he or she thinks fit.

This TV drama inspired me to include similar elements in the current story – as in some of the earlier stories too. I have a natural inclination not to dismiss the inexplicable in *my own life nor, consequently, in the lives of the characters I have created.*

Despite the gravity of the main plot, there are many lighter moments too. I am confident you will remain entertained by the very Italian 'feel' of the storyline. Buona lettura! Happy reading!

Richard Walmsley *(2020)*

PS A note – about footnotes. Since the characters in this story are all Italian, it seems to me quite natural that they use some Italian in the course of conversation. It adds a bit of local colour. In the paperback version of this novel, the translations should appear at the bottom of each page. You are welcome to ignore them, if you choose.

In the Kindle version, footnotes are at the back. But a single touch on the footnote reference number brings up the translation on the page you are reading. The technology is impressive!

To Nadia – who inadvertently launched my career as a writer.

My thanks to all the readers – and proof readers – who have enjoyed, criticised, praised and appreciated the previous novels.
Without you all, writing books would be nothing more than an act of self-indulgence.

Richard Walmsley (2020)

Prologo

The *Santo Spirito*[1] hospital in Pescara had been alerted at two o'clock in the morning that the ambulance bearing two young patients was on its way. Its precious cargo was a brother and sister who were being transferred from the local hospital in L'Aquila suffering from some illness which the medical staff there had been reluctant to diagnose. They wanted a second opinion, fearing that the treatment required might challenge their resources. It was touch and go, it had been implied, as to whether the children would survive the lengthy ambulance journey to Pescara.

Not for the first time in his career, *Il Dottore* Bruno Esposito had been woken up in the midst of dreams of a premature retirement in some mountain location with an unpolluted stream rushing past his house. The voice of a younger colleague on night duty at the *Santo Spirito* had begged him to come to the hospital as soon as he possibly could.

His official designation was that of Chief Toxicologist. But he was a man of many talents and was often called upon simply to diagnose medical conditions when everyone else was at a loss. More often than not, he needed a single glance or a minute or two with the patient before giving his opinion. His reputation at the *Santo Spirito* was based, in part, on the fact that he usually turned out to be right on these occasions.

"Drive carefully, *amore*," said Bruno's wife before turning over and falling asleep again. He kissed her forehead and was out of the house within minutes, unshaven and feeling in urgent need of a coffee.

---

[1] Santo Spirito = Holy Spirit

The distressed voice of the female colleague who had phoned him twenty minutes previously had remained in his head.

"I'll be waiting for you, *dottore*, outside where the ambulances stop," she had said anxiously. He had a premonition that the circumstances of this case would prove to be abnormal.

The sight of the two diminutive children, wrapped up in over-sized bio-hazard suits, was heart-rending. One pair of frightened eyes was looking at Bruno. It had to be the elder brother, thought Bruno. The smaller of the two figures had her eyes closed, seemingly unconscious. Bruno had glanced briefly at their medical notes.

"Get them into the isolation ward immediately," Bruno ordered the ambulance crew. "We don't know yet if it's a biological or a chemical problem. Either way, we have no time to lose."

1: A change at the top...

Commissario Beppe Stancato was still at home with Sonia, his wife, and their two children, Veronica and Lorenzo. His 'punishment' period of three months' suspension – without pay – had only two weeks left to run.

His chief, the *Questore*,[2] Dante di Pasquale, had reluctantly imposed this sanction on his colleague as a result of Beppe's clandestine action involving the entrapment of three American agents, whilst faking the death of one, Giada Costa, simply to save her from being forcibly deported back to the United States against her will.[3] His period of suspension was enforced despite his success in rescuing Donato Pisano, a notable physicist, illegally abducted by the same American secret agents.

Beppe had accepted his period of exile at home with good grace. The *Questore's* act had, in point of fact, been one of kindness. It had enabled Beppe to spend time, which he would not ordinarily have allowed himself, with Sonia and their two very young children. His chief, the *Questore*, had publicly appeared to be observing official condemnation of his colleague's unauthorised venture – thereby keeping his bosses in Rome happy.

It was with some surprise, therefore, when he was called from down below by Sonia's mother telling him he was wanted on the *fisso*.[4]

"It's your chief on the line, Beppe."

"*Pronto?*"[5] he said on picking up the receiver.

---

[2] Il Questore - the rank of Chief of Police
[3] Reference to the previous Beppe Stancato novel, 'The Vanishing Physicist'
[4] fisso - landline (= *'fixed'*)
[5] Pronto – it's what Italians say when answering the phone = 'ready'

"Good morning, *Commissario*. This is Dante di Pasquale speaking. I trust you haven't forgotten who I am!"

"Of course not, *Signor Questore*. You gave me a three-month holiday as a reward for carrying out my duty as I saw fit! You know there are no hard feelings."

"I'm glad to hear that. I hope you will not think any the worse of me when I tell you that I am terminating your period of suspension. You are back on full pay as from today."

Beppe remained speechless for several seconds. A pang of secret joy became mingled with a feeling of disappointment that the time spent with his family would be cut short. Dante di Pasquale continued implacably.

"There is an important matter which I need to discuss with you – and regrettably it cannot wait. Would you be so kind as to present yourself back in *Via Pesaro*[6] tomorrow morning by 10 o'clock?"

"Of course, *Signor Questore*. It will be a pleasure to be back."

"I trust you will be of the same opinion after tomorrow," said the *Questore* enigmatically, before bringing the brief phone call to a close.

Beppe went upstairs to their spacious apartment occupying the top two floors of the house.

He was turning over in his mind all the likely scenarios which would have prompted Dante di Pasquale to cancel his suspension. He broke the news to Sonia who tried valiantly to look pleased for him.

"I bet he needs you to work on some investigation that no one else wants to touch," ventured Sonia.

---

[6] Via Pesaro. The name of the street in Pescara where the *Questura* – the main police station – is situated

"I'm not so sure about that, *amore*[7]. It sounded more like a personal matter."

"Maybe you could persuade him to let you work part time for a while, Beppe."

"I'm sorry, Sonia. I know you'll miss me after all this time at home…"

"I was going to suggest *I* go back to work instead of you, *amore,* while *you* stay and look after the children."

Beppe managed a guilty smile in return. He should have recognised Sonia's teasing tone before assuming *his* absence had had anything to do with her request.

"I'll mention it to him – if I get the chance," said Beppe. "Just to see what his reaction is."

* * *

As soon as Beppe stepped into the *Questore's* office the following day – a mere ten minutes after the appointed time – he knew that the reasons for his recall had nothing to do with any investigation.

There was a well-dressed woman in her thirties standing next to Dante di Pasquale, who was himself seated behind his desk. The woman was busy reading a document on the desk over the *Questore's* shoulder. She did not look up immediately when Beppe entered.

The thought occurred to Beppe that she might be a police lawyer – who had come to reassess his rash action of a couple of months ago. This would explain his boss's reluctance to recall him to the *Questura*[8] at such short notice.

Beppe identified the 'class' of lady that she represented within one second of seeing her – the new, up-

---

[7] Amore = 'my love' and other terms of endearment.
[8] La questura – the main police station in an Italian city.

and-coming managerial class of woman finding her feet in what had for centuries been a male-dominated world. She would have attended some prestigious business school or university faculty such as the *Università Bocconi*[9]. Her appearance at the police headquarters did not bode well.

The *Questore* was looking uncomfortable as he stood up to shake the hand of the colleague whom he had not seen for over two months. He reached across his desk, whereas he usually walked round to the front of the desk. He always attached great importance to the human touch in his dealings with those in his charge.

The lawyer, or whoever she was, looked impatiently at the time on her wrist-watch and then at Beppe, making her displeasure at his lateness very clear. She sat down on a chair next to Dante di Pasquale.

"I'm sorry I'm a bit late, *Signor Questore.* The *Carabinieri* have set up a road block to the north of Pescara. Cars were only filtering through slowly. I guess they were on the look-out for someone."

Beppe addressed his apology exclusively to his chief, and pointedly ignored the 'lawyer'. His permanent dismissal was, doubtless, one step closer as a consequence.

"Beppe, may I introduce you to *Vice-Questore* Mariastella Martellini – from Bologna. Mariastella, this is Commissario Beppe Stancato, my second-in-command."

Beppe was taken aback by this revelation. He started to think he had misread the situation and - more importantly – the reason for this smart young woman's presence behind his chief's desk.

---

[9] A prestigious university business school in Milan

There was no escaping the handshake demanded by normal courtesy. But he was now aware he also needed to show a measure of deference in the presence of a more senior officer.

The lady stood up a split second before Beppe and thrust a rigid arm in Beppe's direction. Her gesture reminded him more of someone aiming a pistol at point blank range. He shook the proffered hand which briefly held his own. The hand was warmer than he had expected and the grip firm and confident. He felt at a sudden disadvantage.

"Molto lieto, signora,"[10] he managed to articulate.

When Beppe finally looked directly at her face, he realised from her eyes that she had been assessing him and was taking some pleasure in the fact he was ill-at-ease. He stared back at her.

She was exactly the same height as Beppe and her cool grey-blue eyes caught him off guard. He was less sure that his famously steady stare would unsettle her.

Beppe was relieved when she broke eye contact a split second before he did. But immediately afterwards, he regretted the cheap point-scoring. He sensed she still had the upper hand. She had *chosen* to look away from him.

The whole exchange had lasted less than ten seconds and now the *Questore* was talking again.

"Beppe, Mariastella will be taking over my duties in a few days' time. As my second-in-command, I know you will make her feel welcome and support her. I have told her you are my most experienced and effective officer – and how the rest of our team take their lead from you."

---

[10] 'Pleasure to meet you' – Beppe uses a very formal expression.

Beppe stared speechless at both of them. The *Questore* filled the brief silence.

"I have taken the decision to begin my retirement – I have been putting off the move for the last three years. It has already been agreed by Rome that *Signorina* Martellini[11] will be taking over my post."

"You will be sorely missed, *capo*," muttered Beppe without looking at the soon-to-be promoted *Vice-Questore*.

"I called you back early, Beppe, because I wish it to be *you* who gives the news of my departure to your team. I might break down in public if I attempt to tell them in person," stated this dignified man with sad irony in his voice.

"Please come back and see me later today, Beppe," he continued. "I have many more things to say to you."

"And *I* would like to see you at 9 o'clock this coming Monday morning, *commissario* – assuming that fits in with your plans," said Beppe's newly appointed *capo*, pointedly. Her voice was soft - yet she spoke with calm self-assurance.

Beppe gave a bow in her direction and left the room. After he had closed the door, he fancied he heard Dante di Pasquale laugh briefly in reply to some comment from his replacement. But it might have been a sigh...

* * *

After a rapturous reception from the entirety of Beppe's team of officers, an attentive silence had fallen on the assembly. Something about their leader's unsmiling face warned them that the reason for his premature return might

---

[11] Martellini is a common Bolognese surname.

have been brought about by some other set of circumstances.

Pippo was looking at his chief – and friend -with a puzzled expression on his face. They had only spoken to each other over the phone the day before. Surely Beppe would have told him if he had known he was going to return to work the following day?

"There is no point in beating about the bush, *ragazzi*," Beppe began. "Dante di Pasquale called me yesterday afternoon and told me to come in today. He has asked me to tell you that he is retiring from his post as *Questore* with immediate effect."

There was a stunned silence. Finally, Pippo Cafarelli broke the tension by asking:

"Do we know who his replacement will be, *capo?*[12] Have you met him?"

The *commissario* was careful to stifle any hint of facial expression before replying.

"Yes, about thirty minutes ago. Her name is Mariastella Martellini – from Bologna," added Beppe, as if her home town was a mitigating factor to be considered.

There was gasp of shocked surprise from all the officers – with the exception of two of them.

Lina Rapino, the only woman left on the team, gave a secret smile and nodded her head in silent approval. Beppe's oldest officer, Giacomo d'Amico, had instinctively looked at his watch.

Beppe smiled at him.

---

[12] Capo = head : chief

"I'm not sure whether you can make time stand still, by consulting your wrist watch, Giacomo. The moment has already passed, I fear."

Giacomo laughed uneasily, realising that Beppe had caught him off guard.

"It was a purely irrational reaction, *capo*. I was wondering how long it was before *I* could retire."

There was a general outburst of laughter at their colleague's explanation. It broke the ice and lessened the blow of this unexpected piece of news.

Outside the conference room door, a very smart lady from Bologna was frowning. Laughter was not the reaction she had been expecting. What had that maverick *commissario* told them to provoke such an outburst of mirth? She would make it her business to find out over the next few days. She walked towards the reception desk – where nobody had been left on duty, she noted. Thus, she did not overhear *Commissario* Beppe Stancato's closing words to his team of officers.

"She is a highly intelligent lady, *ragazzi.* We are all going to give her the respect and support she deserves."

2: *Subject to the new regime...*

Sonia's reaction to the news when Beppe returned home was low-key.

"I thought you looked a bit subdued, Beppe. I take it you have reservations about the appointment?"

"Not just because she is a woman," Beppe said. "But because any change is inevitably going to alter the dynamics of the way the *Questura* works."

"I don't want to cast aspersions on my own sex, *amore*. But in my experience, women bosses feel the need to assert their authority more than some men. Much more so when they are in a new situation. I'm just afraid it might cramp your style..."

"I think I have gained that impression already, Sonia. But time will tell."

Beppe gave Sonia a lucid account of his first impressions.

"If I looked a bit despondent, I think it is more because I shall miss Dante di Pasquale's presence. I also gained the distinct impression that our *Questore* was secretly concerned about his health. He might have a more personal reason for leaving. I couldn't press him on the issue."

It was Sonia's turn to look despondent.

"Come on Sonia, let's enjoy the last moments of my freedom. I don't need to go in again until Monday morning. I have an appointment with our new lady *Questore* at 9 o'clock. She appears to be a stickler for punctuality."

"Well, she *is* from Bologna – so that makes her a Northerner, I guess," said Sonia with a smile.

Beppe spent more time than usual in the garden with Veronica teaching her to walk, which seemed to be even more important to her than speaking. Each fall she had usually provoked a happy outburst of giggles. But she did manage seven independent steps before her father caught her in his arms.

Beppe and Sonia lived his remaining forty-eight hours of family life as if it was their last for some time. He was phoned by Pippo Cafarelli wanting to know what he really thought of their new leader. Beppe rigorously maintained his neutral position.

"It'll work out just fine, Pippo. You'll see."

* * *

On Monday morning, Beppe arrived at the police headquarters before eight o'clock. Well before Mariastella Martellini put in an appearance at 8.30.

Beppe felt this would give him a psychological edge. Everything seemed reassuringly normal at that early hour.

"In bocca al lupo,"[13] his colleagues had wished him, almost to a man, as he set off to climb the stairs to reach Mariastella's office. On his way to the top floor, Beppe was surprised to run into his one remaining female officer – after a young officer called Valentina Ianni, transferred to Pescara at her own request - had implored Dante di Pasquale to let her return to L'Aquila on the grounds of chronic homesickness. Her real motive for wanting to go back home, she admitted only to herself, was her discovery that her

---

[13] Best of luck! Lit. 'In the mouth of the wolf'

'hero', *Commissario* Stancato, had been inexplicably granted three months leave of absence.[14]

Lina Rapino was on her way back downstairs. Usually a very dour but alarmingly honest person, she surprised Beppe by giving him a broad smile as they passed each other on the stairs.

"*Buongiorno,* Lina. I see you have beaten me to it!" said the *commissario,* returning the smile.

"Mariastella is waiting to see you, *capo,*" said Officer Lina – almost smugly.

Beppe was frowning as he continued on his journey upstairs. He would have liked to ask Officer Rapino a question, but realised that satisfying his curiosity would have made him thirty seconds late for his appointment.

Beppe's fingers were bunched, ready to knock on the door. It was precisely 09.00 hours.

"*Avanti,*"[15] said the voice from within.

The new *Questore* was dressed in full regalia – just as Beppe had predicted she would be.

Mariastella smiled kindly at him and gestured to him to sit down. She did not stand up nor attempt to shake hands. She patently did not wish to repeat the experience of their first encounter. She looked disturbingly at home, thought Beppe, still perplexed as to why a junior officer had been summoned to her office before him. Perhaps the new *Questore* had felt duty-bound to make the acquaintance of the only lady officer as a priority? Beppe was looking at his new boss with barely-concealed suspicion.

"Thank you for coming to see me today, *commissario.* I'm sorry to have been the cause of your early return to duty.

---

[14] See 'The Vanishing Physicist'
[15] 'Advance': i.e. Come in.

But I thought it important to meet all the officers in my charge without any delay."

"I notice that you have met one of them already," Beppe said, rather too abruptly. He was unsure how the new *Questore* wanted to be addressed.

She seemed to sense Beppe's dilemma but continued talking anyway.

"Yes, I asked *Agente* Rapino to come and see me because I had fifteen minutes to spare before you were due to arrive. Apart from sounding her out about her feelings at being the only lady on the team, I had one particular question to put to her."

Beppe looked at her quizzically. But her expression gave little away.

"Let's just say I wanted to ask Lina what her impression was of the meeting you had with your team last Friday. I imagine that most of them were shocked by the discovery that Dante di Pasquale was to be replaced by ME, *vero,*[16] Beppe?"

Beppe's mind was hard at work – replaying the events of the meeting with his colleagues. The truth came to him in a flash. Mariastella Martellini must have been listening outside the door. She would have heard the outburst of laughter caused by Giacomo d'Amico's unconscious reaction to the news. She would have misconstrued what she had heard. Beppe said nothing, but felt a twinge of sympathy for his new boss. She was only a human being and not pretending to be otherwise.

"You will be pleased to hear that Officer Rapino was full of praise for your handling of the meeting, Beppe,"

---

[16] Lit: True? In this context 'Weren't they?'

continued the new *Questore*, with a knowing smile on her face at what had been left unsaid.

Beppe raised a surprised eyebrow in response. It explained the radiant smile on Officer Rapino's face when they had passed each other on his way upstairs – she had been pleased to give Beppe her support. Human nature was a strange thing and should never be underestimated, he thought.

"And what was Lina's reply to your *first* question?" continued Beppe, needing to find a way to continue the conversation without embarrassing Mariastella.

"She merely told me she would welcome another woman on the team – just so she didn't feel outnumbered. What do you feel about this, Beppe?"

"I entirely agree with Lina. We did have three lady officers on the team until quite recently..."

"You may call me 'Mariastella' when we are on our own, Beppe. It's so much easier," said the lady *Questore*, simply, correctly interpreting the pause in Beppe's reply.

He nodded his head by way of reply, secretly admitting to himself that her offer had caught him off guard.

"I expect the *Questore*... I'm sorry, I meant Dante di Pasquale, has filled you in on the recent history of changes within our team...Mariastella?"

There was a twitch of a smile on the new *Questore's* face as she registered the brief hesitation before calling her by her first name for the first time. Beppe was unsure about this woman. He had had the fleeting sensation that he was beginning to like his new boss. That would never do!

"Not really, Beppe. I understand you *married* one of them – but Dante di Pasquale suggested that it would be better for you to fill in the details. I had the impression that his departure was causing him some pain."

"I had the same impression, Mariastella. We lost our other young lady officer – Oriana Salvati – who asked for a transfer to L'Aquila. Another romantic attachment, I fear," said Beppe with his first smile to his new boss. "She was sorely missed by the whole team. She was noted for her cutting tongue. She alone went a long way to restoring any gender imbalance that existed within the team."

Mariastella laughed – it was a pleasant sound Beppe was forced to admit.

"You must tell me more about her one day when we have more time, Beppe. I'm not sure what you think about gender imbalance, but in my experience, any team suffers if there is a preponderance of *either* sex..."

"*Sono d'accordo con Lei,* Mariastella – *a cento percento!*"[17]

What else could he have done but to agree with his new *capo* entirely? Her words enshrined an undeniable truth – in *any* walk of life, except in the context of a convent.

"You may be interested to learn that a lady officer from L'Aquila by the name of Simona Gambino has requested a transfer to *Via Pesaro.* Apparently, she needs to attend courses for further training – because of the irregular manner of her appointment. Does this mean anything to you, *Commissario?*"

The *Questore* was looking meaningfully at Beppe.

Could it be that Dante di Pasquale had really *not* explained to his successor how Giada Costa had become Simona Gambino, and joined the police force? Or was she

---

[17] I agree with you – 100%

playing cat and mouse with him to test his readiness to come clean over this decidedly unofficial episode in his recent career?

"I have to be frank with you, Mariastella. Simona Gambino is the name of the lady whose rescue led to my period of suspension. It's a long story. I would rather tell you when we have more time. She is a very competent officer, I am sure – but her training was a rather hurried affair in the circumstances..."

"She has particularly requested to be transferred to Pescara to be near you, Beppe."

"I am flattered, of course, Mariastella. But all I would say is that the presence of Officer Simona Gambino here in *Via Pesaro* would give us another highly competent team member. I know you will understand why when you meet her."

Mariastella sighed unexpectedly.

"We still have such a lot to talk about, Beppe. I would love to talk to you about the other team members. But perhaps I should meet them all together before I see them individually? What do *you* think?"

To Beppe's embarrassment, his mobile phone rang before he could answer Mariastella's question. He looked apologetically at his *capo.* She waved a hand at him to tell him to take the call.

Beppe looked at the screen. It was his friend, Bruno Esposito, the chief toxicologist from the hospital. Beppe frowned. It was rare for Bruno to ring him during working hours. But, of course, he must have assumed that the *commissario* was still on leave.

"*Pronto,* Bruno?"

As soon as Bruno began talking – without any preamble – Beppe sensed that his friend had an urgent matter to share with him. He looked at Mariastella and gestured that he was going to switch his mobile to loudspeaker mode. The *Questore* nodded.

"Just a minute, Bruno. I would like the *Questore* to hear what you have to say... *Va bene.* Carry on."

The edge in Beppe's voice told the Chief Toxicologist that something fundamental had changed. He began to repeat what he had said previously, delivering his account in a more formal manner.

I thought I should get in touch with you, commissario, because of something very unusual that happened here at the hospital a few days ago.

Beppe smiled at the use of his official title coming from the mouth of his friend.

"We're listening, Bruno."

These two young kids – a brother and his little sister - were brought to us in an ambulance from the hospital in L'Aquila. They had come in from a remote village called Pazzoli,[18] *some 20 kilometres to the north west of L'Aquila. It was heart-breaking to see them. We rushed them straight into an isolation ward because it was obvious that they had come into contact with something toxic. They arrived with a dangerous level of dioxins in their bloodstream. They were both petrified, poor kids, and couldn't tell us anything.*

"Are they going to survive, Bruno?" asked Beppe fearfully.

I am hopeful we have saved the life of the boy but his younger sister is still critical. I cannot yet say whether they

---

[18] Pazzoli – a name I adapted simply to avoid using a real town name. Pronounced 'pAtzoli'.

will suffer from after-effects – even if they do survive. Both the parents are here at the hospital. We have given both children blood transfusions and rinsed their insides out as far as we can. It's heart-rending to see these kids side by side in oxygen tents – and just as painful to see the parents peering through glass panels at their children without being able to go near them..."

Beppe and the *Questore* were moved by the signs of grief exhibited by the chief toxicologist. His voice had become tearful.

"I'm so sorry, Bruno. I have to ask the obvious question – although I think I already know the answer."

You don't need to ask me any questions, Beppe. I am sure you have already worked it out for yourself. These innocent kids have been in close proximity to toxic waste – some of which may be radioactive. We must assume, therefore, that it has been illegally dumped in sufficiently large quantities to be a danger to human life. And that, somewhere near Pazzoli, the toxic waste is still there – waiting to be discovered by other children. This has all the hallmarks of the mafia clans at work again. It has become a matter for the police. I'm sorry, Beppe, but you are the one person who I felt I could turn to...

"You did the right thing, Bruno. I will discuss the matter with the *Questore* and let you know."

I am sure we shall have his total support, Beppe.

"Our new *Questore* has been listening to our conversation Bruno. She is not going to let this matter rest - you can be quite sure of that."

Ahhh! said Bruno Esposito as if to himself and hung up.

3: In at the deep end...

Beppe and Mariastella looked at each other in silence. It was the *Questore* who spoke first, her voice on edge.

"*Mi getta nella mischia, commissario?*[19] she asked half-seriously. "What would you have done first in response to this situation, Beppe, if I had not been here?" she asked simply.

Beppe smiled, fighting off the desire to admire his new chief's tactful approach.

"I would probably have shot up the mountains to some town called Pazzoli – which I have never even heard of," replied Beppe with candour.

Mariastella looked grateful for his reply. He had given her back the initiative.

"May I suggest, *commissario*, that you go to the hospital and talk to the children's parents first? You can reassure them that the police are on their side in these distressing circumstances."

"Thank you," said Beppe quietly, nevertheless choosing his next words with great care. "I think that would be a much more sensible first step, Mariastella."

"Come back and see me when you've spoken to this Bruno – and the mum and dad. I think I should meet the whole team together later on today, Beppe. Can we say 3 o'clock this afternoon?"

"I'll ask Giacomo D'Amico to organise it – he is our unofficial liaison officer."

The *Questore* stood up at the same time as Beppe. They looked each other straight in the eye.

---

[19] Are you throwing me in at the deep end, commissario?

"Thank you for coming in this morning, Beppe. I'm glad we've met up."

"*A più tardi, Signora Questore,*"[20] said Beppe. "I'm pleased to be back again."

* * *

"So, Beppe," said Bruno Esposito as they shook hands. "That came as a bit of a shock, I imagine - after your lengthy 'holiday'! What are your first impressions of your new leader?"

"My first impressions were formed last Friday. I spent the whole weekend trying very hard not to form impressions."

"And today?"

"It's early days yet, Bruno. But I am in the process of revising my opinion. I think she may be easier to work with than I feared. *She* was the one who implied I should come and see you without delay – although possibly because I managed to manoeuvre her into making the suggestion."

"I think you should meet the children's parents, Beppe. I haven't managed to get much out of them about how the children became ill. They are simply too scared about losing them both – with very good reason."

Just as Beppe had anticipated, the parents both had their faces pressed to the glass partition which enclosed the isolation rooms. The man, stocky but short in stature, had his arm round his wife's hunched shoulders. She was clutching a handkerchief tightly in her hand as if to wring

---

[20]A più tardi - See you later.

the tears from it – tears which she was too tensed up to shed.

Beppe sighed audibly. He dreaded moments like this when children's lives were in the balance. He felt a burden of responsibility on his shoulders not to let them or the parents down.

Bruno went up to the couple and gently laid a hand on the father's shoulder.

"Mi scusi, Signor Ianni – Diego..." I would like you to meet Commissario Stancato from the Pescara police force. He would like to ask you a few questions – to help us find out how Alessandro and Ginevra became so ill."

Diego did not want to abandon his watch over their children. He cast a resentful glance in the policeman's direction with a look which clearly stated that the matter could easily wait.

But Diego's eyes met those of the *commissario* from Pescara. There was an expression of appeal on the inspector's face, coupled with a steady stare from a pair of kindly brown eyes. It was strangely difficult to ignore him.

The father turned to his wife to tell her that he would only be a minute.

"I would like to talk to both of you together," said Beppe quietly but firmly. In any case, he imagined that the wife would not be able to bear the prospect of a lonely vigil. Bruno Esposito made the formal introductions and led them to his office.

Beppe sat down at Bruno's desk and gestured to the couple to be seated. Bruno raised an eyebrow in Beppe's direction.

"Please stay, Bruno," he suggested. "I won't keep you from your patients for more than five minutes, I promise."

The *commissario* turned his gaze to the parents.

"May I call you Diego and Adele?" he asked. They nodded. Beppe reckoned they would feel indifferent to whatever form of address he decided on.

"Very briefly, *signori,* I need your help in trying to locate the source of Alessandro and Ginevra's affliction. It is very likely that the mafia clans from Naples - or even Calabria[21] - are starting up their old trade of dumping other people's toxic waste in *our* beautiful countryside. We will need to go to Pazzoli with a clean-up team..."

The mother and father were looking horrified at Beppe's words.

"We had no idea, *commissario*..." began the mother.

"Have you any idea where they usually go and play?"

Diego looked at his wife to reply.

"They go all over the place. There's this boy called Dario – a couple of years older than Sandro[22] who often takes them further afield than they would usually go on their own. I always thought he was the sort of boy who would lead them astray..."

Beppe was looking expectantly at Adele, willing her to say more. She seemed to have dried up.

"They often go and explore along the river, *commissario,*" interjected the father. "It's usually safe and has wide grassy banks on both sides. It's not very deep at this time of year..."

"Thank you, Diego. We'll begin our search there. Do you remember the surname of this other boy – Dario – by any chance?"

---

[21] The Camorra (Naples) or the 'ndrangheta (Calabria)
[22] Sandro – short for Alessandro.

They both shook their heads. Beppe had the impression that they were not able to focus on such banal matters.

"We shall need to speak to you again when you're all home, Diego, Adele. Can I ask you for your address?"

They both appeared to be thinking hard about the question. Beppe continued to look at them expectantly, until the father finally delved into his coat pocket and fished out from a battered-looking wallet an equally frayed calling card.

"Ah, you're an electrician, are you, Diego? *Bravo!*"

For some reason, Beppe's reaction to his profession brought a strained smile to Diego's face.

"You should go and talk to our mayor, *commissario*. *She* knows about everything and everyone in Pazzoli..." stated Adele, without malice.

Beppe had to stifle the thought that men might soon become redundant.

"I don't suppose you have *her* name, do you?" he asked the couple.

Before they could answer Beppe's question, an alarm sounded from somewhere inside Bruno Esposito's white doctor's coat. He shot to his feet and looked wildly at the mother and father, who had turned white with fear.

They followed Bruno out of his room and all three ran up the corridor towards the isolation rooms. Beppe followed them at a more thoughtful pace. The anxiety on his face was patent.

The little girl called Ginevra was being wheeled out of the isolation room.

"We're taking her to the emergency theatre," stated a green-gowned pair of nurses, their voices muffled by the masks they were wearing. Bruno Esposito made a gesture to Beppe as if in apology for deserting them.

"I'll call you, Beppe…"

The remaining nurse looked through the window and, in alarm, noticed Alessandro's arms waving about in a frenzy. She ran into the room to calm him down as he fought to remove the breathing tube covering his nose and mouth. He was trying desperately to say something to the nurse. From the other side of the glass petition, she beckoned the mother and parents to come in, as she thrust face masks, latex gloves and overalls into their hands.

"Put these on first, *signori!* Then you can go and talk to Alessandro…"

Beppe suddenly felt powerless, redundant. He reluctantly went downstairs and out of the hospital – aware that his heart was beating much faster than it should have been.

"*O Dio!*"[23] he muttered as he reached his car and drove back slowly to Via Pesaro.

* * *

He headed towards his own office for the first time that day. He suspected that his reluctance to have made it his first port of call that morning was due to a subconscious delaying tactic. If he had sat down behind his desk, he would have to admit that his 'holiday' was truly over. In Mariastella's office, *she* was in charge and he was not responsible for the course of events.

---

[23] O Dio = Dear God

It was lunchtime and he could not face food after his distressing visit to the hospital. He wandered back to the reception area and found *Agente* Danilo Simone on desk duty. The downcast expression on his chief's face caused Danilo to comment.

"Well, *commissario,* we are pleased to see *you* back. It doesn't look as if you are so pleased to see us."

Beppe apologised to his young colleague.

"It's not like that, Danilo. I've been to the hospital this morning to see the parents of two very sick children from a place called Pazzoli. Do you know where it is?" Beppe asked tentatively. Usually, when Beppe asked that kind of question, he was greeted by a chorus of native *Abruzzesi*[24] all chanting: "Oh, *commissario,* everybody knows where…"

Beppe was thus relieved when Danilo replied:

"Never heard of the place, *capo."*

"I'll tell you all about it during this afternoon's meeting with the *Questore. A proposito,*[25] I suppose she has gone to lunch, Danilo?"

"No, *capo.* She's still in her office. She asked me to send you up as soon as you returned."

Beppe nodded at Danilo and headed towards the stairs.

"Should I call her to tell her you're …?" began Danilo.

"No, don't bother. She doesn't seem to be the type to be excessively correct."

"Grazie a Dio!" muttered Danilo as if to himself.

When he arrived on the upstairs landing, Beppe decided to phone Sonia before knocking on the *Questore's*

---

[24] People from Abruzzo. Beppe is originally from Calabria.
[25] A proposito = by the way

door. He needed to share his harrowing experience of that morning with her before he could face the world.

Mariastella Martellini was looking more comfortable with the situation than on the previous day. She greeted Beppe with a smile. She was on the telephone and gestured to him to sit down.

"I need to call you back in five minutes, *signorina*. Please stay near the phone."

She turned to her second-in-command.

"I really want to know how you got on at the hospital this morning, Beppe. You look as if your visit wasn't all that easy. I need to call this person back again immediately. I was wondering if we could possibly meet up after our three o'clock meeting? I shall feel a lot more relaxed at that stage," she said with a rueful smile. "Would you indulge me if I asked you to accompany me downstairs just before three o'clock?"

"*Ci mancherebbe altro, Mariastella,*"[26] said Beppe as he stood up to leave.

* * *

Mariastella Martellini, accompanied by their *commissario* walked into the meeting room. Their arrival provoked a spontaneous round of applause from the entirely male gathering - Mariastella had assigned Officer Lina Rapino to desk duty.

The massive form of Luigi Rocco was the first to stand up whilst still applauding. The rest of the team immediately followed suit. Beppe felt embarrassed for his

---

[26] "Of course, I will, Mariastella" His choice of Italian expression cleverly implies that he would have done so without being asked.

new leader. She might well assume that the applause was for his return to the fold.

Beppe need not have been anxious on her account.

When everyone had settled down again, the new *Questore* began to address the assembled officers with a smile on her face.

"I thank you all for the warm welcome. I am very aware that you must all be delighted and relieved to see Beppe back again in your midst. I am simply pleased to know that I have the support of such an unusual and competent leader. It instantly gives me the security of knowing that I have someone upon whom I can rely without any reservations."

Her opening words were, somewhat to her gratification, greeted by a brief but sincere round of applause.

"You *were* included in our greeting, *Signora Questore*," said Giacomo D'Amico in his habitually courteous manner. The other officers nodded their heads and murmured their agreement.

"Then I thank you all on behalf of Beppe and myself," she added, barely catching the knowing look which Danilo Simone gave his friend Gino Martelli at the use of their *commissario's* first name.

"I am going to ask you over the next couple of days to indulge me by coming up to my office individually – or in pairs, if you prefer – so that I can get to know you better."

The fleeting glance which she bestowed upon officers Simone and Martelli as she spoke those words was quite sufficient to signal to them that she was not the kind of person to be trifled with. Danilo graced her comment with an embarrassed grin of acknowledgement.

"Nice one, *Signora Questore!*" thought the *commissario*, who was taking in every little detail of his team's reactions.

"I have no intention of being the 'new broom' who sweeps away what is, mercifully for me, a police headquarters that is running smoothly," continued Mariastella. "Except in one aspect alone. I am sure you will agree with me that you have lost two outstanding team members due to the departure of officers Oriana Salvati and Sonia Leardi..."

The assembled members of Beppe's team broke into quiet laughter at Sonia's name.

"Yes, indeed," said Maristella. "I am of course aware that it is your *commissario* who is entirely responsible for the disappearance of Sonia Leardi!"

This earned her a brief outburst of laughter accompanied by an equally brief round of applause.

Beppe was forced to admit that their new *capo* was handling her overture meeting with consummate skill.

"Over the next week, I shall be appointing three new recruits to be shared between our team here in Pescara and the police station in L'Aquila. Two of the recruits are young ladies – I shall explain to you all later how I intend to distribute the new staff and my reasoning behind the decision. You may not all be aware of the fact that *Agente* Oriana Salvati is about to go on maternity leave..."

At that moment, Beppe's mobile phone rang. He looked apologetically at his boss.

"It's Bruno Esposito," he explained. "May I...?

Maristella nodded as Beppe went out of the meeting room.

"Do any of you have any questions you would like to ask *me*?" she invited.

Only Giacomo D'Amico asked a question to fill the embarrassed silence.

"It would be interesting to know where you were before you joined us, *Signora Questore*," he asked in his dignified manner.

Mariastella had hardly begun telling them about her post as *Vice Questore* in her native Bologna when Beppe came back into the room. The mood of the meeting changed radically as everyone noticed that Beppe was manfully supressing tears.

Mariastella sat down and gestured to Beppe that he should address the team.

He gave them a brief résumé of the events surrounding the two children who had been admitted to Pescara's hospital.

"We shall be investigating the suspected dumping of toxic waste, *ragazzi*. I have just learnt that the medical team at *Il Santo Spirito* hospital has been unable to save the little girl, Ginevra, So, this is now a murder enquiry."

4: Different ways of proceeding...

Mariastella took one look at Beppe's face and took pity on him.

"*Commissario* – please go home! You have had a deeply harrowing first day back in the harness. I shall feel less guilty if I know you are with your family for the rest of the day. I also need time to think about how we should set about investigating this outrageous death..."

"What is there to think about, *Signora Questore?*" asked Beppe brusquely.

"You mean I should pack you off to Pazzoli tonight and let you get the investigation underway at once, Beppe?"

"The sooner we start the better," replied Beppe, whose anger and frustration at the sins of the modern world – and those of the mafia clans in particular – were vying for supremacy over his suppressed grief for a little girl called Ginevra.

"I understand your anger and impatience," said the new *Questore*. "Please let me sleep on it until tomorrow. I cannot send you off immediately because I need you here on Wednesday when our three new recruits are arriving for the first time..."

"Surely you can cope with them without my help, *Signora Questore?*" replied Beppe, all too aware that he was clearly overstepping the mark.

Mariastella Martellini sighed and looked calmly at her second-in-command.

"Yes, I'm quite sure I could cope, Beppe. But that is not the reason why I would like you to be present when the new recruits arrive."

Beppe stared at his new boss.

"What you do not know, Beppe, is that two of the three recruits are local girls from Pescara. Apparently, their desire to join the police force has been inspired by you and the reputation you have earned since your arrival in Pescara. They are in their early twenties and are fired with enthusiasm for police work thanks largely to the respect you have inspired in others. Can you imagine how they would feel if you were not present when they first set foot in the *Questura?*"

Beppe remained speechless.

"Yes, I too was a little overwhelmed when I learnt of their reasons for joining the police force, Beppe. As to the matter of the tragic fate of Ginevra, I agree that we should act immediately."

"How do *you* suggest we set about the investigation, Mariastella?" asked Beppe with a degree of contriteness which surprised even him.

"Well, as I said already, I would like to work out the details. But it seems sensible to me to send out the L'Aquila team on a preliminary visit. After all, they are a mere twenty kilometres away from Pazzoli – instead of our one hundred and twenty. And then, I need to think about *Agente* Simona Gambino's request to be transferred to Pescara in light of our new recruits arriving. You see my problem, Beppe?"

The recalcitrant *commissario did* see his new boss's dilemma. He had to admit to himself that she was right.

"*Mi scusi, Mariastella,*"[27] Of course, you are right. And I think I would like to call it a day. Thank you for being so understanding."

---

[27] Mi scusi = I apologise

"If you wish, Beppe. We could both drive out to L'Aquila tomorrow morning so that you can brief the team on this investigation in person. And I could get to know the officers in L'Aquila first hand. What do you say to that?"

"I would say it is a very sound course of action, Mariastella. *Due piccioni con una fava,* so to speak."[28]

"*Appunto,* Beppe."

On his drive back home to Atri, Beppe was forced to admit that his new chief had shown outstanding management skills during that long day – not to mention a large measure of forbearance and sympathy towards himself. He might even have to admit to Sonia that their new *Questore* had handled her first day brilliantly.

"*Una colpa di scena!*"[29] were the words that sprang to mind. He might even end up liking her!

* * *

"I think I would like to meet this Mariastella," stated Sonia from deep within the intimacy of their bed just before sleep overtook them.

Beppe had relived every moment of his first tumultuous day as he gave Sonia a full account of events. She had giggled with amusement at the exchanges between the new *Questore* and her somewhat maverick husband.

"It seems as if she has got the measure of you very rapidly, *amore!*" she said teasingly.

Beppe had merely grunted in reluctant acknowledgement of the truth behind her words.

---

[28] Two birds with one stone – Lit. Two pigeons with one broad bean
[29] Una colpa di scena = A turn-up for the books

But Sonia had hugged him tightly as he related the scenes at the hospital leading up to Ginevra's last breath. She heard the catch in his voice as he relived the terrible moment when Bruno Esposito had broken the news of his failure to save the little girl's life.

Sonia had said very little after that, limiting herself to a muttered imprecation: *"Catch the bastards who did this, Beppe!"*

Thus, Sonia's suggestion that she should make the acquaintance of the new *Questore* came as a surprise.

"Is that because I told you we are driving up to L'Aquila together tomorrow, by any chance?" asked Beppe, sensing a chance to retaliate.

"Absolutely, yes!" she replied.

"Let's make it this Thursday, then. We'll be busy with the new recruits the day after."

Beppe was strangely reassured by Sonia's impulsive desire to confront Mariastella. Sonia would undoubtedly put the new situation at the *Questura* into perspective for him. And Mariastella *had* said she wanted to meet ALL the team members! After all, Sonia was only on leave.

"Do you think your parents will mind if we leave the kids with them for a whole day, *amore?*"

"Oh, Veronica and Lorenzo are coming too!" said their mother before falling asleep.

Beppe wondered if his new *capo* liked children. The question opened up a whole new set of conjectures regarding Mariastella. There was still a lot to learn.

* * *

Once again, Beppe had intended to arrive at the police headquarters before Mariastella. He did not bother to analyse his motives – to him, it was obvious, and completely unworthy of him, he had to admit. It was just to give himself the fleeting impression that he was still wholly in charge of his team.

It was his friend, Pippo Cafarelli whom Beppe ran into as he walked into the *Questura* just after seven-thirty. Beppe looked at Pippo quizzically.

"I've just spent the last half hour with our new *Questore, capo.* Luigi Rocco is with her now. After that, she asked me to tell you, she will be ready for your trip to L'Aquila…"

Beppe was looking resentfully at his friend – as if Pippo's summons to Mariastella's office had been of his own choosing.

"And what did *she* have to say for herself?" he asked sharply.

"Well, she asked me why I walk with a slight limp. So I had to tell her the story of how I got shot instead of you, Beppe."[30]

"And how did Mariastella seem to you, on a one-to-one footing?" asked Beppe – in what was intended to be a challenging tone.

Pippo was looking guilty. He knew his chief's personality quirks all too well.

"*Sinceramente,* Beppe? It is difficult not to like her."

Beppe looked hard at his friend and nodded noncommittally.

---

[30] See 'A Close Encounter with Mushrooms'

"*Buona giornata,*[31] Pippo," he said and left his friend standing there.

"You too, *commissario,*" muttered Pippo to Beppe's retreating figure. "And by the way, she's not in uniform today, *capo.*"

Beppe made as if he had not heard his friend's last comment.

During the drive to L'Aquila, seated side-by-side with his new boss, who was, significantly, in the driver's seat, Beppe was about to learn far more than he had bargained for. First and foremost, was that she owned a two-seater sports car with only nominal passenger room in the rear – and that she drove it very fast.

"I can drive more slowly, if you wish, Beppe," she had offered on seeing the way that her second-in-command was clutching onto anything within reach that protruded.

"I learnt to drive on a racing track with my father," she went on to say. "He used to be a *pilota da corso.*"[32]

Beppe simply waved his spare left hand in a dismissive gesture, intended to imply that he was not nervous.

When he had got used to Mariastella's driving, he reckoned it might be a good idea to bring up the matter of Sonia's intended visit to the *Questura* in two days' time.

"She seems to be very determined to meet you, Mariastella."

His chief's reaction to the suggestion took his breath away.

"*Ho capito, Beppe!* [33] She was worried about us two being in a car together. Am I right?"

---

[31] Buona giornata = Have a good day.
[32] Confusingly, 'pilota' is also a racing car driver in Italian.

"I wouldn't say that..."

"*I* have the advantage over *you* here, *commissario*. I'm a woman!"

Beppe remained silent. It was not worth him commenting on the obvious - in an obvious way.

"You may reassure your wife, Beppe, that she has nothing to fear. I have a predilection for younger women."

Beppe had to stifle the only repost which came to mind.

"What a waste!" he thought secretly to himself. However, he managed a sideways glance of respectful surprise in his chief's direction, but he made no comment. There had been something about the manner in which she had delivered this revelation which did not ring true. It was as if she was simply taking great delight in muddying the waters. He concluded that Mariastella had many strata to her personality. She had compounded the complexity of the inner workings of her mind rather than simplifying them.

"I think we are almost there, Mariastella," he told her. "I'll give you directions to the police station."

* * *

"Down to business then," stated Mariastella Martellini after formal introductions had been made to an astounded group of police officers. Apparently, they had been only partially informed about the change of leadership. Beppe had deliberately omitted to mention one vital aspect when he had phoned the officer in charge of the L'Aquila police force, *Ispettore* Fabrizio De Sanctis, to set up the

---

[33] Ho capito = I get it! Lit: I have understood.

meeting. He had wished to reserve for himself the mischievous pleasure of observing their reactions at first hand.

The inspector had hardly batted an eyelid. Giovanni Palena, his second-in-command had only registered mild astonishment, suppressed well before he shook hands with Mariastella.

The other three police officers – all women – looked with varying degrees of surprised curiosity at Mariastella. Officer Valentina Ianni, the youngest member of the team, was too busy looking at her 'hero', Beppe Stancato, to register more than passing surprise – a reaction duly noted by the new *Questore*. Officer Simona Gambino – the lady 'rescued' by Beppe from abduction by the American secret services – smiled openly as she shook hands with Mariastella.

Only an obviously expectant mother, Oriana Salvati, was displaying signs of a series of multi-layered reactions, which Beppe had secretly predicted would be the case. She first of all looked fleetingly at her partner, Giovanni, with a glance that implied she had had a narrow escape by transferring to L'Aquila. Her expression changed as she looked briefly at Beppe – a cheeky grin which clearly said: *'That's given you something to think about, Beppe Stancato.'* She smiled openly at Mariastella with self-evident admiration.

"Congratulations, *Signora Questore*," she said as she shook her hand.

"How are you coping with pregnancy and police duties, Oriana?" asked Mariastella kindly.

"I can assure you, ma'am, the day after delivery, this child," she said pointing at her belly, "will be in a papoose and we'll be doing our policing together!"

The general outburst of laughter was spontaneous. Mariastella glanced at Beppe as if to say, "I see what you mean about Oriana."

The atmosphere changed to solemnity as Beppe began to explain to the assembled officers the reason for their visit to L'Aquila.

There was scarcely a dry eye in the meeting room by the time Beppe had finished talking. Even Mariastella was obviously suppressing tears on what was her first total exposure to the unabridged version of events.

"I subsequently learned from *Il Dottore* Esposito that the boy, Alessandro, had called out from his oxygen tent the words "Gina, Gina, she's gone forever!" as the nurse was desperately attempting to stop his arms flailing around..." concluded Beppe.

"So how do you want us to proceed, *commissario?*" asked Inspector De Sanctis when he had regained his composure.

Beppe had the courtesy to raise an eyebrow in Mariastella's direction, aware of Fabrizio's unintentional lapse of professional etiquette.

Mariastella Martellini simply nodded at Beppe, encouraging him to continue.

"*Grazie, signora Questore.* I have to warn you, *ragazzi,*[34] that what we are about to ask you to investigate has the stamp of the mafia all over it..."

---

[34] Ragazzi = lads (and lasses if women are present) Italian is grammatically 'sexist'!)

5: Reluctant delegation...

"What criminal act *doesn't* show the hand of the mafia these days, when you look more closely!" stated Oriana Salvati, the black belt in most forms of martial art, already looking as if she was preparing to do battle against the forces of evil.

"*Appunto,*[35] Oriana. However, at this point, we are only asking you to carry out a preliminary investigation. A vital first step! The town, or village – I had never heard of it until a few days ago – is called Pazzoli..."

Beppe was mildly astonished when the team of four officers sitting round the table let out a collective groan, replaced by knowing smiles. Mariastella raised a quizzical eyebrow.

Inspector Fabrizio De Sanctis resumed his serious face, as he addressed the new *Questore.*

"We joke about that particular *comune* as deserving its name – they all seem to be slightly mad there.[36] The lady mayor of Pazzoli is called Eugenia Mancini. She has her finger on the pulse of that community. We joke about *her* because she always claims to be ambidextrous."[37]

"There's little that goes on in that town that she doesn't know about, *Signora Questore,*" added officer Giovanni Palena, at pains to address Mariastella directly.

"Well, that should help to set you off on the right path," concluded Beppe. "We're treading on unchartered territory here. You'll need to contact your lady mayor straight away – as well as the mother and father of Ginevra.

---

[35] Appunto = precisely
[36] 'I pazzi' means 'mad people'
[37] Her surname is Mancini. Mancino = 'left-handed'

Their son may be the only one who knows exactly where this toxic waste site is situated. The parents mentioned an older boy who might have taken them there. They knew his first name was Dario but..."

Eugenia Mancini will soon root *him* out, *commissario*," said officer Valentina Ianni.

"Good – she sounds as if she will be a great help to us. Bear in mind that there might turn out to be other toxic waste sites involved which nobody knows about," warned Beppe.

"Do we know when the little girl's funeral will be held?" asked Simona Gambino, speaking for the first time. "We will need to tread very gingerly when we talk to the parents."

"Thank you, Simona. I agree. No, we don't know yet. As soon as you find out, please let me know when the funeral is. I would like to be there too, if possible..."

Beppe gave Mariastella a side-long glance, but the *Questore* remained detached.

"This is the parents' address," Beppe said, handing Diego's business card to Officer Gambino. "There's very little to go on, *ragazzi*. But I am sure your intervention will be crucial."

"When will *you* become involved, *commissario?*" Valentina Ianni asked out of the blue. Beppe had been afraid that someone would bring up the issue of his presence at the scene of the crime. He was not surprised that it had been Valentina Ianni, after her manifest frustration that she had asked for a transfer to Pescara – only to learn that her 'hero' had been suspended for three months.

"This is not the moment to decide, Valentina," Beppe replied brusquely.

Mariastella coughed politely.

"Don't worry, I have no intention of imprisoning your *commissario* in Via Pesaro until he reaches retirement age," she informed them gently.

The gathered officers grinned and relaxed visibly.

"There, I think that's all I need to say to you all, *ragazzi*. Except *"in bocca al lupo"* and keep me updated as often as possible. Is there anything else you would like to add, Mariastella?"

Her first name had just slipped out of his mouth naturally. He could see from the assembled officers' faces that their minds were busy at work. It was pointless to attempt to cover up his minor gaffe.

The *Questore* did not show the slightest hint of embarrassment.

"No, Beppe, you have been refreshingly succinct and crystal clear in your assessment of this awful business. I would only like to add publicly that it has been a real pleasure to meet you all so soon after my arrival. You are obviously a team who works well together. May I take this opportunity to invite anyone present to tell me a bit about what it is like being police officers in L'Aquila three years after the earthquake?"

The officers remained thoughtful for what seemed like minutes on end.

Inspector Fabrizio De Sanctis felt the onus was on him to answer for them all. But it was Oriana Salvati who pre-empted her senior officer. Imminent motherhood certainly hadn't detracted from her sharpness of mind, thought Beppe.

"It's as if the city has been struck by some pernicious virus, *Signora Questore,*" began Oriana. "You can feel it in the air. Outsiders keep on telling us it will soon get better. It's true that the physical discomfort is easing – people have got new houses to live in on the outskirts of the town. But it's the town centre that feels abandoned, struggling to find its identity again..."

L'ispettore Fabrizio De Sanctis had found his tongue.

"Yes, it's just as Oriana says. The original spirit of the town has still not returned. There are too many reminders, too many buildings still in ruins..."

It was Giovanni Palena's turn to contribute his perspective.

"And there are increasing drug problems among teenagers. There's one derelict house – an old *palazzo*[38] - which has been taken over by homeless or parentless kids. We are constantly being called out because of their rowdiness and drug habits. But where else can they go? It's a fulltime job trying to block the clandestine supply of drugs..."

"But the kids themselves almost treat us as comrades when we go there. You have to feel some sympathy for them. If the police cannot reassure them, nobody can!" added Oriana – as if she had been personally challenged on the issue.

"And then there's the money lenders who've set themselves up. So many people lost their jobs as well as their families," added Valentina Ianni.

"But our team sees the worst aspects of the town. In many areas, people are finding their feet again, regrouping, starting new ventures..." said Simona Gambino.

---

[38] Palazzo = an apartment block

"Thank you all for what you are doing," concluded their new *Questore*. "I hope you can spare the manpower to cope with the Pazzoli problem! I can promise you a new recruit within the next few days. Perhaps you and I could have a brief chat, *Ispettore,* before Beppe and I head back to Pescara?"

* * *

"You drive please, Beppe," said Mariastella handing him the keys to her yellow Alfa Romeo Spider, as if they had known each other for months. It sounded more like an order than an offer, so Beppe did not demur.

"I don't feel like driving all the way back to Pescara. And I'm hungry," she added.

Beppe's usual tendency – not yet entirely overcome - to overlook his team's need to eat at lunch time would not work with his new *capo,* apparently.

"I know just the place, Mariastella," he said. For the first time in three years, he was not the 'newcomer'. He felt a hint of self-satisfaction, as he set off with a reassuring burst of acceleration towards *La Bilancia,* just outside Loreto Aprutino.

"Aren't we too late for lunch?" asked Mariastella as they drew up in the tree-lined car park.

"Ah, but this is a special restaurant. It belongs to Oriana Salvati's uncle."

His new-found superior local knowledge made him feel well-disposed towards his new boss. An aspect which did not escape her notice.

"I'm impressed, *commissario,"* she said.

"Wait until you've tasted the food, *Dottoressa!"*[39]

* * *

Back in Via Pesaro, some two hours later, Beppe regretfully handed back the car keys to Mariastella.

Not having the need to concentrate on the road, she had talked more freely on the short drive back to Pescara from Loreto Aprutino.

"I had an interesting talk with the Inspector after our meeting. He is reluctant to allow Officer Simona Gambino to transfer to Pescara for now, especially as Oriana Salvati will soon be away for a time – despite her determination to sideline motherhood. You were right, Beppe. She is a remarkable young woman..."

"I talked to Simona Gambino, too," said Beppe. "I convinced her that she did not need any extra training. Reading between the lines, she is likely to end up in the same state as Oriana before too long. She is living with her scientist boyfriend..."

"I should really like you to fill me in on that episode some time, Beppe. If only to satisfy my own curiosity!"

"You should get Officer Luigi Rocco to tell you all about the vanishing physicist, Mariastella. He played a major part in solving that mystery. He's a man of hidden talents..."

"He reminds me of, I don't know, a mountain bear or a Sumo wrestler..."

"That's what he used to be called by all the others. Now, he is accepted and admired by the whole team."

They stepped out of the car and entered the police station.

---

[39] Dottore/Dottoressa: a frequently used courtesy title – not restricted to the medical profession.

"Will you come up to my office, Beppe? I want to give you the dossiers on the three young recruits who are coming tomorrow morning. I told them to be here at nine o'clock. And thank you for making my task so easy today. I know you are anxious to be involved in the Pazzoli case, but let's see what the L'Aquila team can achieve under their own steam for a few days. *D'accordo,* Beppe?"

"*Sissignora Questore,*" replied Beppe. "I thank you for allowing me to drive your rather special car."

"I *was* tired – really. By the way, just to clear things up, I am not going to stand in your way just because I am new to the job. If there's one thing I have learnt over the last few years, it is that respect has to be earned in this life, patiently step by step. It does not automatically come with rank."

"I am sure you will have no difficulty in winning the respect of all concerned in Via Pesaro – and beyond, *Signora Questore.*"

Beppe could not quite believe he had uttered those words. What had come over him in that single unguarded moment?

"I was right to let him drive me back," thought the new *Questore* with a secret smile on her face – invisible to the *commissario,* who was walking upstairs just behind her.

6: *Nelle ore piccole...* *(In the small hours of the morning)*

Whenever Arturo Annunzio heard the phone ring at 1 o'clock in the morning, he was filled with dread. This was already the fourth time it had occurred. He knew who it was on the other end of the line. He was also aware that each time he reluctantly yielded to pressure from *those people,* he was, quite literally, digging a deeper hole for himself. He had neither the courage nor the vision to resist. His frequent brushes with the law in his younger days had led him to mistrust policemen in any shape or form. Asking the police for help or protection was simply not an option, to his way of thinking.

His wife was equally aware who was calling them in the middle of the night. She sat up in bed, looking fearful. The blood had drained from her cheeks.

"Non rispondere, Arturo!"[40] she begged him.

But he had tried ignoring this sinister caller on a previous occasion. It hadn't helped. It inevitably made matters worse when the convoy of two or even three vans arrived, with headlamps dimmed, despite the total darkness of the Abruzzo countryside.

The sound of the telephone ceased as he began his descent to the floor below. But that was their ploy. If he went back to bed, the phone would ring again - its jangling tone, intended to be heard when they were working outdoors, made sleep impossible. The din it made, he was certain, was enough to be heard by their nearest neighbours some 800 metres away.

---

[40] Non rispondere – Don't answer it.

Sure enough, the caller waited just long enough for him to be lulled into a false sense of security before the noise began all over again. He picked up the receiver.

"*Pronto,*" he growled, "*chi è?*"

"*Signor* Annunzio...Arturo. *Buongiorno!* Did I wake you up? *Mi 'spiace...*"[41]

The heavy Neapolitan accent was exaggerated, mocking, and devoid of pity.

"I told you last time, I don't want to do this anymore. It's too risky. You promised you wouldn't..."

"And I am a man of my word, *dottore!* But this consignment was unexpected. I just didn't know who else to turn to."

"I won't do it, *Signor...?*"

The man had never once given him a name. This time was no exception.

"My drivers will be with you soon...Arturo! You have that lovely new digger we gave you. So, I suggest you get out there and make a nice deep hole. My boys become very nervous if they have to hang about..."

"This is the last time - or I go to the *sbirri.*"[42]

The derisive laugh on the other end of the line was spine-chilling.

"Then we shall have to start dumping our stuff on the surface of your land ... Arturo."

The speaker had a way of accentuating his name so that it sounded as if he was being scolded like an uncooperative schoolboy by a teacher who was barely suppressing his temper.

---

[41] Mi 'spiace – I'm sorry (said sarcastically, in this case)
[42] Sbirri – cops *(slang)*

"Don't worry yourself to death. We can deal with *any* problems. *Buona notte...* Arturo."[43]

The man, without a name, without a face, had spoken derisively and hung up.

There was nothing Arturo could do except go out and dig another hole as quickly as he could - as near as he dared to the other three pits, which he had been left to cover over with the soil he had excavated. His wife, Maria Pia, made him a coffee and then stood looking on in quiet despair. She made the sign of the cross as she muttered a prayer, which she hoped the Virgin Mary would listen to more attentively this time.

Arturo turned on the motor of the machine that *those people* had delivered before their first visit. It was a compact machine but, despite it being the latest design, was still driven by a diesel engine. The wind would carry the noise of the engine in the direction of the neighbouring farm, he was certain. Indeed, he noticed that a downstairs light had come on as he began to remove the top soil.

"Merda! Porco puttana!" he swore out loud.

Within thirty minutes, he had made a hole which was perhaps three metres deep and almost as wide. That would have to do for those bastards, he decided.

Then came the anxious wait for *them* to arrive. It was always the same – he had been scared into believing that the drivers would be arriving imminently, whereas it was almost half past three before two white vans were driven into his field with engines being revved up impatiently as soon as the vans were stationary.

---

[43] Buona notte - Goodnight

Arturo scowled at the drivers and gesticulated at them to make less noise. Their only response was to rev the engines even more aggressively. The vans had been reversed up to the edge of the pit. Four men leapt out of the vans. The engines were left running.

Three of the men began to offload the plastic bags hurriedly, carelessly - not going to the trouble of making sure they were properly sealed. They were chucked unceremoniously into the hole he had dug. As on previous occasions, Arturo was disturbed to see how much of the waste had the yellow and black skull and crossbones symbol on the outside.

The man who was the obvious gang leader, tattoos covering every part of his arms and torso under a sweaty T-shirt, had gesticulated without words to the fourth man to go off into the darkness. Arturo assumed he had gone to relieve himself. He felt his stomach churn at the thought of everything he would have to clean up after their departure.

It was all over in less than ten minutes.

The three men who had done the unloading, the swarthy tattooed man in the middle, took a few menacing steps towards Arturo. He was fearful for his own safety, but he remembered his own childhood and teenage days in the back streets of Naples. it was fatal to show fear - an invitation to be knifed.

"Our boss is angry with you, Arturo. You threatened him over the phone. That wasn't a wise move."

Arturo understood the almost forgotten dialect words easily enough.

"You told him you would go to the *sbirri* next time, didn't you...Arturo!"

Arturo continued to glare at the man, whose words were full of suppressed menace. The fourth man was returning from out of the shrouding darkness of the countryside. All Arturo's false bravado vanished in an instant. The man was dragging a pregnant ewe along by the wool on its neck. The animal was bleating in fear. The man took out a knife from his belt and slit the animal's throat. Its brief scream of agony and terror rent the air.

"No more threats of going to the police, Arturo. *Capito?*"[44] said the ringleader.

He threw an envelope on the ground at Arturo's feet.

"That should keep you quiet for a bit," said the man with a sneer on his face. "*Andiamo, ragazzi!*"[45]

The two vans were driven away with revving engines and eventually were inaudible, swallowed up in the stillness of the nascent dawn.

Maria Pia came out to join her husband. They both looked on in despair at the bloody carcass at their feet. Arturo handed the envelope to his wife without checking the wad of banknotes it contained.

"We have to go to the police, Arturo," she muttered unconvincingly. She had repeatedly tried to persuade her husband to break the habit of a lifetime and turn to the law for help.

"No police, I tell you! We'll end up in jail anyway if the cops get involved!"

Maria Pia knew it was a waste time insisting. He would dig his heels in even more.

---

[44] Capito? – Understood?
[45] Andiamo, ragazzi – Let's go, lads.

The only form of justice Arturo understood was the carcass lying at his feet. He felt impotent in his anger and despair.

***

Two days later, while her husband was occupied milking the sheep in the modern, pre-fabricated milking shed, Maria Pia had the weird sensation that her silent prayer to the Virgin Mary had been answered in a way she had not been expecting. She had been peeling a few desperate vegetables to put into a mutton stew.

She looked out of the window on hearing a car pull into the courtyard. It was a police car. If the police had somehow found out what they had been doing, then the matter was out of their hands. She felt relieved rather than fearful about the possible repercussions.

A youthful-looking male officer accompanied by two uniformed female officers – one of whom was seemingly in an advanced state of pregnancy - stepped out of the police car and headed casually towards the farmhouse. She should ring the bell to alert her husband. But for reasons known only to her, she decided not to.

"Let's wait and see why they are here first," she decided all on her own.

7: Without the guiding hand of Commissario Stancato...

Ispettore Fabrizio De Sanctis had wasted no time in dispatching his team to Pazzoli the morning after Beppe and Mariastella's visit to L'Aquila. On the *commissario's* advice, he had sent all of his team of four officers to carry out the initial enquiries, leaving only himself in charge in L'Aquila. After all, it was assumed that the team would return to L'Aquila at the end of each day, should some urgent matter arise.

The inspector had been buoyed up by the news that a new recruit would be arriving soon. The new *Questore* had also clearly inferred that his promotion to *vice-commissario* was a distinct and well-deserved probability. Maristella Martellini had struck him as someone who was very forward-looking.

When he had mentioned possible promotion to his friend Beppe, the *commissario* had grinned and restricted himself to saying: *"Ah, Fabrizio – scopa nuova spazza bene!"*[46]

The inspector had telephoned the lady mayor of Pazzoli, Eugenia Mancini, and told her about the death of Ginevra Ianni in Pescara's main hospital.

Shocked to the core about the news of the tragedy which had befallen one of the youngest inhabitants of her town, Eugenia Mancini had pledged her willingness to become wholly involved in helping the police.

"We shall be truly grateful to you, Eugenia. Your local knowledge will be invaluable."

---

[46] Scopa nuova spazza bene. Almost literally as in English 'New mop cleans well' New brooms sweep clean, of course.

"I'll be up tomorrow at the crack of dawn to meet your officers, *Ispettore,*" she had reassured Fabrizio.

His own junior officer, Valentina Ianni, had been particularly upset by the news of the little girl's death because of their shared surname - even though she was fairly certain she did not have any close relatives in Pazzoli.

"I just cannot begin to imagine the heartbreak of losing a child so young," she explained to her *capo.*

"I agree, it's a tragedy beyond imagination, Valentina. We must simply make sure that whoever is responsible for the death of this little girl is brought to justice."

"Oh, they will be, *capo.* We shall make sure of that."

The Inspector admired her enthusiasm. He hoped that her first encounter with the 'real' criminal world would not stifle her enthusiasm.

***

The team of police officers had not arrived at the crack of dawn, even though the mayoress had been quite prepared for this eventuality. Eugenia Mancini had taken her only daughter to school at seven-thirty and left her at the gate with the head teacher, who had burst into tears at the news of Ginevra Ianni's tragic end.

"She was the sweetest child you could imagine," she sobbed. "But how could a healthy little girl like Ginevra...?"

"Mamma?" said Eugenia's daughter, grabbing her mother's hand in perplexity. She was visibly upset at the sight of the lady who ruled their little scholastic world shedding uncontrollable tears.

"Mamma, what's happened to Ginevra?"

"A terrible thing, Alice.[47] I'll tell you later, *amore."*

Eugenia could not take her leave until the head teacher had recovered, dried her tears and, with her emotions under control, taken Alice's hand and led her into the school building, chatting as they went. Eugenia had not mentioned that the police were treating Ginevra's death as murder - that would have been the last straw. Eugenia would leave it to one of the L'Aquila team to tell the head teacher later on that day.

"That's the best way to go about it," she succeeded in convincing herself.

A text message from a police officer called Giovanni Palena informed her that the police from L'Aquila would arrive in Pazzoli by nine-thirty. She sent him a reply naming a bar – the only one of two in the town's high street – where they would find her at the appointed time.

The mayoress had just under an hour to go before the police officers were due to arrive.

"Come on Eugenia," she said out loud. "You must pay the Ianni parents a visit. I know you don't want to face them right now, but that's no excuse!"

Having audible conversations with herself was an established habit. She found she could sort out problems much more readily if she had someone to argue with – even when it was only with herself. It had earned her the reputation of being mildly eccentric, but that did not particularly bother her. It had driven her husband mad – he had used this foible of hers as an excuse to leave her soon after the birth of Alice.

"It's bad enough that you talk your way through the cooking of every meal you prepare, Eugenia. But talking to

---

[47] Alice – pronounced *'a-LEE-chay'* in Italian.

yourself in your sleep is just going too far!" he had scolded her.

Eugenia Mancini was quite convinced that her husband had made that bit up and used it as a pretext to abandon her. He worked in Pescara and had got fed up with commuting every day from a village 120 kilometres from Pescara, which his wife was inordinately attached to. The talking in her sleep, however, had been subsequently confirmed by Alice on the occasions when she shared her mother's bed – too upset by her *papà's* act of desertion to sleep on her own.

With a heavy heart, Eugenia walked down to the lower end of Pazzoli. As chance would have it, she arrived just as the Ianni parents and a devastated nine-year-old boy arrived from Pescara in their large but antiquated estate car. There was a tiny white temporary hospital coffin in the boot-space where Diego's electrician's equipment was usually kept. Eugenia was about to turn round and walk back up the hill, but she knew this painful moment would have to be confronted sooner or later.

"It might as well be right now, Eugenia," she told herself.

Eugenia was one of those rare individuals whom people never felt uncomfortable with. The sad smile on her face was both sympathetic and reassuring as she walked towards the little group of three, trying to suppress tears that did not need to be induced.

* * *

The four police officers arrived punctually. Eugenia Mancini was waiting for them on the terrace, which was just a narrow section of the pavement with a few metal tables and chairs set out.

The sight of a police car arriving and disgorging an army of uniformed *sbirri* provoked looks of utter disbelief if not outright suspicion from shopkeepers and passers-by alike. Were the cops after their beloved lady mayor for some reason? That would be typical!

Oblivious, or quite indifferent, to the reaction of her citizens, the mayoress was introduced to each of the officers in turn. She suggested they go inside the dark interior of the bar. Their arrival provoked a collective choking fit from the old-timers downing their early morning glasses of white wine at the bar.

An invisible sign from Eugenia to the bar owner produced five coffees and a plate of croissants. Eugenia took one look at Oriana Salvati's belly and asked the bar owner to bring a carafe of fresh water to the table too.

This earned her a grateful look from the pregnant officer.

Eugenia's eyes must have displayed a residual redness, which caused an observant Simona Gambino to raise an eyebrow in her direction.

"I've just seen a miniature coffin containing Ginevra Ianni arrive at the family home," she explained. "Where would you like to start, officers?"

"We have very little to go on, Eugenia," began Giovanni Palena. "We need to find out where the toxic waste was discarded near the river so we can make sure it is cordoned off and removed. Ginevra's brother, Alessandro, should know…"

"Sandro is too traumatised by his sister's death to be of any help at present," said Eugenia. "I've just come back from seeing the family about thirty minutes ago."

"But there's another boy involved too, so we gathered from the parents, Eugenia. He was the one who took Ginevra and Alessandro down near the river in the first place. We only have his given name, Dario, to go on…"

A heavy sigh from the mayoress as soon as she heard the name Dario stopped Officer Palena in his tracks.

"Dario Tondino!" she exclaimed with a note of exasperation in her voice. "That comes as no surprise! Well, we can find *him* for you in no time at all. He's a problem child in a class of his own. He is repeating a year – so he is stuck in a class with pupils who are younger than he is. I feel sorry for *them!*"

The four officers looked at each other covertly and then smiled at the mayoress. It was obvious that Eugenia Mancini was going to prove to be a great asset.

"Our *commissario* from Pescara, who met the family at the hospital just before Ginevra passed away, is convinced that somebody else in Pazzoli will have become involved with the mafia in burying toxic waste in the countryside."

The mayoress looked anxiously at the police officer in charge.

"That is a deeply disturbing revelation, *Agente* Palena. But nothing like that has ever come to *my* attention…"

"But there must be hundreds of outlying farmsteads in the countryside. We shall need to do a lot of footwork to cover them all…"

Giovanni Palena was just beginning to feel disheartened by the enormity of the task before them.

"Let's make a start with this boy Dario," said Eugenia Mancini. "Don't worry, officers, if something sinister is going on in or around my town, it will come to light sooner rather than later. It always does!"

Her optimism was infectious. They finished their coffees and croissants and, at Eugenia's suggestion, parked the police car in the main *piazza* just outside the little town hall.

That's my reserved space," she explained. "But I don't have a car, so you are welcome to use it whenever you come to Pazzoli."

"How on earth do you manage without a car, Eugenia?" asked Simona Gambino, genuinely concerned for their guiding light's mobility.

"Because I ride a motorbike," replied the mayoress as if that was the most obvious explanation in the world. "My daughter rides pillion if we are both going to the same place. Normally, we walk everywhere – or even take a bus."

And indeed, Eugenia led the four officers on foot down to the school, which, she explained, was only a short distance away from the bereaved family's home.

"Two birds with one stone," declared Eugenia Mancini cheerfully.

* * *

Eugenia was addressing the whole school – there were only three teachers including the headmistress – and not many more than forty pupils of various ages. Simona Gambino was looking at Eugenia Mancini in fascination as she spoke. The mayoress was slim and shapely, short in stature, not obviously beautiful, but she had a vitality about her which made her far more attractive than superficial good looks would impart.

"A terrible thing has happened, *ragazzi,*" she was saying. "In a minute, I shall ask these lovely police officers to share the news with you. I want you all to promise to be courageous. We shall be needing your help, you see. All of you are going to become our secret agents."

The whole school – teachers and pupils alike – were holding their breath.

It had been Eugenia herself who had come up with the idea of involving the children in the investigation as they walked to the school.

"They come from homes which are scattered all over the area. It would take you a week to visit all the properties. If we take the tiny risk of asking them to keep their eyes and ears open, it might save you days of fruitless interrogation in a neighbourhood which you are unfamiliar with. *Che ne dici, Giovanni?*"[48]

"It's a good idea, Eugenia. It certainly can't do any harm," Giovanni had replied. Beppe Stancato, he felt sure, would not have entertained any scruples about harnessing the natural talent and curiosity of children – especially if it led to the arrest of the potentially remote perpetrators of this particular crime.

On the way down to the school, the police officers had held a rapid straw poll to decide which of them should impart the tragic news to the children. The majority decision was that the painful task should be carried out by Officer Simona Gambino.

---

[48] Che ne dici? = What do say to that? What do you think?

She stood in front of the group of teachers and children and told them what had happened to Ginevra Ianni – and to her elder brother. Grief is infectious and the tears and shock gripped the gathering. Simona waited until a stunned silence had settled again before she began to talk to them about the toxic waste which had been dumped near the river bank.

"This is where we believe that Ginevra must have touched something dangerous which poisoned her body..." Simona was saying.

What happened next took everyone by surprise.

Oriana Salvati had been observing a boy sitting in the back row. He looked larger than the other children and wore a sullen expression on his face, in marked contrast to the shocked or tearful looks on everyone else's.

"I bet I know what *his* name is!" Oriana was thinking, as a flash of enlightenment dawned.

One second later, the boy had broken ranks and was heading at breakneck speed for the door at the back of the hall. He was outside the school and heading for the gate before anyone had time to react.

"DARIO!" shouted the head teacher – to no avail.

Oriana was the first to react. She was out of the door in pursuit of the escapee within seconds.

The next to react was Officer Palena, who told Simona to stay with the teachers and children. He signalled to Valentina Ianni to follow him as he ran after his partner, Oriana – who should not be running *anywhere,* he had repeatedly told her. Eugenia did not wait to be invited. She followed on the heels of the departing police officers.

The children in the hall were all talking at once. The fugitive youth had sparked off a very different reaction to the grief and tears of a few minutes previously.

The head teacher looked quizzically at Officer Gambino as if to say: "Do you want me to quell the rebels?"

Simona shook her head and smiled. She was catching fragments of the children's conversation which told her a lot more about Dario Tondino than their silence would ever have done. In the end, Simona saw two of the older girls in the back row tentatively raising their arms in the air. They had something to say - apparently with some reluctance.

Simona Gambino clapped her hands together once.

"Va bene, ragzzi!"

The authority in her voice brought the children back to order. But the two girls at the back had lowered their hands as soon as silence had fallen.

"Anything you want to say will be treated seriously, *ragazzi*. This is a very grave matter. So, now's the time to speak up."

The head teacher intervened.

"Federica and Gloria," she said addressing the two girls in the back row. "I think you have something to tell us."

One of the girls stood up reluctantly and began talking.

"It's Dario, *signora*. We don't want to get him into trouble but..."

"We only want to talk to him, er...?" said Simona, hinting that the girl should give her name.

"Federica, ma'am," said the girl. "It's just that he's a bully sometimes, and he picks on younger kids like Sandro and Ginevra and dares them to do silly things..."

"Yeah, that's right. He's been boasting how he got Ginevra and Sandro to go down to the river and play with some stuff he had found near the water..."

The other girl, Gloria, had decided to join in too in support of her friend.

"He told us there was stuff down there with, like, a skull-and-crossbones on it..." continued Federica, gathering pace.

Officer Gambino decided to stop them so as not to upset the younger children.

"Thank you, Federica – and Gloria. Perhaps we could have a word in private. And anyone else who wants to tell us anything they know.

One boy put his hand up. He was a solemn-looking eight-year-old who looked very sure of himself.

The head teacher took over.

"Marco?" she asked.

"I know where he may be hiding, miss!"

The head teacher brought the assembly to a close. She instructed the children to look out for anything unusual that happened near where they lived.

"Especially if you live out in the country, *ragazzi!*" she insisted. "You are our eyes and ears."

The children filed out, looking very subdued.

* * *

Officers Palena, Ianni and Salvati were looking dispirited. Eugenia Mancini tried to buoy them up.

"He can't have gone far, *agenti*.[49] He'll turn up sooner or later. His mum tells me he's scared stiff of the dark."

Oriana's phone was ringing. She took one look at the screen and listened to what she was being told with a grin on her face.

"That was Simona on the phone," she said. Turning to the mayoress, she asked:

"Can you take us to his home, Eugenia? Simona thinks we might find him there."

Oriana had a mischievous smile on her face.

"It's not far to walk," explained Eugenia. "But what makes your colleague think he'd go straight home, Oriana? He's a cunning little so-and-so at the best of times. Even his mother says so."

Giovanni Palena took one look at his partner. Two years living with Oriana had taught him that she was enjoying leaving them in suspense and would impart nothing.

Oriana merely smiled and said:

"Let's just see if Simona is right, Eugenia."

* * *

Dario's mother opened the door to find the mayoress in the company of three uniformed police officers. She was a harassed, rather overweight lady in her forties.

"What's he done this time?" she asked wearily.
"I can't cope with him anymore. He's not even thirteen and already I have no control over him."

"What about his father, *signora?*" asked Officer Palena.

Eugenia Mancini coughed politely.

---

[49] Agenti = Officers

"There *is* no *Signor* Tondino, *Agente* Palena."

"'e buggered off as soon as Dario was three years old," stated Dario's mother.

"I'm sorry, *signora,*" said Giovanni contritely. "May we speak to Dario? He's not in trouble – we just need to talk to him."

The mother looked at Giovanni in patent disbelief.

"'E ain't 'ere! He's at school!"

Out of the corner of his eye, Giovanni noticed that Oriana was disappearing round the side of the house.

Oriana spotted the dog compound immediately. A Great Dane was standing looking at her – passively, idly wondering who she was.

The floor of the compound was covered in excrement and bits of bone. A bowl of dirty water was almost empty. Oriana felt disgust and anger at the same time.

"Why do Italians treat animals like this? Locked up, no exercise and as little food as possible! Small wonder they become aggressive!" she was thinking.

Behind the compound was a large hut-like kennel with a doorway big enough for a human being to crawl into.

"Come on out, Dario. We know you're hiding. There's nothing to be afraid of. We just need to talk to you."

No response! Oriana's hand was on the bar which kept the door closed. Instantly, the dog moved towards her, growling at the back of its throat.

Oriana, the black belt in almost every form of martial art was not sure whether any of her manoeuvres would work on a dog this size. Besides, the idea of stepping inside the filthy compound brought on a sensation of nausea. For the first time, being pregnant made her feel vulnerable.

She needed to call for back-up.

Giovanni and Valentina were there within seconds.

"Dario's hiding in the kennel at the back," she stated with a degree of certainty she was not feeling. "At least, I'm pretty sure he is…"

To Oriana and Giovanni's amazement, it was Valentina who opened the door of the compound and stepped fearlessly inside. She was talking quietly to the animal. Giovanni and Oriana had instinctively taken their revolvers out of their holsters.

The huge animal had reared up in silence and placed its front paws on Valentina's shoulders. It began licking her face. Her colleagues burst out laughing.

"She's a secret dog-whisperer, *amore*," stated Oriana to Giovanni. Valentina had revealed an aspect of her character they would never have guessed at.

Half a minute later, Valentina was leading a bewildered twelve-year old out of the kennel. His hide-away had been breached for the first time in his life. Not even his mother had worked out that he often took refuge in the dog's kennel when he wanted to escape from life's tiresome demands.

"I'm hungry," he stated rudely, as soon as he was back in his mother's presence. She always caved in when he wanted something.

"First of all, you're going to show us where you took Ginevra and Alessandro that time," stated Giovanni.

"I'm hungry. I need to eat something first," argued Dario, looking to his mother for back-up.

"If you prefer, we can put handcuffs on you, Dario, and frogmarch you down to the river. Then all the kids in town can have a good laugh!"

That was Oriana's contribution. Giovanni winced. His beloved partner had obviously spent too many years in the company of their *commissario,* he was thinking. But the threat had worked.

Dario went as meekly as a lamb for the kilometre-long walk to the dumping site, where Ginevra had been robbed of her precious young life.

What was upsetting Dario more than anything else was the fact that his mother had not uttered a word in his defence – nor even given him his usual on demand *panino.*

He was also wondering how the police had found his hiding place so easily. One of his classmates must have snitched on him.

8: *Commissario Stancato on his best behaviour...*

Was it possible that *Commissario* Beppe Stancato was feeling a little piqued that the L'Aquila team had identified the boy called Dario *and* unearthed the toxic waste site in the space of one day? Entirely without his assistance!

He dismissed the notion as absurd. He had spoken to Inspector Fabrizio De Sanctis much later in the day:

"Please pass on my warmest congratulations to your team. They have worked wonders in the space of one day."

He had been highly amused at the account of Officer Valentina Ianni taming the Bloodhound – or whatever make of dog it had been. The ability to distinguish one breed of dog from another was not one of Beppe's strong points. As far as he was concerned, the only difference between a Chihuahua and a Great Dane was their size.

Beppe had spent Wednesday morning interviewing the new recruits in the company of Mariastella Martellini. Or rather, he had had the impression that *she* had interviewed the recruits in *his* company. He had, at times, felt redundant, despite assurances from his *capo* that his presence and his contributions were invaluable.

Admittedly, his first contact with the three *novellini*[50] had been gratifying. The two young ladies had shaken his hand warmly and told him how they had followed his career in Pescara and beyond with fascination since his arrival three or so years ago. They repeated what Mariastella had already told him: that it was he who had inspired them to train as police officers. Beppe was very good at remembering names. He had memorised their names and

---

[50] Un novellino – a newcomer to a job

photos well before they had presented themselves at the *Questura.*

"Thank you, Cristina and Emma," he said addressing the correct face as he spoke.

Cristina Cardinale and Emma Campione gave the impression that there existed a long-standing friendship between the two of them. Beppe wondered how they would react if the *Questore* ever decided to send one of them to another police station.

"I may not have followed your career so ardently, *commissario.* But I am sure I shall learn a lot from you."

It was the young male recruit, Claudio Montano, who had spoken, without waiting to be addressed by the *commissario.*

Beppe smiled at him. He looked intelligent - *in gamba.*[51]

"I hope for your sake you will avoid copying any of my many defects, *Agente* Montano," added Beppe, shaking the young man by the hand.

The new male recruit looked as if he had some witty reply on the tip of his tongue – but decided that he should keep it to himself. Beppe had liked the look of this lad from the outset.

Mariastella and Beppe had an informal chat with the three new arrivals together. They were then interviewed one at a time. Mariastella gave them a thorough grilling – "just to see how they react under pressure," she had explained.

Beppe was impressed by the procedure. She entirely avoided asking them clichéd questions. She asked each

---

[51] In gamba – (lit. 'in leg') meaning 'with it', alert etc

recruit one particular question which she claimed she had invented especially for such an occasion.

"And how do you imagine you will fill your time when not on duty?" she asked each one in turn. She had assigned Danilo Simone and Gino Martelli the task of looking after the two recruits not being interviewed, with the aim of ensuring they could not compare notes or pre-empt any of the questions.

Claudio Montano gave the smartest answer.

"Free time, *Signora Questore?* Will there be any?"

When no reaction was forthcoming, he smiled and said he would probably be out playing football with his team.

"It's a question which always takes young would-be officers by surprise, Beppe," the *Questore* explained. "It reveals a great deal about their preconceived notions of what they imagine police work is like."

Beppe was 'invited' to ask the recruits questions whenever he wished.

"How would you deal with a situation where you are interviewing a child who is reluctant to talk freely with the parents present?" Beppe asked Cristina Cardinale. He had not really thought up any questions beforehand. His old friend, Dante di Pasquale had always conducted these interviews with Beppe acting as a silent partner and attentive observer.

Cristina Cardinale looked taken aback by the question but rose to the occasion.

"Out of context, that's a somewhat hypothetical question, *commissario*. It would depend on the child's age, for example. As a last resort, I might give the child a large glass of water and wait for him or her to want to go to the bathroom. That way I could get the child on its own!"

The girl had certainly showed spirit with her slightly risqué reply.

Cristina was relieved to note that the *Questore* had smiled at her impromptu solution.

Beppe considered it would be advisable to think up a different question for the next interviewee.

Three slightly dazed recruits all met in the *Questore's* office together at the end of the morning. Each one would be assigned to an experienced officer for two weeks. "You'll be shadowing them whatever they do and wherever they go," explained Mariastella.

She told them she had decided on a flexible approach during their first few months.

"I'm assigning you, *Agente* Montano to the police station in L'Aquila. But I intend to move the three of you about from time to time. I trust that will not be a problem?"

The two young women looked a bit crestfallen, but Claudio Montana took it in his stride.

"Officer Rapino will take you to get your uniforms now, *ragazzi*," explained Mariastella. "We shall meet up here tomorrow at eight o'clock. Your careers as police officers have begun. *In bocca al lupo!*"

Before taking leave of each other, Beppe reminded his chief that his wife, Sonia, would be accompanying him to Via Pesaro the following day.

"I hadn't forgotten, *commissario*. I'm looking forward to meeting your other half," she added. "By the way, what do you think about our new recruits?"

Beppe detected a note of anxiety in her voice. She was unashamedly showing just a hint of vulnerability.

Beppe's heart very secretly went out to her. It was the first time in her career, no doubt, that she had been solely responsible for recruiting new personnel.

"They'll fit in just fine, Mariastella. I liked their youthful enthusiasm – it was very refreshing. And they acquitted themselves very well during their individual 'grilling'. We'll all look after them and help them through those first crucial weeks..."

Beppe had been sincere but cautious in his choice of words. He still had an instinctive feeling that he and she might clash in the not too distant future. He did not feel that mutual trust had been fully established between the two of them. With his recent departures from strict adherence to the rules of the game, he could hardly blame her.

* * *

Sonia carried out her threat of bringing Lorenzo and Veronica with them the following morning, despite the necessity involved in carting a trunk-load of the accessories required for two young children's needs with them. For the children at least, it promised to be a day to remember.

Beppe and Sonia marched into the *Questura* arm-in-arm, Beppe holding Lorenzo in the crook of his spare arm and Sonia holding Veronica's hand as she toddled into the police head-quarters on her own two feet. The whole team – including the three uniformed newcomers – had greeted their arrival with an outburst of spontaneous applause. They had all assembled by the reception desk.

Sonia was treated like a celebrity - even the usually dour *Agente* Lina Rapino had a broad smile on her face. Mariastella Martellini appeared from upstairs at some invisible signal. Maybe she had heard their noisy arrival from upstairs – or she had arranged for Officer Rapino to send her a surreptitious text message as soon as the family arrived.

The *Questore* was not wearing her uniform, for only the second time since her arrival, Beppe noted with interest. She mingled in with the other officers, looking completely at her ease. She introduced herself to Sonia after the briefest nod of approval in Beppe's direction.

"Congratulations on your choice of partner," she appeared to be intimating.

"Please come up and see me whenever you feel like it, Sonia," she invited.

"With or without the children, *Signora Questore?*" asked Sonia.

"With!" replied Mariastella, as if surprised that the question had even been asked.

Beppe grudgingly admired her reaction to Sonia's curt question. He had the uncomfortable premonition that the two of them would hit it off. Another one of his defences laid bare!

***

Sonia and children were ensconced on a large sofa. Mariastella had drawn up an armchair facing the little group. Lorenzo was mercifully asleep again, whilst Veronica was more interested in exploring her new surroundings with her recently acquired ability to set one foot in front of the other. Mariastella had held Veronica's hand and walked her over to the window, from which she could see the River Pescara flowing out to the nearby Adriatic.

"Well, Sonia, how does it feel to be back in your old surroundings once again?" asked the *Questore* once Veronica's wanderlust had been temporarily sated.

"I was happy working here for all those years, Mariastella." Sonia had been instantly forbidden to address her by her title. "I loved the routine of policework and contact with the public. But life in Via Pesaro became immediately more interesting – and unpredictable – as soon as Beppe arrived from Calabria – by boat! Did you know that, Mariastella?"

The *Questore* shook her head.

"Yes, he has the knack of not allowing one to relax for too long," agreed Mariastella with a wry smile. "That much I have already discovered."

The two women had quickly overcome the initial reserve of meeting for the first time. Out of sheer habit, Sonia could not escape the feeling of deference owed to a person of the *Questore's* rank. But Mariastella rapidly disabused her of any notion that she set store by matters of status.

At Maristella's instigation, Sonia filled her in on some of Beppe's more notable exploits. In particular, the *Questore* had been fascinated by Sonia's account of his rescue of the vanishing physicist – and the part played by the Archbishop of Pescara in their lives.

"You should make the acquaintance of Don Emanuele as soon as you can, Mariastella. Beppe considers him to be the most remarkable man he has ever met."

"I will certainly make a point of it – as soon as I get the chance, Sonia. Even though I am a firmly believing atheist."

"What? As well as being a lesbian – as you claimed to my husband?" asked Sonia without restraint.

Mariastella laughed out loud at this.

"I'm not really quite sure why I said that, Sonia. Just to see what his reaction would be, I guess."

"I don't think my husband believed you, Mariastella."

Mariastella smiled, quite unembarrassed.

"I am sure that being a lesbian and an atheist are not mutually exclusive – where applicable," Sonia added.

"Well, I never told Beppe that I didn't believe in God," stated Mariastella, choosing deliberately to misinterpret what Sonia had said. "That *would* have been a step too far!"

They both broke out into gales of laughter at the unlikely direction their conversation had taken.

Beppe, who had been instructed to come and rescue Sonia after a couple of hours, was outside the door, his fist poised ready to knock politely.

He noted the unbridled mirth from the other side of the door. His worst fears had been realised, he thought ironically.

* * *

Friday morning. Beppe set off again to Pescara, sad to be leaving his little family behind. Their company had been reassuring.

"Be patient with Mariastella, *amore*," was Sonia's parting comment. "She's really quite vulnerable beneath her official skin. I sensed it, yesterday. Don't be too hard on her!"

Beppe had no desire to be hard on his new boss. She was not a conventional character at all – in fact he quite liked her, he admitted grudgingly to himself. But it was not her as a person that troubled him. It was her rank. She was the one who, if she so wished, could keep him at the *Questura* whilst other officers would be responsible for finding Ginevra's killer. Her cruel death had affected him deeply. He dreaded the thought of not being free to pursue the scum of humanity who were indirectly – no, directly - responsible for this cynical outrage. He desperately wanted to be in Pazzoli.

Sonia had understood exactly how he was feeling. "She always does," thought Beppe fondly.

But, how to manoeuvre the course of events in his favour was a challenge.

In the car heading to Pescara, Beppe did what he always did on these occasions. He appealed to his own invisible deity. He had long ago rejected any conventional notion of a fatherly God looking down from heaven. If there was anything out there at all, it was a spirit, a force so powerful as to be totally incomprehensible; an omnipresent being who pervaded the unthinkable depths of a mysterious universe where every living creature accidently found itself. Just occasionally, Beppe thought he had detected the invisible presence of something ethereal which, at a whim, would listen to him and possibly intervene on his behalf. There had been too many of these silent interventions in his life to allow him to deny their admittedly illogical existence.

"Just provide me with some irrefutable excuse which even Mariastella will not be able to argue with," he said out loud as he arrived at the police headquarters.

The day was filled meaningfully enough. The new recruits had had their first taste of the routine life of police officers – following up reports of domestic violence, petty thieving from supermarkets, frantic calls from people living in apartments whose peace and quiet was being shattered by deaf neighbours with TV sets turned up to maximum level. It had been agreed that Claudio Montano would be transferred to L'Aquila the following Monday. Beppe had offered to take him in person – seeing this as a possible excuse to escape from captivity. But it was the new recruit who had politely declined the offer, explaining that he lived in Penne and had his own car.

Late in the afternoon, Beppe was contacted by his colleague in L'Aquila, Fabrizio de Sanctis.

"What news, *ispettore?*" Beppe asked.

"Two things, *commissario*. First of all, you asked me when Ginevra's funeral would take place – well, it's been arranged for this coming Tuesday morning. Everyone is likely to be there – including all of the school children. The headmistress is closing the school for the day. It's become an emotionally charged event, as you can imagine. The whole town has gone into mourning. I know you wanted to be informed, *commissario*..."

"I shall find a way to be there, Fabrizio," Beppe said, with a confidence he was not feeling. "And the second thing?"

"Ah, well that is something completely different – and very relevant to the case we are dealing with..."

"Yes?" snapped the *commissario*. "*Dimmi tutto, Fabrizio.*"[52]

Fabrizio had enjoyed keeping his colleague and friend in suspense for a few precious seconds – to increase the significance of what he was about to impart.

---

[52] Dimmi tutto = Tell me all!

"I've just had a phone call from our amazingly smart lady mayor in Pazzoli – Eugenia Mancini, she's called, for your future reference."

He paused simply to draw his breath. But Beppe's impatience could not wait that long.

"Ispettore!" he said with a note of threat in his voice.

"She phoned me to say that she has had a report from one of the remoter farmsteads out in the hills. A few nights ago, the couple who live there heard disturbing noises coming from their neighbours' farm. Apparently, this Eugenia Mancini had had the bright idea of getting the school kids to act as informers, if they witnessed any unusual activity in the countryside. To save my officers from trudging round the hundred or so small-holdings, you understand..."

"What kind of noises, Inspector?" interrupted the *commissario*.

"Some vehicles driving up to the farm at three in morning, the sound of a mechanical digger at work, then they claim they heard the terrified scream of an animal as if it was being..."

"Bravo, Fabrizio! I knew it! You and your team have done brilliantly."

"What about my new recruit?" asked Fabrizio De Sanctis.

"Oh, you'll like him! He's a bright lad, *in gamba*. He'll be arriving on Monday morning."

"That's good – because everything seems to be happening at once out here in L'Aquila. I've sent Officers Palena, Salvati and Ianni to go and visit the farm where the noises were heard. I'm keeping Simona Gambino with me – because something odd has come to our attention."

"You seem quite determined to keep me in suspense today, *ispettore*," Beppe chided his colleague, after another significant pause.

"Well, it's so outlandish. I'm not even sure if it comes under our remit, Beppe. But to satisfy your curiosity," continued the inspector hurriedly, "we've been asked to investigate a rumour that a valuable painting stolen from a gallery in Venice has turned up in a house in Monticchio. You'll remember the house because it's the one just opposite Remo's *agriturismo* which we used to spy on Don Alfieri just before we rescued the Sleeping Beauty…"

"Best of luck with that! Be careful how you proceed - it sounds as if it might be a mafia job. They've taken to stealing works of art to give away in return for favours carried out – or so I've been told. That way, they avoid handing out traceable cash. You should be wary how you go about investigating that."

"I've never heard of *that* before. Thanks for the warning, Beppe … *commissario*," he corrected himself.

"And I have to thank *you*, Fabrizio – for everything you're doing. You'll deserve your promotion by the time you've finished," Beppe added.

"Maybe, *commissario*. But I am sure we are going to need you with us very soon. Is there any chance you'll be able to…?

"Escape from the lady *Questore's* grip, you mean?"

"Well, I cannot imagine that she would stop you…"

"I'm working on it, Fabrizio," said the *commissario*. He apologised to his colleague. "It's a touchy issue, Fabrizio. She's already queried whether it is truly essential that I attend Ginevra's funeral."

"*Ho capito, commissario.*"[53]

* * *

Beppe was back home with Sonia and his children. It was nine o'clock in the evening. Lorenzo and Veronica were fast asleep.

Beppe had related everything that had happened that day to Sonia. She understood without words what Beppe was feeling. He still had no idea at all how he would bring about his full involvement in this investigation. Mariastella was not the kind of person who you could manipulate easily. His attempts at appealing to his invisible spirits had not born any fruit.

Sonia did not want to say anything trite, but her soulmate needed some solace.

"Be patient, Beppe. Something will happen. It always does with you."

They were actually in bed, half toying with the desire to make love, when Beppe's mobile phone interrupted the first tentative kiss.

Beppe's feeling of mild frustration was transformed instantly into wakefulness at the first words of his caller.

"I'm sorry to disturb you at a moment like this, Beppe," said the gentle voice of Don Emanuele, the Archbishop of Pescara.

How does he always KNOW?" thought Beppe.

"It's just that I need a favour, you see. I've been asked by the mayoress of some obscure town called Pazzoli to conduct the funeral of a little girl called Ginevra. I have no idea how to get there and I hate driving. I'm sure you must be involved in this tragic death somehow..."

---

[53] Ho capito – I understand (Lit: I have understood)

"I'll take you there myself, Don Emanuele."

"*Grazie mille,* Beppe. I was hoping you would say that."

"Just one problem, however," said Beppe. He told the Archbishop what the problem was.

"Just you leave that side of things to me, *commissario!*"

Sonia was giggling under the sheets.

"I told you so," she whispered, happy for him – even if she knew it was bound to signal her husband's absence from the family home for the next few hours – or even days. Something that she secretly dreaded.

9:   Unlooked-for interventions...

Officers Palena, Ianni and Salvati were walking towards the open door of the remote farmhouse with a certain degree of trepidation. This visit could prove to be the first positive step in an investigation that would take them one step nearer the sinister world of organised crime. The importance of what they were doing was daunting – especially for *Agente* Giovanni Palena, who was nominally in charge of operations.

They could see the startled face of a woman whom they assumed must be the farmer's wife peering at them through the worn, yellow-stained net curtain covering the lower half of the kitchen window. At her own suggestion, they had left Eugenia Mancini at the farm further down the road with the couple who had reported the sinister nocturnal goings-on. It had been their nine-year-old daughter, Gaia, who had urged them to contact the mayoress.

"We were told by this *simpatica*[54] police officer called Simona to tell the mayoress about *anything* strange we've noticed out here," Gaia had insisted.

Reluctantly, they had taken the rash step suggested by their daughter. It went against all their deep-rooted instincts to poke their noses into what went on in other people's homes. It inevitably led to trouble. However, their daughter's tearful appeal had worked simply because she was so visibly upset by the loss of her school mate.

"You did the right thing," Eugenia Mancini was reassuring them.

---

[54] Simpatica = nice : kind (f)

"They've always struck us as being like outlaws," the farmer's wife added. Her husband had frowned severely in her direction. It was bad enough to grass up one's neighbours to the police, but to pass judgement on them as well was a step too far.

At the neighbouring farm, the face behind the net curtain vanished and the whole person reappeared framed in the main doorway a few seconds later. The woman was wiping her hands on a filthy apron, whose two strings barely made it round her ample waist. She smiled at the police officers nervously. Her hand was automatically reaching up towards the bell pull - obviously to summon her husband from somewhere beyond their line of vision.

Oriana shook her head imperceptibly at Giovanni. He cottoned on immediately to what she was thinking.

His hand shot up in one reflex action and held the tongue of the bell to prevent it ringing.

"We would like a word with you alone first, if you don't mind, *Signora...?*"

"Maria Pia...Farina." She whispered her name – and her surname as a kind of afterthought. Officer Valentina Ianni suppressed a giggle.[55] The state of the woman's apron showed signs of almost every culinary ingredient possible in its unwashed state.

"May we come inside, Maria Pia?" requested Officer Palena, since the woman appeared to have become frozen into a state of indecision. "We can send for your husband in a minute," he added reassuringly. The farmer's wife simply turned round and walked back into the kitchen. The three officers looked at each other and followed her without being

---

[55] She suppressed a giggle – Farina means 'flour' in Italian.

invited in. The pungent smell of mutton stew intensified as they entered the kitchen. Maria Pia sat down heavily on one of the chairs round the spacious wooden table. The three officers remained standing, looking at the farmer's wife with varying degrees of expectation.

"*Signora* Farina – Maria Pia," began Giovanni Palena kindly, when it became apparent that the lady was not going to be forthcoming. "We are going round all the farms in the countryside surrounding Pazzoli asking if there have been any unusual events over the last few days. You know, unexplained night time visits or disturbances of any kind…"

The expression on Maria Pia's face was telling. *Agente* Ianni exchanged a meaningful glance with her colleague, Oriana. Officer Giovanni Palena continued to look at the lady.

She gave the impression of wanting to open up – yet she could not seem to muster the powers of speech. Oriana was the one to break the verbal deadlock.

"You're scared of what your husband will do if you tell us, aren't you, Maria Pia?"

Maria Pia nodded. Giovanni Palena looked gratefully at his partner. Yet he feared he would get nowhere without the husband being present. But he did not want to give up so easily. He sat down on one of the chairs near Maria Pia and patted her reassuringly on her shoulder.

"Don't worry, *Signora* Maria Pia. Your next-door neighbours gave us some idea as to what happened the other night. They were woken up by the noises, you understand…"

Oriana Salvati was looking nauseated by the odour of fatty mutton emanating from the cooking pot. She signalled to Valentina that she was going to go outside for some fresh air.

Valentina nodded in understanding – there was no point, she thought, in both Oriana *and* her unborn child being subjected to the overpowering intensity of Maria Pia's meat stew. Valentina sat down at the table opposite her colleague.

"Did those men who turned up kill one of your sheep, Maria Pia?" Valentina asked.

Giovanni Palena was looking aghast at the newfound boldness of his hitherto compliant colleague. It must be born of the realisation she was about to step into Oriana's shoes, reckoned Giovanni. He dutifully frowned at Valentina for the rashness of her outburst.

But tears had appeared in Maria Pia's eyes at Valentina's words. The shock to her system that these young officers seemed to know already about the arrival of 'those crooks from Naples' loosened her tongue. She began tentatively to talk about that horrific night.

Outside, Oriana was walking beyond the confines of the farmhouse. As she climbed up a gentle slope towards the open countryside, her attention was caught by a piece of machinery which looked brand new – the only thing she had seen on the farm which did not show signs of old age. The vehicle parked outside the farmhouse was an ancient FIAT diesel truck loaded with empty milk churns. The mini-digger which she had spotted struck her as being out of place. The grass underfoot gave way suddenly to an area of bare soil which looked as if it had been recently dug up.

She paused only long enough to reflect that her impulsive desire to set the digger in motion was simply because she wanted to see some result in this investigation before the child inside her body brought her life as a police woman to a temporary halt.

The sound of an engine being started up and the unmistakable sound of the scoop on the digger sinking into the earth brought Arturo Annunzio at a run out of his milking shed.

"*Che cazzo...?*" he muttered.

His alarm turned to fury when he saw 'his' mini-digger being manned by a young woman dressed in a police uniform.

He flung open the door of the mini excavator and made as if to grab Oriana's arm. Instead he met the flat of a shoe under his chin and fell backwards on to the earth.

Oriana switched off the engine, jumped nimbly to the ground and stood over the supine form of the farmer with arms akimbo.

"My apologies, *Signor Annunzio*. But I just saved you from assaulting a police officer. That's one less charge you'll be faced with," stated Oriana, going straight into attack mode.

She was all too aware she might have acted impetuously, but was not going to let that stand in her way.

Arturo Annunzio was hauling himself to his feet with some difficulty but refused this chit of a girl's proffered hand. A second such humiliation would be too much of a blow to his pride. He resorted to verbal aggression instead.

"What the hell do you think you're doing driving *my* mechanical digger?" he began.

"What the hell do you think *you're* doing digging holes in our countryside?" retorted Oriana equally aggressively.

"I have to dig a new well shaft," replied Arturo Annunzio. He had prepared this excuse as soon as he had been forced to dig the first pit.

"I trust you have the necessary planning permission from the town hall, *signore?*"

He had not thought far enough ahead to have a ready-made answer to that question.

"I'm waiting for permission," he said feebly.

"So..." began Oriana, getting into her stride, "you dug a hole, realised you needed permission for a new well – and promptly put all the earth back into the hole you had already dug. Is that about right, *signore?*"

The farmer merely glowered darkly in her direction.

"*Va' all'inferno!*"[56] he muttered after a pause in their exchange, during which Oriana had furiously outstared her adversary.

"No, let's head for the house, shall we, *signore?* You can meet my colleagues, who are talking to your wife about what happened a few nights ago."

With a look of total panic on his face, the farmer lurched towards the farmhouse. Oriana stayed outside, as much as she would have liked to listen to the exchange which she was sure would take place in the kitchen. She could not face the stomach-churning smell of that stew again – it could be detected even outside the house.

Arturo had burst into the kitchen with the words:

"Don't believe a word that woman has told you! She fantasises about everything. We don't have any problems out here!"

Giovanni Palena remained unruffled by the violent intrusion.

"So, you are obviously aware of the reason for our visit, *Signor Annunzio?*"

---

[56] Va' all'inferno! – Go to hell!

"She had a bad dream and imagined all sorts of things which never happened," replied the farmer belligerently.

"Show some respect for your wife, *signore!* She has a name," *Agente* Ianni interjected.

"I hope you are not going to pretend that nothing happened a couple of nights ago, *Signor Annunzio.* Your neighbours can attest to the disturbance – the noise woke them up."

This comment from Giovanni Palena.

"It was nothing, officers," said Arturo Annunzio. "A couple of drunken youths turned up and started messing around with the digger. I had to go out and chase them away."

"And you are going to pretend they didn't kill one of your sheep, I suppose?" added Valentina Ianni.

"That was a fox – or a wolf, *signori.* That's all that happened…"

Officer Giovanni Palena was aware that insisting would get them nowhere. He signalled to Valentina that they should leave as he stood up to go.

"Do not think for one minute that this is the last you will be hearing from us, *Signor* Annunzio," added Giovanni Palena.

"And don't even think of taking it out on your wife, *Arturo!"* added Officer Ianni for good measure.

On the way to the police car, Giovanni said quietly to his colleague:

"We need the *commissario* with us on our next visit. Arturo Annunzio isn't going to budge from his version of events. He's obviously more scared of *them* than he is of us – whoever they are."

They found Oriana Salvati already sitting in the police car.

"I went back to take one more look, *ragazzi*," she said. "Playing with that digger, I must have begun to uncover some of the waste. There was a bag just beneath the surface with a skull-and-crossbones on it."

Oriana had wanted to take a photo of what she had seen, but an image of a little girl called Ginevra came to mind as she thought of the child in her womb. She had run from the site without once looking back.

Officer Ianni had another disturbing thought passing through *her* mind. Her clothes smelt of that mutton stew. What if the couple's lunch had been made from the remains of the slaughtered sheep? She felt her stomach churn.

"Well, we certainly found out what we wanted to know," said Giovanni. "Thank you both for your magnificent performances!"

He would get his *capo* to contact Beppe Stancato as soon as he got back to L'Aquila. They stopped to pick up Eugenia Mancini from the neighbours' farmhouse and left her outside the little town hall in Pazzoli.

"Mission accomplished – more or less. Thank you, Eugenia, for all your help."

The mayoress had gleaned very little about what had transpired during their visit to the other farm. The police were being reticent, she thought. That means they discovered something important.

"Ah well! *Che sarà sarà!*"[57] she informed herself. "You'll find out sooner or later, Eugenia."

---

[57] Che sarà sarà – What will be, will be. (A lovely phrase from the cradle of European civilisation!)

* * *

A knowing smile played across the lady *Questore's* face. She detected a whiff of conspiracy in the air.

It seemed more than mere coincidence, she decided, that she should have a conversation with Sonia Leardi about this supposedly illustrious clergyman on Thursday and, lo and behold, she receives a phone call one day later from the Archbishop in person, requesting an appointment with her the coming Monday – 'at a time to suit you, *Signora Questore'*.

She could hardly accuse a man of God of conspiracy – whether she believed in a deity or not – without running the risk of embarrassing herself if the request turned out to be benign. Besides which, Mariastella admitted, he did have a very soothing voice. She suggested 10 o'clock in the morning. It would be easier to determine face to face whether her *commissario,* or even Sonia herself, had had a hand in arranging this encounter. But why would *either* of them attach so much importance to setting up a meeting between two such diverse officials? An archbishop and an atheist *Questore* make very unlikely bedfellows. She would just have to wait and see what this Don Emanuele had to say.

A second telephone call a few minutes later from *Ispettore* Fabrizio De Sanctis put thoughts of scheming archbishops out of her mind.

Mariastella listened without interruption to every word concerning the L'Aquila inspector's report on his officers' visit to the farmstead outside the town of Pazzoli.

"That is a great step forward in this investigation, *ispettore. Congratulazioni!* Have you told Beppe about this yet?" she asked, seemingly in all innocence.

"No, *Signora Questore*. I thought it right to tell you directly."

"Your diplomacy is much appreciated, Fabrizio. And for heaven's sake, call me Mariastella – it should not detract from your respect for my position of authority."

There was no reply from the inspector. She had obviously faced him with a dilemma in police etiquette.

"Just think of the name Mariastella as being part of my title – if that helps.

She was gratified to hear Fabrizio De Sanctis laughing on the other end of the line.

"Very well. I'll remember that in the future," he concluded. The inspector took a deep breath and asked with some trepidation:

"My officer, Giovanni Palena, has requested the presence of the *commissario* on their next visit to the Annunzio farm. Beppe's skills may be required to loosen the farmer's tongue. So far, he is in a state of denial that he is helping the mafia dispose of toxic waste. Beppe has the knack of..."

"Well, *ispettore*, I was just thinking how admirably you and your team are dealing with the situation without our famous *commissario's* intervention. But of course, I shall consider your request without prejudice. By the way," she added hurriedly to bring the discussion about Beppe's presence in Pazzoli to a close, "the forensic team is arriving in Pazzoli on Monday to clear up the toxic waste by the river. I wonder if your team can be there to lead them to the river bank where the first lot has been dumped."

"Of course, we will. It will be a pleasure."

"I would suggest you might also like to direct them to the Annunzio farm so they can deal with the waste dumped there – to save a double visit," said the *Questore*.

Mariastella Martellini was greeted by an embarrassed silence.

"May I tactfully suggest you talk to Beppe about the waste on the farmland, *Signora Questore?* The *commissario* may have a different angle on that aspect of the investigation," said Fabrizio De Sanctis after a significant pause.

"Your sense of diplomacy is noted, *ispettore*," replied Mariastella and brought the call to an abrupt end by hanging up.

It was time for a face-to-face encounter with *Commissario* Beppe Stancato, she considered.

* * *

The *commissario* in question, had just received a phone call from Inspector Fabrizio De Sanctis.

"I've just been speaking to the *Questore,* Beppe. I think you should know that..."

After Beppe had been filled in on all the details, and lavished praise on the effectiveness and imagination displayed by the inspector's team of officers, he looked at his watch and decided it was time to make a tactical withdrawal. At the reception desk, he told Officer Danilo Simone that his son, Lorenzo, was having teething problems. He would be heading home a few minutes early – should anyone ask for him.

A terse text message from Maristella, minutes after he had left the *Questura,* informed him that they needed to meet urgently at 8 am on Monday morning – just before the Archbishop was due to come and see her, the message stated.

Beppe had been right. The first conflict of interest between him and his boss was imminent. The honey-moon period – such as it had been – was over.

10: A dilemma for the new Questore?

On arriving home, Beppe hugged Sonia and held her close to him for longer than usual. He had been unsurprised to discover that Lorenzo really was suffering the pains of teeth forcing their way through his tender gums. But it was, he realised, the first time he had made his own children the excuse for escaping early from the *Questura.* His former boss, Dante Di Pasquale, had practically begged him to go home to be with his daughter whenever she had been unwell.

"Difficult day at the office, *amore?*" asked a solicitous Sonia.

"Not for me, it has to be said," Beppe told her. He related the day's events in great detail.

"Please don't worry about Mariastella, Beppe. I'm sure she will see things your way when you explain what is at stake. And you have certainly behaved completely correctly towards her – throughout your brief acquaintance! So, stop being anxious. Have faith in Don Emanuele."

Sonia always managed to restore his optimism. He kissed her warmly – and they lived their collective domestic life in peace for two whole days.

* * *

By Monday morning, Beppe felt almost serene when he announced his presence at eight o'clock. Mariastella's door was open so he went in with only a discreet knock on the door to announce his arrival. Mariastella was looking out over the river Pescara and had her back to the door.

She sat down behind her desk and looked intensely at Beppe. She was not smiling.

"Is there a problem, Mariastella?" he asked in all innocence.

"I'm not sure whether I have your trust, *commissario*."

"So far you do, Mariastella. It's early days yet."

"Very well. I'm not entirely sure whether I trust you."

"I can understand that from your point of view. I have the reputation of being a bit of a maverick. But might I know more precisely what is troubling you? I may well be able to set your misgivings to rest."

So far, the dialogue was going according to plan – a well-rehearsed scenario worked out in great detail with Sonia over the weekend.

"Your Sonia recommended I should make the acquaintance with the Archbishop of Pescara. Only one day later, I get a call from this...Don Emanuele, wanting to come and see me at ten o'clock today. It feels just a bit too much of a coincidence, *commissario*. Did you know about this beforehand?"

"Yes, he phoned me last week with a request. I told him he should get in touch with you."

"Does this have anything to do with your desire to go to Pazzoli, Beppe?"

"I would rather he explained the reason for his call *di persona*, Mariastella."

Beppe, under instructions from Sonia, was sticking religiously to calling his boss by her first name. She was obviously fluctuating between his official title and his first name. A sign of her fragility, maybe? Once again, he had to resist the urge to be sympathetic.

"Were you contacted by *Ispettore De Sanctis* last week?" asked the *Questore*.

"Yes, I was. He called me just after he had spoken to you. Why do you ask, Mariastella?"

"He seemed to defer to you as soon as I suggested we should send the clear-up team to the Annunzio farm to remove the toxic waste from his land, as well as the site near the river."

"Ah, now I understand what you are driving at, Mariastella. You sense we might be conspiring behind your back."

The *Questore* allowed herself a smile – and a slight shrug of her shoulders by way of acknowledgement.

"When you meet the Archbishop, you will discover that his interventions border on the uncanny. But I can assure you that his visit today is purely coincidental. As to the toxic waste on the Annunzio property, I have to say that I suspect there will be far too much to clear away in one visit to Pazzoli. Besides which, if the waste is removed and the police intervene, Arturo Annunzio will simply wash his hands of the affair. We shall lose the only lead we have to link Ginevra's death to whoever dumped that poison. We shall need to trace this foul deed back to the real culprits. They are almost certainly members of a Camorra clan. And I suspect I already know which clan is involved. But I need proof. I am sure Fabrizio De Sanctis had this in mind when he spoke to you last week."

"Thank you, Beppe," said Mariastella quietly, as she stood up to indicate the 'interview' was at an end. "What a pity I didn't manage to catch you on Friday afternoon before you shot off home…"

It was Beppe's turn to smile.

"*Touché, Signora Questore!*"[58]

"I would like you to come up and see me when Don Emanuele has gone. I just hope he won't try to convert me!"

"He won't, Mariastella. Have no fear of that!" said Beppe. "But, prepare to be taken by surprise," said Beppe as he took his leave with his integrity intact.

* * *

Beppe looked at his watch – still a long time before the Archbishop was due to appear. Beppe told his friend, *Agente* Pippo Cafarelli, on duty at the reception desk, to call him as soon as Don Emanuele arrived.

The imposing form of Officer Luigi Rocco emerged from behind the desk area flanked by the two new recruits. They appeared dwarfed by Luigi's stature.

The two ladies smiled on seeing their 'hero'.

"Where are you three off to?" asked Beppe. It was apparent that Luigi Rocco had been assigned the task of looking after Officers Cardinale and Campione for the day.

"We are off to our old *scuola media, commissario,*[59]" said Cristina Cardinale. "One of the teachers has had her car vandalised."

"It was always a bit of a rough school," added Emma Campione.

"What – even after you two had left?" teased Beppe.

This produced girly giggles of pleasure and a smile from Luigi Rocco – who looked secretly self-satisfied about being in charge of the newly appointed 'girls'.

---

[58] Touché – Italians use the same French expression as we do.
[59] Scuola media – Middle school

"*In bocca al lupo!*" Beppe wished them. "School kids are always a challenge."

Beppe did the rounds of all the other officers who were not out in the town. The Archbishop arrived at five minutes to ten.

"The *Questore* is expecting you, Don Emanuele. She has guessed you might have an ulterior motive for your visit. She is quite worried that you might try and convert her," warned Beppe.

Both the Archbishop and Pippo Cafarelli let out a peel of laughter.

"Just you leave your new boss to me, Beppe!" said Don Emanuele. "I shall make her feel spiritually at ease. The rest I shall leave to the Holy Spirit!"

It was almost 11.30 by the time Don Emanuele emerged from the *Questore's* office. His expression gave little away. Beppe looked anxiously at him.

"Will you pick me up from the presbytery tomorrow morning, Beppe – or shall I meet you here?" was all the Archbishop said.

Beppe headed upstairs as pre-arranged with Mariastella. How had Don Emanuele achieved this impossible outcome?

His conversation with Mariastella did not enlighten him to any degree.

"At one point of our conversation, Beppe, I told Don Emanuele that I did not believe in a God that looked down benignly on every single living creature on Earth, bestowing his favours on whoever he felt well-disposed towards. God is a myth created for the weak-minded, I suggested. And can you guess what his reply was?"

Beppe merely shook his head.

"He told me it was very sensible of me not to believe in a God who was so totally unbelievable in the first place."

Beppe laughed.

"That sounds just like the sort of thing he is famous for saying, Mariastella."

He is a remarkable man, Beppe. That much I *will* concede!"

* * *

The moment had come, on Tuesday morning, when Beppe, Sonia, Veronica and Lorenzo had to separate. Sonia was putting a brave face on for Beppe's benefit. His three month 'punishment' period under the previous *Questore's* jurisdiction had brought them all closer together. Now, it was much harder to endure the idea that he would not be returning home the same evening.

"I'm not sure how long I shall be away, *amore*," said Beppe. "I didn't like to ask Mariastella how long she was prepared to let me be absent from Via Pesaro. And Don Emanuele...well, I haven't had a chance to speak to him yet."

"Just keep in touch - at least twice a day, Beppe," pleaded Sonia. "And *don't* try to be a lone hero again!"

"I promise, *amore*. I shall make sure at least one of our officers is with me at all times."

It was plain to see that Veronica was old enough to be aware there was something different about her father's leave-taking. She bestowed a wet kiss on his face and looked as if she was about to cry.

"*Senti, amore,*[60] if you're away for more than five days, we'll come up and stay near you," promised Sonia.

Finally, Beppe managed to get into his car and drive back to Pescara. He had promised to pick up Don Emanuele from outside the Cathedral in Pescara.

* * *

"So, how did you succeed in persuading our new *Questore* to let me go?" was the first question Beppe asked as they set off on the road to Pazzoli.

"I didn't really have to say anything, Beppe. She accepted the idea that your presence was needed at Ginevra's funeral without any qualms. I think she was bowing to the inevitable. Underneath, I have the impression she knows that she will have to give you some freedom to choose your own path over the coming years."

"But for how many days, Don Emanuele? Shan't I be driving you back to Pescara this evening?"

Don Emanuel chuckled. Beppe realised that, yet again, his unusual companion had thought through the whole situation beforehand. He had an uncanny ability to understand what was going on in the minds of other people.

"I assured your *Questore* that you would drive me back to Pescara as soon as I had attended to the spiritual needs of my flock in Pazzoli. I imagine that might take me a bit longer than one day, Beppe."

Beppe smiled. Sonia had been right. He should have trusted Don Emanuele.

"Besides, I need a break from my episcopal routine. Religion can be quite a bore, you know."

"So can police work, Don Emanuele."

---

[60] Senti... Listen...

The journey went smoothly, seamlessly – until Beppe asked the Archbishop a question:

"So, what do you think of our Mariastella Martellini, Don Emanuele? I think she is quite a difficult person to read, don't you?"

Don Emanuel's reply was so unexpected that Beppe had to concentrate furiously on the winding road ahead.

"No, I think she is like an open book – not the Bible, I am glad to say. I have known so many people who claim to be atheists, Beppe – and they all have one thing in common. A deep desire for something – or someone - to turn up and persuade them they are mistaken. Beware of those who pay lip-service to their belief in God and never have the courage to admit to themselves that we humans might just be fragile nobodies hurtling round the sun on a path to nothingness."

"And Mariastella Martellini?" asked Beppe, after he had recovered from the emotional jolt of the Archbishop's apocalyptic utterance. He was curious to know how the Archbishop's words applied to her.

"She is a sensitive person who *is* frightened by her own fragility. And I would predict that you will see her inside a church in no time at all, Beppe."

"I remain to be convinced about *that*, Don Emanuele," Beppe laughed. The remainder of the journey to Pazzoli was accomplished in a comfortable, composed silence.

Beppe let out an involuntary sigh, which evinced a smile and a knowing nod from his companion. Beppe felt at peace for the first time in days. He was heading in the right direction at last.

11:   A farewell to Ginevra…

It's as if someone has wrenched your heart out with their bare hands…

Don Emanuele was standing on the steps leading up to the altar. As usual, he had refused to use the pulpit, on the grounds that anything Jesus Christ had ever uttered had been done at ground level. He was addressing a church which provided standing-room only for the majority of the townsfolk of Pazzoli. The children with their teachers and Eugenia Mancini had been seated at the front of the nave, sharing their places with Ginevra's parents and her brother, Alessandro.

Adele Giuliani, Ginevra's mother, was nodding silently, tearfully, at the Archbishop's words. Yes, it was just like that, she thought.

The church had been filled to bursting point. Flowers of every colour filled the air with their sweet scent. The local florist had refused to accept any money from the parents or the *comune*, Beppe had been told by his colleagues from L'Aquila before the mass had started. The floral display must have represented a whole month's income for the florist, reckoned Beppe from the back row of chairs – which he was sharing with the police officers from L'Aquila. The majority of the congregation was standing in any available space. An even larger number of the townsfolk were gathered in the little *piazza* outside the church, straining to hear Don Emanuele's words. One woman, her head shrouded by a dark veil, stood out from the crowd. She stood head and shoulders above most of the others. She had edged forward imperceptibly so as to be as near as possible to the wide-open doors of the church.

The elderly parish priest was sitting just behind the Archbishop, wondering nostalgically what it would feel like if his congregation ever reached such multitudinous numbers at a normal Sunday mass. He had never met his Archbishop before. He had been held spellbound by his words from the outset.

What should you all be feeling at the moment? Grief, sadness, anger even? Cling on to what you are feeling, because it is right that you should have these feelings. But remember, all of you, that your emotions are dwarfed into insignificance by what Ginevra's mum and dad – and her brother – are feeling at this very minute.

Diego, Adele and Sandro, there are no words that I can say to compensate you for your loss. May time and the Holy Spirit heal your suffering over the years to come.

But I say to you now...

Don Emanuele had stepped towards the minute oak coffin and laid his hand on the wood.

...the earthly remains of this wonderful little human being are NOT the thing you must think about today. Think of the way she smiled, wept, played. Think of the way she spooned her breakfast cereal into her mouth to keep up with her big brother. Think of her laughter. Think of her sleeping peacefully at night because she was the daughter who you created and on whom you bestowed safety and happiness. This is the way you will keep her alive. And I say this to you all. Never let this thought go – because I am telling you that what we remember of those we have lived with and loved is not just a cosy thought to make you feel better. It is literally what keeps us all alive.

We cannot hope to understand the nature and meaning of life and death. But inside this little wooden box is not the child who has been lost.

I have spoken to many wise men – physicists of great renown - about life after death. They tell me in total seriousness that when each one of us dies, a huge amount of the energy that fills the universe escapes from our bodies. Only God understands how the lives of those we love are perpetuated into eternity. But never allow yourselves to forget that the gift of life is still an ineffable mystery. Keep Ginevra alive in your hearts, in your minds – and in your daily lives. Because she is still here somewhere, somehow. Rejoice, dear friends, and God bless you one and all!

There was a stunned silence inside and outside the church. Nobody knew who it was who had first begun to applaud. It might even have been Beppe himself. Within a split second the whole congregation was clapping their hands together in admiration of this godly man's extraordinary words.

But Don Emanuele had not budged. He wanted to say something else, it became apparent.

There is a different aspect to the earthly loss of Ginevra which you should be aware of. Most of the children I have had to say 'farewell' to in my life have suffered illnesses that have stolen them from their families. This is not the case with Ginevra. Her death should never have happened. The culprits belong to the evil and corrupt members of Italian society whom we Italians usually refer to as 'la malavita'.[61] The mafia, in other words. Ginevra – and to a lesser extent, her brother Sandro too, suffered because they came into contact with toxic

---

[61] La malavita – the underworld : gangland

waste - some of it almost certainly radioactive - dumped in your beautiful countryside by the clans.

Earthly justice is not my domain, but I believe firmly that those who have caused this family – and so many other families in Italy - suffering and grief because of their vile crimes, should be held to account. I am therefore going to ask someone present here today to tell you all that Ginevra's death will neither be forgiven nor forgotten.

Don Emanuele seemed to be beckoning to someone at the back of the church. It must be himself, thought Beppe, who had instinctively risen to his feet. But the tall woman who had been waiting outside was walking up the aisle. She turned towards the congregation with the words:

"My name is Mariastella Martellini. I am the new *Questore* based in Pescara. The Archbishop has asked me to say a few words to you all on this occasion."

Beppe, who had recovered from his initial shock, was feeling a mixture of annoyance at having been caught out so easily, followed by the desire to laugh at the way Don Emanuele had played such a trick on him.

"Can he *ever* resist the temptation?" Beppe wondered, as the Archbishop's prediction during their car journey from Pescara had become so 'unexpectedly' true.

Mariastella told the whole congregation that she would leave no stone unturned to bring those responsible for Ginevra's death to justice.

"My team, ably led by our own *Commissario*, Beppe Stancato, present in this church right now, will not rest until these criminals are behind bars," she promised them. "I trust you will give him and his team every bit of help you can."

* * *

Almost the whole of *Pazzoli* had turned out to say farewell to Ginevra. Many of them followed the procession to the cemetery, where the parish priest went through the sad formalities of laying Ginevra to rest. The coffin, looking even more diminutive amongst the massive slabs of carved marble, was gently slid into place next to another, older family member. A smiling photo of Ginevra was placed on a little ledge nearby. Many of the townsfolk had taken flowers from the church and placed them around the modest Ianni family tomb. The priest completed the ceremony and everyone made the sign of the cross and turned around and walked slowly back along the way they had come. Only Ginevra's father, mother and brother lingered on the spot, desperately clinging onto the words of assurance uttered by Don Emanuele during the mass.

Only two of the inhabitants of Pazzoli were missing as far as she could tell, Eugenia Manicini informed Beppe when they had been introduced to each other after the ceremony.

"Neither Dario nor his mum are anywhere to be seen," said the mayoress.

"Perhaps they *both* went into hiding in the dog compound, Eugenia," suggested Beppe.

Eugenia laughed at the image conjured up by Beppe's words, surprised that even this minor aspect of the case had already been absorbed by the *commissario*.

"This is the man who's going to get the investigation moving!" Eugenia informed herself as she headed home with her daughter by her side.

"*A più tardi,*[62] *commissario,*" she said.

Beppe caught up with Mariastella, her hands on the steering wheel, just as she was about to drive off on her return journey to Pescara.

She had a triumphant grin on her face.

"I trust you won't get into any trouble over the next few days, *mio caro*[63] *commissario?*"

"*Grazie infinite*, Mariastella," Beppe replied sincerely - but with an ironic bow thrown in for good measure. The *Questore* shot off at speed. He remained where he was, still looking at the departing Alfa Romeo Spider, with the dawning of real respect for his new *capo.*"

Looking thoughtful, Beppe went off in search of Don Emanuele.

---

[62] A più tardi – See you later.
[63] Mio caro commissario - My dear inspector. (Spoken ironically)

12:   Forza, Commissario Stancato![64]

Beppe tracked down the Archbishop in the *canonica*,[65] deep in conversation with the elderly parish priest.

Formal introductions were made.

"This is my good friend, *Commissario* Beppe Stancato, father. I think he has come to chide me. Beppe, this is my host, Don Francesco."

"That was cheating, Don Emanuele," said Beppe without preamble, waving an admonishing finger from side to side.[66] The priest was looking perplexed at Don Emanuele and then at Beppe in turn.

Just as Beppe had predicted, Don Emanuele was unrepentant. He had been expecting this visit.

"I suppose it *was* a bit naughty, Beppe," admitted Don Emanuele. "But I just couldn't resist it. I truly wanted you to be agreeably surprised by Mariastella's appearance. It was entirely her idea to attend Ginevra's funeral - and I didn't want to tell *you* just in case she didn't make it, you understand. I think she wanted to show you her support. And I bet your respect for her went up by a notch or two. Am I right?"

Beppe attempted to look stern but he couldn't keep it up when faced with his friend's affable countenance – coupled to his unerring logic.

"To make amends for my deception, Beppe, may I say now that I shall agree at once to assist you with your investigation – just as soon as you make the request."

---

[64] Forza! = Get cracking!
[65] Canonica – the Italian equivalent of a vicarage.
[66] A very Italian gesture when you are mildly chiding someone.

Beppe was staring in bewilderment at Don Emanuele. His words sounded more like a prediction than an offer of help.

"But I didn't have any intention of involving you in..." he began.

"I think I ought to be back in Pescara on Friday at the latest, Beppe. I would love your company on the journey back. Would that give you enough time in Pazzoli, *amico mio?*"

Beppe was looking nonplussed at the Archbishop. He had come across this extraordinary man's apparent ability to foresee future events too many times in the past to be dismissive. But he could not envisage a situation where the Archbishop's intervention could ever be needed in the hunt for those responsible for Ginevra's death.

He gave up conjecturing. Don Emanuele had played a key role in helping him solve cases in the past. Why should he be surprised by anything which might happen in the future?

Don Emanuele was smiling at Beppe's puzzlement. The parish priest offered the *commissario* a cup of herbal tea. But Beppe excused himself, saying that he was already late for a meeting with his team. He also realised at that point that he had no idea where he would be sleeping that night – or on any subsequent night.

The Archbishop took up his theme again with the parish priest, just as Beppe was leaving the room.

Because, father, as I was saying, God did not create us to be robots. Can you imagine how unexciting and meaningless life would be, if we knew we were never going to die? What I can *tell you is what my physicist friend, Donato Pisano, assures me - that the atoms you and I are made of are virtually indestructible. And they, after all, are OUR atoms! So, don't worry, father – God has got something in store for us mortals that we shall never understand until..."*

"Until it's too late?" said the priest with a sad smile.

Beppe would have liked to linger – but the L'Aquila team would have already been waiting for him in the bar for some time. He reluctantly took his leave, apologising to Don Francesco for the interruption.

"You are welcome to stay with us for a few nights, *commissario,* if you are ever stuck for somewhere to sleep. The *canonica* was intended to house three clergymen when it was originally built."

"Thank you, Don Francesco. I might well take you up on your kind offer next time," said Beppe.

* * *

The atmosphere in the *Bar Commercio* was charged with anticipation when Beppe entered. The whole of the L'Aquila team – including the new recruit, Claudio Montano – was waiting expectantly for his arrival.

A handful of locals were drinking at the bar – in uncomfortable defiance of the presence of so many policemen in *their* familiar drinking establishment. The owner, trying to balance the needs of his new guests with those of his regular clientele, tactfully suggested that Beppe and his team might feel more comfortable in the almost redundant dining area at the back of the bar. Beppe nodded.

"Fill me in on all the details, before we begin, please, *ragazzi.* Did the clean-up team arrive yesterday?" Beppe asked.

"Yes, they cleared the site near the river, *commissario*. It's still cordoned off – until they are sure it's not contaminated. There was a considerable amount of low-level radioactive waste there, as well as traces of some really toxic stuff. They'll come back in a few weeks' time before they give the site their official blessing," explained Inspector Fabrizio De Sanctis.

"So, our investigation will be concentrated on the farm above Pazzoli for the next few days," said Beppe. "It's just about the only lead we have. Do I understand the farmer is reluctant to cooperate with us at present?"

"That is correct, *commissario*. We are looking forward to seeing how he reacts when confronted by *you*," added Giovanni Palena with a grin.

Beppe was feeling anxious about the high expectations of his team – as he always did on these occasions. But he had wanted to be in the frontline, hadn't he? That's what all the fuss had been about, surely? He stifled his self-doubts with as little effort as possible. *"Forza, Beppe!"* he told himself.

"I suppose I ought to begin by admonishing one member of the team, who might have overstepped the mark. I understand that one of you had the idea of starting up Arturo Annunzio's mechanical digger?"

He knew perfectly well that it had been Oriana Salvati – and he secretly admired her for her act of impetuosity.

As on many past occasions, Oriana was quite convinced that the severity of her chief's accusation was just for show.

"I apologise, *capo*. It was an impulsive reaction, I admit. But don't worry – I knew what I was doing. My dad's a builder and he taught me how to operate those machines.

And if I hadn't started up that digger, we almost certainly wouldn't have got anywhere at all…"

Beppe merely gave Oriana a hard look, but said nothing. Based on her experience of working with Beppe back in Pescara, she reckoned her assessment of the situation had been correct.

"All we have to do this evening, *ragazzi*, is decide which of you will come back tomorrow and accompany me to the farm. I suspect, Fabrizio, that you will have to have sufficient officers with you to man your police station. How did you get on with the stolen painting, by the way?"

"That was weird, *commissario*. It turned out that the house where the stolen picture was reported to be was the same house that we used to spy on Don Alfieri during the Sleeping Beauty case. You remember – the one opposite Remo Mastrodicasa's amazing *agriturismo*…"[67]

"How can I forget it?" said Beppe.

"Well the odd thing was, when we got there, the house was occupied by a family of Chinese – who apparently couldn't speak a word of Italian. We shall have to go back there with a search warrant – and an interpreter."

After much discussion, it was decided that Officer Oriana Salvati and her other half, Officer Giovanni Palena, should stay in L'Aquila. The imminent arrival of Oriana's child was reason enough not to be too far from the hospital. Oriana did not protest. The lingering memory of Maria Pia Farina's mutton stew was enough to quell Oriana's desire to return to that farm.

In the end, Beppe – in consultation with his colleague-in-charge, Fabrizio De Sanctis - decided to take

---

[67] Agriturismo – a brilliant Italian invention. A farmhouse-cum-restaurant, where the food eaten has to be locally sourced.

Officers Valentina Ianni, Simona Gambino and the *novellino*, Claudio Montano, who had practically begged Beppe with his eyes to allow him to join the investigative team.

"Thank you for what you have done so far," said Beppe to the whole team, before they dispersed. "Your help has knocked days off what might have dragged on for ages. Now we can get on with the real investigation!"

"We shouldn't forget the contribution of Eugenia Mancini, *capo*," said Giovanni Palena.

As if she had been waiting in the wings, the mayoress appeared as if from nowhere.

"I just wanted to be sure everything was alright," she said. "It also occurred to me that the *commissario* might be needing somewhere to sleep tonight. I have an enormous house, which has only two people living in it. What do you say, *commissario*?"

"I say *grazie mille, Signora Sindaco.* That would solve a big problem."

Beppe had not been looking forward to sharing the presbytery with two clergymen overnight. Didn't they get up at four in the morning to say Prime? Or was that only for monks? Maybe they slept on planks of wood rather than mattresses?

Eugenia Mancini gave Beppe instructions on how to get to her house and shot off on her motorbike to prepare a dinner for three.

"Won't it be odd to have a man in the house again?" she observed out loud over the noise of the engine. She even nodded in total agreement with herself.

Later that evening, after a convivial meal with the mayoress and her talkative nine-year-old daughter, Alice,

Beppe retired for the night and finally found the time to phone Sonia before he fell into a deep slumber.

Eugenia Mancini went to bed disappointed that she had not managed to winkle any details out of her guest as to what course the investigation would take.

"But it *IS* comforting to know there's a real man in the house," she admitted happily to herself before slipping into unconsciousness.

"You talked a lot in your sleep last night, *mamma*," Alice accused her mother over the breakfast table.

"Oh? And what was I talking about, may I ask?"

"I can't tell you now, *mamma*," she replied *sotto voce*. Beppe had just entered the kitchen.

Eugenia Mancini felt herself blushing – even though she could not remember any of her dreams, let alone the running commentary that must have accompanied them.

* * *

Beppe and his three uniformed companions had arrived unannounced at the sheep farm well before nine o'clock. It was Maria Pia Farina, the farmer's wife, who had greeted them. She only recognised two of the officers from the previous visit. She appeared to find the change of personnel disconcerting, reckoned Valentina Ianni. Maria Pia was looking in awe at the only non-uniformed policeman present. He had announced himself as *Commissario* Stancato from Pescara – that far-away town she had never set foot in. The *commissario* did not smile at her. He had a way of looking fixedly into her eyes – not in a hostile manner, but as if he was endeavouring to read her mind.

"I think we should summon your husband, don't you, Maria Pia?" said Beppe, finally relenting.

His voice was gentle but left her with the impression she had no choice in the matter. She scuttled off out of the kitchen and rang the bell that was hanging outside the entrance door. The sound seemed to carry all the way to the distant mountain peaks.

Agente Claudio Montano was grinning broadly at the almost wordless comedy that was being played out before his eyes. He was going to enjoy working with the *commissario,* he sensed. He stored away in his mind his new chief's mesmerising stare, thinking he should practice this technique by himself using the mirror in his bedroom, before he tried it out on the public at large. He had usually found himself grinning inanely at everyone he had had dealings with during his one-week-old career. The *commissario's* approach would be far more effective in most of the situations he had so far encountered.

"I should warn you - it takes years of practice to perfect, Claudio," Beppe would confide in his tenderfoot recruit some days later, when the subject came up in conversation.

Valentina Ianni had felt sorry for the farmer's wife – and thought it her duty to share her impressions with the *commissario.*

"She's completely under her husband's thumb, *capo*. It's *him* you need to be putting the fear of God into," she chided.

"Yes, sorry, *Agente* Ianni, replied Beppe. "I might have unintentionally overdone the act a bit."

This young officer had recently become far more forthright. It was a good sign, Beppe conceded.

Rather than return to the kitchen, Maria Pia waited outside for her husband to appear. He often ignored the bell, assuming that his wife was panicking over some womanly bagatelle not worthy of his presence.

Arturo Annunzio's non-appearance was becoming suspicious. Beppe gestured with his head towards his team for one of them to go out and see what was going on.

It was Simona Gambino who took the hint. She found Maria Pia looking embarrassed at her husband's lack of reaction to the sound of the bell.

"He often doesn't take any notice of me at all, *agente*."

"We'll see about *that*, Maria Pia," said Simona kindly. She took hold of the rope hanging down from the clapper and shook it for a good fifteen seconds, only stopping when she saw the surly figure of Arturo Annunzio emerging from the milking shed. Even at a distance of some one hundred metres, Simona could see the sour look on his face. He noticed Simona's uniform and made as if to turn round and disappear into the building he had just left. He changed his mind instantly when he saw the female officer taking a decisive step in his direction. He still had painful memories of his encounter with 'that other one' who had started up his mechanical digger a couple of days previously. He sighed and tramped towards the farm house.

Arturo Annunzio was scowling in irritation as he marched into the kitchen followed reluctantly by his wife, who looked as if she was about to burst into tears.

"I thought we had been through all this a couple of days ago, officers. Whatever *she* has told you, it's all in her imagination. There's nothing going on here. You're wasting your time – and mine."

The other female officer from the last police visit, the pregnant one, was not there, he noted with relief. He recognised the male officer who had been in charge last time. The second uniformed male officer looked too inexperienced to pose any threat. There was nothing to worry about. He could bluff this out.

"Why are you bothering me again?" he said in irritation. "I've already told you what happened..."

"Put the handcuffs on him," said a quiet voice from behind him. "I am considering arresting you, *Signor* Annunzio, for wasting police time."

Arturo Annunzio swivelled round. A man in civilian clothes was standing, so far unobserved by Arturo, up against the kitchen wall. Arturo was disconcerted by the man's calm authority – and his unblinking eye contact.

The youngest male officer was snapping a cuff onto his right wrist.

"Hey! Just a minute! You can't do this..."

"Well done, Officer Montano. Now attach the other cuff to the table leg, please. Sit down, *Signor* Annunzio. Let's begin all over again, shall we? And we'll stick to the facts this time."

"Who are *you?*" asked the farmer, attempting to regain some control of the situation.

"I am *Commissario* Stancato, *Signor* Annunzio. I am investigating the murder of a young girl from this town. She died painfully in a hospital, miles away from home. She was poisoned by contact with illegally dumped toxic waste. Are you getting the picture – Arturo? From now on, YOU are going to help us bring the culprits to justice. *Siamo chiari?*"[68]

---

[68] Siamo chiari? (Lit.) = Are we clear? Is that clear?

13: Beppe sul sentiero della guerra...
(Beppe on the warpath...)

Policemen could handcuff one to table legs, or lock one up in a cell. They could even threaten one with lengthy prison sentences. But the mafia's low-ranking thugs could, within seconds, slit his throat or put a bullet in the back of his head without compunction, on the say-so of some invisible mafioso *boss*. Even when one was safely locked up in a prison cell.

Over the years, Beppe had witnessed this silent reaction to absolute fear from men – usually men – whom he was interrogating. The eyes that darted round familiar surroundings because of the dread that an invisible mafia grass might be listening in to catch the unwary informer off his guard.

Beppe knew he was on safe ground. He would just have to patiently chip away at the man's story until the individual concerned slipped up on some detail.

Arturo Annunzio found himself on the point of telling this *commissario* that no seven-year-old girl had been anywhere near his farm but checked his impulse just in time. Such a gaffe would have been tantamount to an admission of guilt.

"I'm sorry for the little girl, *commissario*. But she must have come across this dumped waste somewhere in town."

"By the river, for your information. But the same species of lowlife who started dumping waste in Pazzoli obviously thought it would be better to find someone local, so they could continue their lucrative activities using someone's private land. It's a common pattern of mafia behaviour."

"I'm sure you know best, *commissario*. But I can't help you, I'm afraid."

Arturo Annunzio should have baulked at the mention of the word 'mafia', or at least expressed surprise, to back up his denial. He hadn't done so.

"Maybe you could tell me what you told my colleagues the other day," continued Beppe, quite unruffled by Arturo's evasive reply. "You know, when you woke your neighbours up a few nights ago with the din you were making in the early hours of the morning."

Arturo Annunzio was putting on an act of being irritated by the request.

"I'm quite sure this officer," he said pointing at Valentina Ianni, "remembers exactly what I told them last time, *commissario*."

In point of fact, he could only remember the gist of the story he had concocted two days ago.

"And I am asking you to tell *me* what you told my colleagues, *Signor* Annunzio."

"Like I already said, these two young guys turned up on motorbikes at three in the morning. They were looking for a camping site, and in the darkness, they mistook my farm for the camping site. That's all. I told them they couldn't camp out here. After a bit of arguing, they rode off on their wretched bikes..."

"And the mechanical digger? Your neighbours heard you using it. Was that before or after the motor bikes arrived?" asked the *commissario* casually.

"It was before, I think. Or maybe afterwards as well..."

"What were you doing digging at night time, Arturo?"

"I have to excavate the land for a new well-shaft. I couldn't sleep. I'm sorry, I wasn't thinking that the noise would carry."

"And when did the sheep get killed?" asked Beppe. "Your neighbours heard an animal screaming, in its death throes, they said.

"It was a lamb in the fields. Some wolf or a fox had been prowling about for several nights."

"Going back to the lads on motorbikes, Arturo. They must have been very specific in what they asked you. How did you manage to understand them if they were speaking in Neapolitan dialect?"

"Oh, that was no trouble, *commissario*. I used to work in Naples. I could understand their dialect easily."

It took Arturo a good five seconds and a malicious smile on the face of the *commissario* before he realised that he had fallen into a trap. Then he looked in fury at the face of this policeman who had so neatly tricked him.

"Arturo, for the love of God, will you tell them what really happened?" shouted his wife before she burst into tears of frustration and anger. At a sign from Beppe, Simona Gambino led Maria Pia outside once again.

The reaction from the two remaining officers was muted but significant. Valentina Ianni was looking in silent admiration at her favourite *commissario*. Claudio Montano was grinning enthusiastically from behind Arturo's back and clapping his hands together in noiseless approval.

Arturo Annunzio proceeded to spill the beans in one long, breathless account, which the quick-witted Claudio Montano recorded on his phone. His deepest regret was that he had not recorded the first part of the *commissario's* interrogation. It would have been a lesson in policing worth several weeks of his tedious training course.

Beppe turned to Arturo Annunzio and said simply:

"Thank you, Arturo. Do not be frightened. We shall make sure no harm comes to you as long as you continue to cooperate."

Beppe gestured to Claudio Montano to uncuff their 'prisoner'.

"Now, you will hand over your mobile phone to us. Just put it on the table, please," ordered Beppe. Arturo complied without quibbling.

At that moment, Officer Simona Gambino entered the room with a grin on her face and handed Beppe a rumpled-looking document.

"This was tucked into a pouch under the seat of the mechanical digger, *commissario*. It's on hire from an agricultural machinery supplier in the Secondigliano district of Naples. I thought it might help identify…"

"Thank you, Simona," interrupted Beppe, smiling proudly at his special *protégée*.[69] What have you done with Maria Pia?"

"She's happy enough now, Beppe – sorry, *commissario*. I think she's a bit embarrassed about meeting her husband at the moment. She's still outside.

Beppe looked sternly at the sheep farmer.

"Your wife has done you a favour, Arturo. From now on, you treat her with respect. *Capito?*"[70]

Arturo nodded, contritely. He was unlikely to be aggressive – as long as the police were still there.

---

[69] Beppe 'rescued' Simona during The Vanishing Physicist case.
[70] Capito? - Understood?

"One more question for you, Arturo," said Beppe. "You say the mob have come and dumped their waste here about three or four times. How long is the interval between their visits?"

"About three weeks, *commissario*. It's quite a long time between their visits."

"Well, take courage, Arturo. I can promise you that the next time will be the last!"

Arturo was not looking particularly reassured by Beppe's words. Beppe patted him on the shoulder.

"Trust us, Arturo. It's going to work out fine!"

* * *

Beppe led his team outside the farmhouse. They found a wooden table with two benches either side, and a weather-beaten sunshade providing some cover from the elements. There were no signs that the couple had shared an outdoor meal there in the recent past.

"I reckon they are well past the stage of having intimate meals *all'aperto!*"[71] said Simona Gambino. Her small audience laughed in sad agreement.

Beppe had taken Arturo's mobile phone for safe-keeping and placed it on the table in front of him. He was looking at it intently, as if he was hoping it would suddenly spring to life.

It was Valentina Ianni who broke the silence.

"But how did the mafia – or whoever it is – find out about this farm in the first place, *capo?*"

---

[71] All'aperto = In the open : Al fresco = in the fridge!

Beppe's was staring at her. She was beginning to wish she had not posed the question.

"*Brava,* Valentina! Just exactly what I was thinking," he replied.

Officer Ianni felt a brief shockwave shooting through her body. He had never addressed her by her first name before. She must be doing something right in her chief's eyes!

"I think you three should try to winkle out the truth from Arturo – or his wife. There must have been some initial contact. See if Arturo – or even people from the neighbouring farms - can remember anyone snooping around asking questions. One of the clans must have done some research into a suitable dumping ground. Ask if anyone with a Naples accent has been in the neighbourhood over the past few months. It might give us a lead of sorts."

"What we must do, in my opinion, *capo,*" said officer Simona Gambino, "is find some way to accelerate the mob's next visit to this place. Otherwise, we could be waiting for weeks."

"Once again, *brava,* Simona! We need there to be another dumping incident so we can catch whoever is responsible *con le mani nel sacco.*" [72]

The group fell into deep thought.

"I am sorry to say I shall have to return to Pescara with the Archbishop on Friday. I hope to be allowed back here by Monday. I may bring a couple of officers back with me to help out the L'Aquila team. I feel certain that Oriana will not be able to resist giving birth for very much longer. That is going to leave your team short-handed."

---

[72] Con le mani nel sacco – with their hands in the bag = red-handed

"I wonder if Oriana will allow Giovanni to be present at the birth?" joked Simona.

This time the laughter was less restrained. Oriana's determination to remain independent was a frequent subject of humour amongst those who knew her well.

"Won't you need someone to stay here on the farm to keep an eye on Arturo Annunzio, *capo?*"

It had been the new boy who had spoken. Beppe looked at him and smiled.

"Are you volunteering, Officer Montano?"

"Yes, of course, *capo*. I could camp out here for the next few days. I might even learn how to milk sheep."

It was agreed that Claudio Montano would return to the farm the next day. Beppe – who was very non-technical – was worried about Arturo's phone. Claudio – who adored technology – offered to take the mobile back to the police headquarters in L'Aquila and extract the information of the calls made to the phone over the last weeks.

"We shall need a tap on this phone, too," said Beppe. "Maybe your Inspector De Sanctis could take care of setting that up with the magistrate?"

It was agreed.

"Any other ideas, *ragazzi?*" asked Beppe.

"Just a thought, *capo*," said Simona Gambino. "If we could find out which of the mafia clans has set up this toxic waste dumping operation, then we could set up our very own contract with the *boss* concerned. That would mean we don't have to wait around until Arturo Annunzio is contacted – and the proof of their crime would be unassailable.

Beppe was thinking hard. He was wondering how his new boss, Mariastella Mancini, would react to this form of entrapment. Maybe, just maybe, they could pull it off.

"For it to work, we would need someone who could understand and speak Neapolitan dialect fluently," added Simona Gambino. "I don't suppose *you* know of anybody who...?

She had stopped in her tracks. Beppe had just clapped his hand violently to his forehead.

"*O Dio!* He's done it again!" exclaimed their leader, obviously deeply shocked.

"Who has done *what* again, *capo?*" begged Valentina Ianni.

"It's the Archbishop of Pescara! He offered to help us with this case while we were driving along in the car. It was as if he was predicting that we would need his help."

"But how could he possibly have known we would be needing a...?" began Valentina Ianni.

"Exactly – he couldn't have known. But it seems he did!" replied Beppe.

"Excuse me asking," said the bewildered *novellino*, "I heard this archbishop's amazing sermon at Ginevra's funeral, but how on earth does he know how to speak in a Neapolitan dialect?"

"He has the gift of tongues," Simona Gambino told him facetiously – just to enhance the sense of shocked disbelief which had affected the group.

Beppe felt sorry for Claudio and did not want to leave him in the dark.

"Your education as a police officer will not be complete until you have met Don Emanuele in person, Claudio. He has the gift of prescience. Ask your colleague

Simona as soon as she has got over her surprise. She will tell you how Don Emanuele helped us locate a missing physicist some months ago. It was all to do with a blue exercise book!"[73]

"I can't wait to meet him in person, *commissario,*" Claudio replied, even more mystified than he had been previously.

"I'll see if we can arrange it for you, *Agente* Montano," said Beppe. "For the good of your soul, of course!"

---

[73] A reference to Beppe's previous case – *The Vanishing Physicist*

14: *Don Emanuele makes his presence felt...*

"I understand you deprived us of the pleasure of the *commissario's* company, last night, Eugenia," said Don Emanuele, who had decided that it was time for him to become better acquainted with the mayoress of Pazzoli.

Eugenia felt her cheeks turning a degree warmer – for the second time that day.

"You mean...?" she began.

"That Don Francesco offered to put Beppe up during his stay in your town."

"The *commissario* didn't mention that to me at all, Your Eminence," replied Eugenia contritely.

"Please, Eugenia. I beg of you not to call me by that cumbersome and very ungodly title! Just call me *padre.* That sounds far more like real life."

"Grazie, padre," she said, smiling. "But I just thought that Beppe might be in need of a roof over his head..."

"Don't let it concern you at all, Eugenia. Your house is much more comfortable than the *canonica.* That house is a penance – even for me!"

Eugenia laughed at such un-spiritual words emanating from an archbishop's lips.

"Did Beppe talk to you about his lovely family?" asked Don Emanuele.

"Oh yes. He even showed me photos of his two children. I offered to put the whole family up here if he has to come back to Pazzoli at any point of his investigation. It's not that I ever imagined for a moment..." She stopped, embarrassed that the Archbishop might have misinterpreted the significance of her flushed cheeks.

"It was just so reassuring to have a man in the house again, *padre*. And Beppe *is* a lovely man!"

Don Emanuele held up his hands.

"I understand your feelings. They are entirely good feelings, Eugenia. You are a very good woman."

This time her blushes were even more obvious.

"You only met me properly half an hour ago! I don't think I'm any different to anybody else, father!" she stated.

"Well, maybe it is your humility and self-effacement which make you special, *mia cara* Eugenia."

"May we change the subject?" said the mayoress almost abruptly.

Don Emanuele laughed.

"Absolutely! Do you think there is anyone else I should go and see in Pazzoli – before I return to Pescara tomorrow?"

"Yes, *padre*. I am sure that Ginevra's brother and parents would find it a great comfort if you went to visit them in their own home. And, I think your presence might make a difference to the dog-kennel boy, Dario Tundo, not to mention his mother. Those two really do have serious social and emotional issues. Not to mention financial ones."

"Thank you, Eugenia. I will visit them – but on one condition."

Eugenia was looking suspicious. She raised an enquiring eyebrow in the Archbishop's direction.

"And what might that condition be, *padre?*" she asked tartly.

Don Emanuele appreciated this unique woman and the manner in which she spoke. He smiled and replied:

"That *you* will accompany me on my rounds, *cara signora!*"

She laughed out loud in relief at his words.

"*Va da se,*[74] Your Eminence!"

"I think we should go and see the Ianni family first," suggested Don Emanuele. "Their need is greater, don't you think, Eugenia?"

* * *

"Do you mind if we go into the church for a few minutes before going to see the family, Eugenia?"

Don Emanuele sensed his companion's aversion to entering churches when there was no specific reason to do so.

"You can wait for me outside if you prefer. I shouldn't be too long. But it's not always up to me, you see."

Don Emanuele placed a hand gently on her shoulder before he went inside the ancient church. It was cool and dark inside.

Eugenia sat on a stone bench in the sunshine and proceeded to hold a whispered debate with herself about why she had not wanted to accompany the archbishop inside the church. She failed to come to any satisfactory conclusion.

"I wonder what the *commissario* would have done if he had been in my shoes?" she asked herself – quite irrelevantly.

When Don Emanuele emerged from the church, Eugenia raised her head and smiled at him.

"I've walked seven times round the town of Pazzoli while you've been in there, Don Emanuele."

---

[74] Va da se – That goes without saying. *(Lit: 'Goes by itself')*

The Old Testament reference to the town of Jericho was not lost on him.

"But I see the town has not collapsed yet," replied Don Emanuele.

"Are you ready to meet the Ianni family now?" she asked.

"Only time will tell, Eugenia," was the only answer she received.

As soon as the front door was opened by Adele, Don Emanuele stepped over the threshold – followed by the mayoress.

They were led into the kitchen, where the father, Diego, and his son, Sandro, were sitting round the kitchen table, looking bewildered and disconsolate. They did not show any hint of curiosity at the sight of the visitors who had just walked into their house.

Don Emanuele raised his right hand in blessing. He stood still, looking at the family group. Eugenia could swear she could see tears in his eyes.

"Will you take me to Ginevra's bedroom?" asked Don Emanuele gently.

Adele, Sandro's mother, found her voice:

"Ginevra and Sandro share a bedroom,"[75] she said. She was stifling the sob in her voice.

"We must all stay together," said Don Emanuele, since Diego Ianni had not stirred.

Sandro's bed had been roughly made but his little sister's bed was immaculate, with clean pink sheets and a hand-made quilt spread over the top. A teddy bear lay forlornly on the pillow with its paws in the air. A vase, full of

---

[75] It is very common in Italy for children – even as teenagers - to share a bedroom – especially in the South.

brightly coloured flowers taken from the church, stood on a bedside table between the two beds.

"Sandro, come and sit with me and keep me company."

Don Emanuele patted the space next to him where he had sat down on Alessandro's own bed.

Alessandro did as he was asked. Eugenia, standing just inside the bedroom doorway was struck by the nine-year old boy's lack of embarrassment. He seemed to be under a spell.

To Eugenia, it seemed ages before Don Emanuele uttered a word.

"What does he hope to achieve by this?" she could not help asking herself.

"You are very close to Ginevra, aren't you, Sandro?" stated Don Emanuele out of the blue.

The boy nodded hard.

"I can tell you are very happy together."

Silence fell again. The Archbishop seemed to be quietly reciting words in a language that was not Italian. In the end, he said one single word in such a loud voice that it startled everybody in the room.

"GINEVRA!"

Sandro shot up so abruptly that he knocked over the pot of flowers. The water from the flowerpot trickled down onto the floor.

Don Emanuele smiled at Sandro, putting an arm around the boy's shoulder as he stood up.

"Your little sister has such a joyous laugh, Sandro! Just like little bells trilling…"

The boy was staring mutely at the Archbishop.

"Ginevra was always laughing," said Adele, in her matter-of-fact voice. "Especially when Sandro dropped things or broke things. *'Sei proprio una foca!'*[76] she used to tell him…"

The father and mother, with Eugenia, led the group back downstairs. They could not be precisely certain about what had just taken place.

Sandro was clutching Don Emanuele's hand tightly as they walked downstairs behind the others. Only the Archbishop was near enough to hear the words which Sandro spoke. The boy was smiling radiantly up at the priest – whose shaven head seemed to be touching the ceiling above them.

"I heard her laughing too, father. But did you see her sitting on her bed? I blinked – and she was gone again."

Outside, Eugenia was looking strangely at Don Emanuele.

"What happened in there, Don Emanuele?" she asked.

"Why are you asking *me* that question, *cara* Eugenia?" he replied. "Shall we go and see the boy, Dario, and his mum now?"

"This way, father. It's up the other end of the town."

Even the mayoress could not find any suitable words with which to explain to herself what she had just witnessed inside the Ianni household. What had struck her was the fact that, as they had all left the bedroom, Ginevra's teddy bear had been sitting upright on the duvet.

"How did it get there?" she wondered. "I didn't see anyone picking it up."

---

[76] 'Sei proprio una foca' = You're a clumsy-clogs. Lit: 'You're just like a seal' i.e. all flippers!

She could not supply a logical answer to her own question.

Eugenia led Don Emanuele along the streets of Pazzoli without a word, walking just ahead of him to lead the way.

Inside her head, she asked herself another question as they trudged up the lane leading to the rustic house where Dario and his mother lived in squalid interdependence:

"I wonder what our meeting with Dario will reveal?"

"Oh, this will be a very different kind of meeting, Eugenia," said a voice just behind her.

The mayoress spun round as if she had been touched by an invisible hand – a mixture of astonishment and awe on her face.

"But I never..." she began, but decided that the rest of the sentence was redundant. She might have to think twice before indulging in her habit of having private conversations with herself whilst Don Emanuele was in the vicinity.

"What a remarkable man he is!" she said to herself, immediately twisting round again to look at Don Emanuele over her shoulder, in case he had intercepted *that* thought as well.

Don Emanuele was simply smiling broadly in her direction.

* * *

Don Emanuele had correctly judged that his encounter with Dario and his mother would be of a very different nature. But even the Archbishop had not foreseen that Dario would open the door, take one look at his visitors, decide that he must be in trouble again and push past them at a run. He headed for the back of the house.

"He'll be taking refuge in the dog kennel again," explained Eugenia to Don Emanuele.

Don Emanuele had a look on his face as if a light had just dawned. If anything, he seemed mildly amused.

"*Buongiorno, Antonella,*" said Eugenia to the unsmiling mother of Dario Tondo who turned up at the front door. She was sure she had not left it wide open.

She looked haggard and ill-at-ease at the sight of the two figures standing in her doorway. She made no move to invite them inside, nor did she register surprise that the mayoress was in the company of some priest.

"What's Dario done now?" she asked in sullen despair.

"He's just run off into the back garden, *Signora* Antonella."

It was the tall clergyman who had answered her stock question – assuming the worst as she had learnt to do from bitter experience.

"May we come in, Antonella?" asked Eugenia. "This gentleman is the Archbishop of Pescara. We have come to keep you company for a while."

"I think it is time you let the Holy Spirit into your home, Antonella. He seems to have been absent for too long."

The gentle voice and the steely grey eyes were irresistible. She felt weak at the knees. She turned round and walked into the house without a word. The mayoress and the Archbishop followed her into a rudimentary sitting room, where a couple of not very inviting-looking sofas were facing a large TV screen, which was tuned into *Canale 5* with the sound turned up to a deafening level. Eugenia waltzed over to the TV and switched it off without a by-your-leave.

"That's better, isn't it, Antonella? Now we can hear ourselves think."

Dario's mother looked as if she was about to protest, but one look at Don Emanuele's face was enough to change her mind. The two-metre tall, bald-headed priest looked as if he was about to announce the Second Coming.

What Don Emanuele actually said, addressing Eugenia was:

"If you are happy with the idea, *mia cara,* I think I should go and rescue Dario. I'll bring him indoors again – so we can all be together. How does that sound?"

Antonella finally managed to utter a few words to Don Emanuele.

"No, sir! Don't do that! Dario has gone to hide in the kennel. The dog will attack you if you try to go into the cage."

Don Emanuele, who had not sat down, merely smiled kindly at Dario's mother. Antonella felt strange. This lofty priest was the first man who had smiled at her for as long as she could remember.

"Do not worry yourself about me, Antonella. What's his name, by the way – or is it a 'her'?"

Antonella looked bewildered by the question. Her first reaction had been to say 'Dario, of course!' She had to think for a few seconds before she grasped what the priest was asking her.

"My ex-husband called him *Achille,*"[77] she reluctantly admitted, as if the animal's existence was entirely *his* fault.

---

[77] Achille – Achilles. Pronounced **a-KEE-lè** A popular dog's name in Italy.

Before Eugenia and Antonella's disbelieving gaze, Don Emanuele was shedding his white cassock with one easy gesture, revealing a pair of long shorts which came to just below the knees. The two women watched fascinated as a pair of shapely male calves strode out of the room heading for the front door.

"Might be a bit grubby out there," said the Archbishop, over his shoulder, "and I don't have a clean cassock with me here in Pazzoli. Excuse me, won't you, ladies!"

A few seconds later, when the two ladies had recovered from their respective shocks, Eugenia said to Antonella:

"I don't think there's anything in the bible to say archbishops can't take their cassocks off, is there, Antonella?"

Getting no reply, Eugenia talked and talked and probed every angle of the mother and son's difficult life. She determined to help them in every way she could. She made up her mind to set up some sort of food bank – she felt sure she had just invented a brilliant new expression - to help out the handful of families in her town who suffered from genuine poverty. She also determined that she would try to find some form of employment for her new *protégée.* Antonella obviously needed to regain some of her lost self-esteem, reckoned Eugenia.

"How have you managed over the last few years, *mia cara?* I am sorry that I have been so neglectful of your needs..."

Antonella, it was revealed, had a small amount of money from her parents.

"My husband sometimes sends me a few euros – when he remembers he has a son," explained Antonella bitterly.

Eugenia looked at her watch. Don Emanuele had been absent for over forty-five minutes. Should she be worried about her companion? She was not usually given to attacks of pessimism about the fate of other people.

"Should I go out and see what's become of him?" she asked herself, having visions of a mangled archbishop being devoured by a semi-starving hound. "Give him another fifteen minutes," was the consoling answer she came up with. "You would have heard barking – or screaming – if anything bad had happened," she reasoned.

* * *

Another hour had elapsed before Eugenia Mancini became concerned enough to 'interfere' with the course of nature, as she put it, and go round to the back of the house to see what had become of the cassock-less archbishop. It was this aspect that troubled her more than anything. She reasoned that it must be because Don Emanuele had gone out without his spiritually protective gear on, leaving him as vulnerable as any normal mortal which worried her most of all. Her anxiety level went up even more when she found the animal cage, meticulously clean, with a bowl of fresh water on the ground - but devoid of archbishop, dog and Dario.

"Where on earth could they all have disappeared to?" she asked herself. The air of mystery engendered by their previous visit to Ginevra's house had cast doubts on her habitual belief in the solidity of terrestrial events.

She went back out into the road where her concerns were partially laid to rest by the unusual sight of an unfrocked archbishop walking uphill holding Dario's hand in his right hand and the collar of a passive Great Dane in his other hand.

Eugenia rubbed her eyes in quiet disbelief. She was trying to ascertain which of the two events she had witnessed that afternoon should come under the category of 'miraculous'. It seemed to her rather extravagant that both manifestations should qualify equally.

"Ma pensa un po'!"[78] she said out loud, by way of resolving her dilemma.

Dario was carrying a plastic supermarket shopping bag in his free hand. He wasn't smiling, but he had lost the sullen, persecuted look which he usually wore when out and about in the town.

It was only when the little group were back inside the house that Eugenia noticed that the Archbishop smelt a bit unpleasant. Dario had led the dog into its super-clean pen and left it happily padding round the confined space of the cage.

"Look, *mamma*. Don Emanuele has bought us some tins of proper dog food."

The mother was looking at the tins as if she was thinking of ways to convert their content into any form of meal fit for humans.

"And he bought some frozen meals for us too, *mamma*," added Dario.

---

[78] Ma pensa un po'! - Well I never!

"Say thank you to the Archbishop, Antonella!" prompted Eugenia when Dario's mother seemed to have relapsed into a state of sullen withdrawal.

"Grazie, padre," she muttered barely audibly.

Don Emanuele understood instantly that she was feeling ashamed and embarrassed. She had her pride.

He donned his white cassock once more. The extra layer of clothing gave him back his spiritual authority but did little to cover up the dog-cage smell that lingered in the air, thought the mayoress.

"I think I should go home and have a shower," smiled Don Emanuele. He gave Antonella a blessing, but went over to Dario and placed an affectionate arm round the boy's shoulder.

"You know what you must do, don't you, Dario? Maybe you would prefer Eugenia to accompany you, if she will?"

Dario was looking thoughtful.

"No, father, I would rather go on my own," he said after a pause. The Archbishop briefly cupped his hand round the back of Dario's head.

"Bravo, Dario!"

On the way downhill, Eugenia was walking by Don Emanuele's side. He gave her a sidelong smile.

"Well, Don Emanuele," she asked pointedly, "are you going to keep me completely in the dark?"

"I think poor old Dario will suffer several lapses before he can be considered one of the good guys. But he is more sinned against than sinning, I suspect..."

"But what did you do with him - apart from taking him shopping?"

Eugenia felt she had so much to learn from her companion – and so little time left before he disappeared with the *Commissario* back to Pescara.

"I promise I shall be returning to Pazzoli very soon, Eugenia," he said, thereby confirming her conviction that he could read minds.

"But as to what we did together... Well, as you can see – and smell – we set about making that beautiful animal's living space more habitable. I think what won Dario over was the fact that *Achille* greeted me like an old friend. After that, we took the dog for a walk down to the river – just where the toxic waste had been dumped."

"Why there, Don Emanuele?"

"I don't know really. Guided by..."

The archbishop jabbed a finger heavenwards.

"At one point, the dog went exploring on its own. It headed straight for the cordoned off site. Dario ran after his dog and physically dragged it away. That's when Dario began to talk to me, Eugenia. He was in tears..."

"It was just like what Ginevra done. She ran off on her own. I couldn't stop her, honest father. I never meant to..."

"That's how I learnt what happened to Ginevra and Sandro. Dario just lost control of the situation. He feels that everybody in the town is against him. He doesn't really have the word power to articulate publicly how it happened."

"But what was it that you told him to do – with my help, if he wanted it?" asked the mayoress, desperately trying to satisfy her curiosity before she would have to leave Don Emanuele outside the *canonica.*

"I would rather wait and see if the spirit moves Dario to do what I suggested, Eugenia. It will take a lot of courage on his part."

Eugenia and Don Emanuele arrived at the presbytery. She was debating whether she could hug the archbishop – smells and all – to show him how she felt about the strange events of that afternoon. She was surprised to see *Commissario* Beppe Stancato in the company of the young uniformed male officer waiting for their arrival.

"This is *Agente* Claudio Montano – who was anxious to meet you and Don Emanuele."

Beppe carried out the formal introductions. Don Emanuele suggested they all go inside the *canonica.*

"I need an immediate shower," he explained and disappeared upstairs. Don Francesco sat everybody round the big kitchen table – where, quite unbidden, Eugenia began relating the extraordinary events of that afternoon in so far as she could interpret them. Thus, Officer Claudio Montano had to be content with learning about the Archbishop second-hand. Beppe merely nodded sagely – he was attempting to appear unsurprised by the Archbishop's contribution to life in Pazzoli.

Claudio Montano looked at Don Emanuele with renewed curiosity when a sweeter-smelling clergyman stepped into the kitchen.

"Well, Don Emanuele, I guess we shall have time to talk on our journey back to Pescara tomorrow morning?" the *Commissario* suggested.

"Yes, Beppe. I must say I shall be sorry to leave this extraordinary little town. But I shall be back sooner than you think."

Beppe explained to Eugenia that he would be sleeping at the farmhouse that night – to be relieved in the morning by his 'volunteer', Claudio Montano. Beppe also promised the mayoress he would be back – with his family in tow.

Eugenia looked pleased and decided that, like it or not, she would hug both Beppe and the Archbishop. Her only internal debate was which one of the two protocol dictated she should hug first. But she came to the conclusion that it didn't really matter either way.

***

Alessandro Ianni was dispatched by his father later that evening to answer a timid knock on their front door. Adele was frowning – they rarely had visitors at this hour.

Sandro stood open-mouthed at the sight of the school bully standing nervously on their doorstep. There was something forlorn about the boy whom he had hated for taking him and Ginevra down to the river on that fateful day. Sandro did not understand what made him do what he did next. He raised an open hand in the air and exchanged a high five with Dario, who was emboldened to say:

"I got something to tell your family, Sandro." He was led shaking into the kitchen where Sandro and Ginevra's mother and father looked hostilely at their uninvited guest. Dario burst into uncontrollable tears. Adele took pity on him.

Later, Sandro led Dario upstairs and showed him his and Ginevra's bedroom.

"I saw Ginevra sitting on the bed this afternoon – and I heard her laughing," he whispered to an uncomprehending Dario.

"Was that bald priest with you?" Dario asked after a pause.

Sandro nodded. Something clicked into place in Dario's head – a dim realisation that he wasn't quite the same person as he had been before. He found himself fingering the silver chain and cross, which Don Emanuele had given him, through the material of his well-worn T-shirt.

15: Don Emanuele's offer of help...

Beppe had not slept well during the night. The only spare bed in the remote country farmhouse had a hard mattress laid out on a wooden board – a penance for turning down Don Francesco's offer of hospitality at the presbytery?

Maria Pia had apologised profusely. It was obvious that Arturo Annunzio resented the presence of a policeman on his farm. Beppe made it quite clear to the farmer that his only other alternative would involve being a guest in a cell in the L'Aquila police station. Beppe hoped for his young recruit's sake that he really intended to bring camping stuff with him – and that his ordeal would be over quickly. That depended on how fast they could set up another waste-dumping trip on the part of an unknown mafia clan.

"But, Claudio, I hope I am not making your private life difficult? Don't you have a *fidanzata?*"[79] Beppe had asked.

"Don't worry, *commissario.* No girlfriend as yet – I'm working on it."

"That'll mean another relationship formed which will lead to staff shortages in L'Aquila," thought Beppe ironically, thinking of *Agente* Valentina Ianni following in the footsteps of Oriana Salvati. Beppe let out a sigh at the potential complexities of life, provoked by human nature.

He had phoned Sonia well after her bedtime. She had helped him through the first hour or so of his solitary confinement. He kept Sonia enthralled by his account of the day's events in Pazzoli.

---

[79] Fidanzata – girlfriend/fiancée

"That man is just not of this world!" exclaimed Sonia, who saw no limits to the spiritual powers of the Archbishop of Pescara.

"How would you like to be with me on the second leg of our investigation in Pazzoli?" Beppe had asked Sonia, telling her about Eugenia Mancini's offer to host the whole family.

"I'll begin packing - but not until tomorrow morning," she added sleepily. *"Buona notte. A domani, amore."*[80]

* * *

Agente Claudio Montano duly arrived at the remote farmhouse at 7 o'clock the following morning – with a tent large enough for at least two people. He had hung up his uniform and holstered pistol on a coat-hanger in the back of his car.

Claudio handed Beppe an envelope with all the incoming phone numbers received on Arturo Annunzio's mobile device over the last few months.

"The most frequent caller is from the dairyman in Pazzoli where they make the pecorino cheese, *Commissario*. I've crossed those numbers out. I've also highlighted the numbers in blue which are no longer in service. There's one number which we tried – highlighted in yellow. It was interesting because it was a kid of about eleven who answered it. He told me his name was Samuele. But get this, *Commissario* - I could hear an older guy in the background with a gruff voice asking the kid who it was calling him. And guess what? He was speaking in Neapolitan dialect."

---

[80] Buona notte. A domani. = Good night. See you tomorrow.

"What did you say, Claudio?" snapped Beppe.

"I just said 'sorry, wrong number' and rang off."

"Bravo! You did the right thing."

Beppe spent the next ten minutes briefing his junior officer on every aspect of what he should do whilst on the farm – until Claudio Montano held up a hand to stop the flow of words.

"Leave it to me, *commissario*. I'll phone you if I have the slightest doubt about anything! Oh, by the way, the magistrate is being difficult about putting a tap on Arturo Annunzio's phone. Something about an unnecessary invasion of privacy."

"It might not matter all that much, Claudio. You'll be monitoring incoming calls, won't you?"

Beppe resigned himself to the notion of delegating such an important role to an inexperienced officer. He had visions of Mariastella wagging an admonishing finger in his direction.

"You cannot do everything yourself, Beppe. Give the youngsters a chance to prove themselves *per l'amor di Dio!*[81] Or how else are they going to learn?" he imagined his new boss telling him.

Beppe sighed and shook his young colleague by the hand.

"In bocca al lupo, Claudio!" he said, taking his leave of the young officer.

Agente Claudio Montano's account of the eleven-year-old boy answering the phone was preying on his mind. It raised intriguing possibilities.

---

[81] Per l'amor di Dio!   For heaven's sake!   (Lit. For the love of God)

Surely a mafia *boss* would not make the blunder of passing on a redundant mobile phone to one of his own family?

"It might be worth following up," thought the *commissario* as he headed back to town to pick up the Archbishop, who would already be waiting for him.

But - Beppe reminded himself - Arturo Annunzio had received the last call from the *mafioso 'boss'* on his landline in the middle of the night.

"Non mi quadra," [82] he muttered as he took his foot off the accelerator.

There was nothing for it – Beppe reversed his car and drove rapidly back to the farmyard. He found a surprised Claudio Montano putting the finishing touches to his tent. In reply to Beppe's question, Claudio pointed a finger down towards the milking shed. Beppe strode off energetically towards his destination.

"Just one more vital question, Arturo..." said the *Commissario* in a tone of voice which brooked no argument.

On his return to where Claudio was standing admiring his own tent-erecting skills, Beppe smiled at the new recruit and gave him a thumbs-up sign.

"Bravo, Claudio! You have got off to an excellent start," he said, shooting off at speed. He was already twenty minutes late for his mission to drive Don Emanuele back to Pescara.

Claudio was left wondering if he was being complimented on the first steps of a new career – or on his ability to put up tents.

---

[82] Non mi quadra = I'm not convinced (lit: It doesn't square up)

***

Beppe drove up with inordinate haste and braked sharply outside the presbytery. Don Emanuele was waiting for him, quite unperturbed by his travelling companion's late arrival. The parish priest, Don Francesco was keeping him company.

"I am – believe it or not – in no hurry at all to return to Pescara, Beppe. I would much rather be staying here for another few days. The break from ecclesiastical routine is as good as a holiday."

Beppe took this to mean that he owed no apologies for his tardiness. So, he simply shrugged his shoulders and opened the passenger door for the Archbishop – who promptly moved the front seat back as far it would go.

After minutes of silence as Beppe drove at a steady pace along the road homewards, it was Don Emanuele who spoke first.

"Well, Beppe, judging by your silence, I would guess you already know the reason why I made my offer of help a couple of days ago. Am I right?"

"Yes, Don Emanuele, you are right. And I have known you long enough not to ask you *how* you knew we would need your help."

"You are right not to ask, *commissario*. I often do not understand it myself."

"It was Officer Simona Gambino who hatched the idea of setting a trap for the mafioso *boss*. We thought we could speed things up if we can tempt the clan into making another delivery of toxic waste to the Annunzios' farm. That was the moment when my memory was jogged. It took my breath away."

"Ah! So that's what you are considering doing, is it Beppe? Fight evil with evil, so to speak."

Beppe was uncertain as to whether this last comment from Don Emanuele was spoken in disapproval of his methods.

"Just what I would have done myself, had I been in your shoes," added Don Emanuele to make his position clear.

"It's merely an idea at the moment. And the ramifications of my scheme are likely to be very complex. I'm not sure how Mariastella Martellini will react to the suggestion. But the operation is bound to be dangerous – if it goes ahead."

The Archbishop looked calmly at Beppe.

"I will do *anything* to make sure that the murderers of Ginevra are brought to justice, Beppe. Besides which, I need a rest from saying mass every day – and preaching sermons, come to that. Just think what a great sermon it will make one Sunday when this despicable bunch of sinners are behind bars!"

"I have some ideas as to how you might become involved, Don Emanuele - without too much danger to yourself..."

"You're already making *my* contribution sound a bit dull, *commissario.*"

Beppe merely gave the Archbishop a sidelong glance – and instantly realised that Don Emanuele was not joking.

"First of all, we need to find out which clan is responsible. We know that the culprits come from the Secondigliano district of Naples but..."

"Ah! Did you know, Beppe, that's where the Alfieri clan lives? The real culprit might turn out to be a descendant of Gianluca Alfieri.[83] I might be able to help you there – if your new *Questore* gives us the go-ahead, of course."

"Did you have a premonition about your involvement in this investigation, Don Emanuele? If you don't mind me asking?"

"Yes, Beppe. I fear I did – and I don't think it will be an easy ride," replied the Archbishop calmly.

But, uppermost in Don Emanuele's mind was the happy trill of laughter he had heard ringing out in Sandro's bedroom. He too had noticed that the teddy bear was sitting upright as they left the bedroom. He made a reverent sign of the cross and gazed in wonder at the not-so-distant mountain tops as they flowed steadily past the car.

---

[83] Gianluca Alfieri – the former mafia boss from The Case of the Sleeping Beauty.

16: With a little help from 'above...'

Beppe would like to have shot off back home without delay. His former chief would have ordered him to do so. But he knew he would have to make the journey upstairs and spend time going over everything that had happened since he had last seen Mariastella, just after Ginevra's funeral.

It was not, he decided, that there was still mistrust between the two of them – maybe, potentially, some conflict of interest over procedure.

But before he came out with the details of the scheme he was hatching, he needed time to discuss the details with Sonia. She always managed to make sense of his ingenious strategies – whilst modifying his more wayward flights of fantasy with her down-to-earth sense of reality. It was much easier to think clearly when he was face to face with the love of his life. He sighed nostalgically as he began to climb the stairs to the floor above.

Mariastella's door was open. She smiled broadly on seeing her second-in-command and beckoned him in. Once again, Beppe felt disarmed by her unreserved welcome.

The *Questore's* opening words were unexpected.

"I've just been talking to Don Emanuele, on the phone, Beppe."

"Really? I've only just deposited him outside the cathedral. What did he have to say for himself?" asked Beppe guardedly.

"Nothing much, really. He merely thanked me for letting you accompany him to Pazzoli. He seemed very pleased with himself."

"He has reason to be pleased with himself. In just a few days, he has worked small miracles in that town."

"I don't suppose you feel up to running me through what has happened since I last saw you?" she asked.

Beppe hoped fervently that Don Emanuele had not revealed any hint of his future plan of action to his boss.

Beppe talked non-stop for over an hour. Mariastella contented herself with interjecting a few questions when she required a point of clarification – especially when Beppe told her about leaving Officer Claudio Montana in charge at the farmhouse.

"Arturo Annunzio is not entirely to be trusted. He is petrified of reprisals from the mafia boss. He would cave in under the least pressure. We felt too that he might take out his insecurities on his wife. She is a very submissive person and not able to defend herself physically," Beppe explained.

Mariastella applauded him as his detailed account finally came to a close.

"So, you reckon you have a clear indication as to which mafia clan is involved in the dumping of the waste?" she asked hopefully.

"Thanks to Don Emanuele's knowledge of Naples, yes, I believe we do. But we shall need to do a bit of surreptitious detective work before we can be absolutely certain."

Mariastella Mancini was looking at Beppe with relief – and more than a hint of admiration.

"I am impressed that you have found out so much in such a short time, Beppe. You were right to insist that your presence was needed up there with the team from L'Aquila."

"Would you like me to tell you about Don Emanuele's small miracles, Mariastella? I am quite sure that he is too modest to tell you on his own account."

She nodded.

"Of course, I would, *commissario.*"

"I am not quite clear myself as to the details. But there were two distinct happenings, strictly speaking unrelated to our investigation. I was told about them by the mayoress, Eugenia Mancini – a truly unique lady and delightfully eccentric by nature..."

Again, the *Questore* nodded to encourage him to go into detail.

Beppe told her about the strange episode in Sandro's bedroom and about the magical transformation of a boy called Dario Tondo. This time, Mariastella did not interrupt Beppe's narrative. Her reaction to the account of what happened in Sandro's bedroom was interesting. Beppe recalled Don Emanuele's words about non-believers - secretly eager for someone to convince them that there exists a supernatural dimension, invisible to ordinary mortals most of the time.

"You may make what you will of these events, Mariastella – but *something* happened in Sandro's bedroom which it is difficult to explain away," Beppe concluded.

"You don't think the mayoress is just being over-imaginative?" asked Mariastella, feeling the need to act the devil's advocate.

"No, she is a meticulously honest woman and has vivid powers of description. I could tell she was having difficulty herself in believing what she had witnessed."

A silence fell in the *Questore's* office, which Beppe did not attempt to break.

In the end, Mariastella's face broke into a wistful smile.

"One more question, Beppe – which I beg of you to answer in complete honesty. May I make the assumption that you have more than just a vague idea as to how our investigation might proceed from this point? And does it include the Archbishop in some way?"

Beppe looked shrewdly at the *Questore*. Don Emanuele must have said something to prepare the ground for their next move, he deduced.

"Yes, to both your questions, Mariastella. But I really would like time to think everything through in Sonia's company first. As to Don Emanuele, it was he who volunteered his assistance - days before the discovery which provoked his offer became apparent to myself and the team."

"He certainly is an extraordinary man, Beppe. I have never in my life heard a sermon like the one he treated us to at Ginevra's funeral. It was quite mind-blowing."

Beppe stood up to leave.

"Yes, go home to your family now, Beppe. I know it's Saturday tomorrow, but I shall be here – at least until midday," said the *Questore* simply.

* * *

'Looking secretly pleased with himself' was an expression which rarely applied to Officer Luigi Rocco. But the smug expression on his face was unmistakable. Beppe had run into his massive team-mate as he was preparing to leave.

"*Ciao,* Luigi. And how is life treating you at present?"

"Very well, thank you, *commissario,*" replied the mountain bear. But the secret, self-satisfied look had disappeared in a trice, to be replaced by Luigi Rocco's normally impassive countenance.

Beppe would have to change tack – or take his leave abruptly.

"How did you and the new girls get on with your school visit, Luigi? I seem to remember the three of you were off to investigate a teacher's vandalised car..."

"They were in their element, *commissario*. I was just a spectator. The headmistress was the same one who was there when Emma and Cristina were pupils there. She didn't recognise them. But when the girls reminded her of their surnames, she nearly had a fit. I had the impression that she was about to cross herself."[84]

"Campione and Cardinale – the two Cs! You spent more time in my office than in your own classroom as I remember. And now you've become police officers! *Incredibile!*"[85]

"I told the headmistress that I thought congratulations were in order. She grudgingly paid tribute to their achievements. By the time we left, the headmistress's attitude towards her ex-pupils had been transformed, *commissario*. They organised everything without my help."

"Well, Luigi?" prompted Beppe, since Luigi Rocco had stopped speaking.

"Oh, you would like *me* to tell you?"

"Yes please, Luigi. I'm sure it will be just as valid coming from you."

"Well, *commissario*. I have to admit I was impressed by their preparation. They had obviously thought out their strategy beforehand. They told the headmistress – she was obviously boiling inside because she had to bow to *their*

---

[84] Cross herself = make the sign of the cross – to ward off evil.
[85] Incredibile - unbelieveable

authority – that they wanted to see no more than fifteen pupils at a time from the *Terza Media* group. 'And there must be no contact between a group we have seen and the one arriving,' Cristina had specified to the head teacher."

"Why year three?" asked Beppe.

"Well, it seemed like the sort of act of vandalism that would be carried out by thirteen-year olds. And the teacher concerned seemed to have got on the wrong side of the whole year group – she seemed a bit too 'mature' to be handling kids of that age..."

"But was there a lot of damage done to the car?" Beppe asked his colleague.

"Oh yes. They had smashed a headlight in, bent the car aerial, broken off the driver's side mirror – and scratched the bonnet."

"Why did Cristina and Emma think there was more than one kid involved?"

"Because it would have taken one person too long to have done that amount of damage, *commissario.*"

"I'm sure you must be right, Luigi," said Beppe, wondering how his own kids would turn out as teenagers.

"Shall I continue, *capo?*" asked Luigi. Beppe nodded.

"Well, we got through only four groups of kids before they got their culprits. It was really neatly done.
It was Cristina who addressed each group – she's already got the authoritative voice worked out. She told each group the same thing and Emma and I had the task of watching the children's reactions.

She informed them that they were former pupils of the school, gave them a lecture on respecting teachers and showed them a picture of the damaged car. It must have been vandalised inside the school car park, probably as everyone was going home for lunch.

'Don't worry, *ragazzi*,' she finished up. 'We think we know who is responsible. We have a fairly clear photo from one of the older students in the school who happened to be passing by. She caught them in the act with a photo on her smart-phone. We just wanted to warn you against any similar acts of vandalism in the future. You may be sure that future offenders will be dealt with severely.'

"That was it, *capo*. All Emma and I had to do was to observe the kids' reactions. Some of them nodded knowingly at each other. Others grinned. As I said, we were seeing the fourth group. These two boys, sitting apart, exchanged petrified glances. A simple trick, but it worked perfectly. They confessed in the end that there was a girl with them too, who snapped off the mirror. So, we got all three of them... *Capo?*"

Beppe looked as if his mind had switched to other matters.

"I've just had an idea, Luigi. Our two smart young ladies could help me with the toxic waste investigation we're involved in at the moment. Get them in tomorrow morning, could you? This is what I want them to think about - I'm sure, with their ingenuity, they will come up with some convincing strategy..."

Even the normally passive Luigi looked askance at his chief's suggestion.

"*Va bene, capo.* What time do you want them here tomorrow?" was all he deigned to say.

Beppe drove home north to Atri - and his family. He remained convinced that his colleague, Luigi Rocco, had been looking far too smug for his thoughts to have been provoked by anything as mundane as police work. He had seen that look on Luigi's face once before.

"There must be a woman involved," he concluded.

* * *

Home at last! Veronica seemed to have mastered the art of toddling and was now concentrating on word acquisition. Amazing what a difference a few days can make! Even Lorenzo showed visible signs of recognition at the return of his *papà*.

"We've missed you, *amore,*" stated Sonia simply as she hugged him tightly. "Should I start packing for Monday?"

Later that evening, after the children were in bed, Beppe and Sonia were holding on to each other, sitting side-by-side on the family sofa as if they had been apart for months.

Beppe was outlining the devious scheme he had been hatching, which involved the Archbishop of Pescara masquerading as the owner of a private clinic, in an as yet undecided location, who needed to dispose of a quantity of toxic waste on the cheap.

"The Archbishop will only need to make an anonymous phone call in his best Neapolitan dialect. He won't be physically at risk at all. I'm just not sure whether Mariastella will run with this scheme. Otherwise, we might have to wait for a month before whichever mafia clan is involved will make contact with the sheep farmer outside Pazzoli…"

"I can imagine you won't be able to wait that long, Beppe – knowing you!"

"The farmer, Arturo Annunzio, is the weak link in all this. If we can't work quickly, he'll lose his nerve. And I've got this young officer, Claudio Montano, camping out on the farm to keep the farmer on his toes. I can't keep him there for too long..."

"So, we won't be going to Pazzoli on Monday?"

"A bit premature, *amore*. But you're going to love Eugenia. She's a real treasure. You two will get on like a house on fire."

"But how can you set up this scam toxic waste dumping if you don't know for sure the identity of the mafia *boss* involved?" asked Sonia.

"That depends on a little charade I intend to play out tomorrow morning, Sonia – with the help of those two new recruits who you must have met when you came down to Pescara."

"So, you're going to desert us again, so soon, *amore?*"

"Only until midday. The *Questore* didn't actually order me to come in on Saturday – but she has an engaging way of making one feel obliged to cooperate."

"Good, Beppe. I'll come down to Pescara at midday. We could have lunch together. My mum is dying for the opportunity to look after Lorenzo and Veronica for a few hours. That'll make sure that Mariastella won't be inviting *you* out to lunch, *amore.*"

Beppe laughed.

"You still see Mariastella as a threat to our unity, do you, Sonia?"

"She's an attractive woman, Beppe. And I don't believe a word she says about preferring other women!"

* * *

Beppe knew that his three-month furlough was definitively over when he was woken up at six in the morning by his phone ringing, rousing him from a deep sleep during which he had dreamt he was wandering round an alien town, which had the nerve to present itself to his subconscious mind as his native Catanzara. It required a good thirty seconds to shake off the potent images of being a bewildered outlaw in a town whose name was the only aspect he recognised.

He was even more disconcerted to discover that the caller was no less a person that Don Emanuele – who would never phone him at this hour without good reason.

The soothing voice of the Archbishop apologising for disturbing him at this 'ungodly' hour was enough to bring him back to reality.

"I do not know what stage you are at this morning, Beppe. But I am sure you will be deeply engrossed in our investigation from the earliest moment possible."

"*Dimmi tutto,* [86] Your Eminence."

"Calling me 'Your Eminence' at this time of day really must indicate the worst-case scenario, Beppe. You must have been having bad dreams."

The Archbishop heard a grunt on the other end of the line which he took to be confirmation of his interpretation of events.

"I am so sorry, *commissario,* but I felt duty-bound to tell you what I have just discovered from a very unexpected source. I have just received a phone call from - of all people - Gianluca Alfieri who, it appears, was not feeling sleepy. You

---

[86] Dimmi tutto = Tell me all

may not know that I hear his confession regularly – via WhatsApp.

He informs me that he – and his wife – have just been kidnapped by his nephew and removed from their safe house in Abruzzo. It seems he has been taken to a remote farmhouse belonging to the clan in the hills just outside Naples."

"That is an incredible piece of news. It means that Gianluca Alfieri has become *un latitante!*" [87]

"Yes – and completely against his own will, he tells me. In point of fact, he might have taken quite a risk phoning me."

"It's an incredibly important piece of news, Don Emanuele. And I thank you for sharing it with me at this hour of the day. But I don't quite see how…?"

"The new *boss* of the clan is one of Gianluca's nephews. He is called Salvatore Alfieri. He lives – in luxury - in the Secondigliano suburb of Naples. He has to be your chief suspect. Knowing you, you will be going into the *Questura* early this morning to get this investigation under way. I am sure you have your initial step planned by now. So, I thought I should bring you up to date. It might help you."

Beppe was fully awake and taking in the significance of what the Archbishop was telling him.

"I thank you, Don Emanuele. And you are right to tell me this piece of news as early as possible. It could be invaluable."

"This Salvatore Alfieri has a fearsome reputation as a mafia boss. His nickname is *Totò u curtu*[88] in dialect. I got this from a local parish priest I know – whom I called just

---

[87] Un latitante – a fugitive from the Law
[88] Totò u curtu. 'Totò is short for Salvatore. U curtu = the short one.

before I phoned you. At least *he* was awake getting ready for early morning mass, Beppe. So, I didn't feel too bad about waking *you* up after that!"

Beppe managed a smile – invisible to the Archbishop.

"My parish priest told me he had heard rumours that this Salvatore Alfieri used to dabble in waste disposal. But the authorities in Naples have managed to clamp down on illegal dumping in Campania in the last few years – after literally hundreds of children have been suffering and dying from brain tumours and Leukaemia. On one site, even the buffaloes' milk for making mozzarella cheese was contaminated. Now, the clans are looking for dumping sites in other parts of Italy, I believe."

"*O Dio!* We'll get them, Don Emanuele. Whatever it takes. *Ti ringrazio di nuovo.*" [89]

"Something else you should know, Beppe: apparently, Gianluca Alfieri was telling me, there is a niece of Salvatore Alfieri who lives in the same village in the Abruzzo mountains where he was under house arrest. I understand she wanted to distance herself and her family from the activities of her relatives, so she moved away from Naples. She visited Gianluca regularly. It wasn't so much of a secret location as the authorities would have liked to believe, it seems. The village is called Cimabianca[90] – and the niece is called Violetta Alfieri. I don't know if this information is useful to you, Beppe, but..." concluded Don Emanuele, leaving his sentence hanging in the air.

Beppe knew precisely how he was going to make use of what the Archbishop had just told him. He was out of the

---

[89] Ti ringrazio di nuovo = I thank you again.
[90] Cimabianca = White Peak. Pron: Cheema bianca

house and heading back towards Pescara before Lorenzo and Veronica were awake.

"See you at midday, *amore,*" he said kissing Sonia. "And I know exactly the place where we can go and have lunch together."

"And I think I know which restaurant you have in mind, Beppe," replied Sonia with a knowing smile. "We haven't been back there since the day we were married."

17: All in a morning's work...

Beppe found the two 'girls' waiting for him in the meeting room. Luigi Rocca was with them, waiting for Beppe to arrive before he took his leave. Was that an expression of disapproval on Luigi's face, wondered the *commissario?*

Officers Cristina Cardinale and Emma Campione were both looking dispirited.

"You think I'm taking advantage of your two *protégées,* don't you *Agente* Rocca?" said Beppe gently.

"You know me too well, *capo,*" he replied.

"Why don't you stay with us, Luigi, to make sure I'm not overstepping the mark?"

"Grazie, commissario. I'll stay if you wish me to. But Cristina and Emma are very anxious that they have not come up with a convincing ploy. They are worried about letting you down. And Cristina thinks she will have to use her own phone..."

Before coming to the meeting room, Beppe had been downstairs to see his two technicians, Bianca Bomba and Marco Pollutri. They had enjoyed themselves, putting on their usual act - just to test the *commissario's* faith in their abilities whilst relieving the 'tedium' of being confined to the basement.

"Pardon me, *commissario?"* said Bianca. "You want us to supply you with a mobile phone device which cannot be traced to the caller! What makes you think such a thing exists?"

"Just imagine how much easier life would be if such a device had been invented!" chipped in Marco Pollutri for good measure.

After teasing the *commissario* for as long as they dared, Marco handed him an orange-coloured phone – which was still sealed up in its original cellophane packaging.

"Put it to good use, *commissario*. These gadgets have only recently become available to us."

"I'm trying to catch the killers of one Ginevra Ianni. Does that sound a good enough excuse for you two?" asked Beppe.

The pair relented with good grace.

"You need have no worries, *commissario*. This phone will display a fictitious number on the recipients' phone. If you want them to reply, you simply press this black key. But your anonymity is guaranteed. It will leave no permanent record. It's special police issue and the signal goes through our own telecommunications system."

Beppe took his grateful leave of the two technicians.

"What would the forces of law and order do without you two?" he said.

* * *

"Don't worry, Cristina. You will be making your call on this gadget – which leaves no traces. I have an idea as to how we should tackle this phone call, based on information I received only this morning. Now, which of you two ladies is the better actress, in your opinions?"

"*Agente* Campione," said Cristina.

"*Agente*, Cardinale," said Emma simultaneously.

"But Emma can do a seductive voice much better than me," said Cristina. "She has a special voice she always puts on for persistent boyfriends whom she wants to ditch!"

Even Luigi uttered a deep-throated laugh.

"Well," said Beppe, "You, Cristina took the limelight while catching the car-wreckers, I understand. So why don't we let Emma have a go at this bit of vital deception?"

"Is this to do with the Ginevra case, *commissario?*" asked Emma.

Beppe nodded. Luigi Rocco had lost his look of disapproval.

Beppe outlined the situation to the three officers in great detail, repeating most of what the Archbishop had told him. Emma began to look excited at the prospect of doing something important.

Beppe made her rehearse the scenario six times before he felt she had got into the role. Cristina pretended to be the boy, Samuele, who was likely to reply if Beppe's diagnosis was accurate. Beppe played the role of the boy's father, putting on a strong Neapolitan accent, in the likely scenario that the phone call would be interrupted. He changed the dialogue each time in an attempt to prepare Emma for whenever the conversation took off in an unexpected direction.

"That will do, *ragazze,*" said Beppe. "We shouldn't over-rehearse. The real conversation might take a very different course. *Allora, siamo pronti?*"[91]

Beppe looked at his watch. It was Saturday and not quite eight-thirty – a time when most Italian families should be sitting around the breakfast table.

Beppe was taken aback when Emma, on an impulse, seemed to be undressing.

---

[91] Siamo pronti? Are we ready?

"It's just a thought, *capo,* but it might reassure the kid if we go visual. I'll just run and get some ordinary clothing to go on top. I don't think it would be a good idea if I appeared as a police woman, do you?"

"I'm not sure whether…" began the *commissario.*

"Don't worry, *capo.* Emma's really good at drama," said Christina. "She knows what she's doing." His two new recruits were 'showing initiative', he tried to convince himself. Was he losing control these days?

"Take a deep breath everybody," he said when Emma had returned with a coloured silk scarf wrapped round her white policewoman's blouse. *"Va bene…*dial that number!"

It was a boy's voice who answered the call within three seconds.

Pronto! Chi è?

Ciao, Samuele. Io sono tua zia Violetta. Come stai?[92] But how come it's *you* answering your dad's phone?

Emma's heart rate had increased despite her efforts to control her nerves. She was afraid that her *capo* must be able to hear it beating against her rib-cage.

It's my phone now… eh, zia Violetta. Papà gave it to me several weeks ago. But I didn't know I had an auntie called Violetta.

Well, Samuele, you must have got so many aunts, uncles and cousins, I'm not surprised you don't remember me. I saw you last when you were just a little boy.

---

[92] Io sono la zia…. = I'm auntie Violetta. How are you?

Most people call me Sammy, zia.

Sammy – that's better. Is your papà there, Sammy?

He'll be down in a minute. I'm having my breakfast on my own. Can I see your face, please?

The *commissario* was frowning. It was risky putting the smartphone on to video mode.

Of course you can, Sammy. But just for a second or two. My battery's low – and I do need to talk to your dad...

Emma Campione looked at her chief and reassured him with a nod. She held the phone well away from herself and switched on the video mode. She waved and smiled at the boy and said:

Mamma mia! Come sei cresciuto, Sammy![93]

Emma was smiling and waving at the boy as if she were an old friend. Samuele must have been reassured – as Emma had correctly predicted.

Ciao, zia! I think I recognise you now. Where do you live?

Officer Emma Campione was getting into her stride. She had relied on the fact that her face was quite typical of

---

[93] Come sei cresciuto - How you've grown

so many Italian women – dark-skinned, brown eyes and long black hair.

"I live in a little town called Cimabianca – near where your great-uncle Gianluca lives.

Oh, zio Ginluca! I know him. I think I can hear my parents coming downstairs now. Shall I pass you over to my papà now?

Yes please, Sammy. It was lovely to see you again. You've grown into such a handsome young man!

Grazie zia. Here's my dad.

Beppe was making a furious gesture of cutting his throat with his hand. Emma frowned at the *commissario* as if to say: 'Stop destroying my concentration' as she touched the green icon to cut off the video camera.

Beppe sighed to himself and decided that he was no longer in charge of this performance. Emma Campione was handling the situation brilliantly. He would just take a back seat. He could see Mariastella in his mind's eye. She was nodding in approval.

The tension in the room mounted as the team waited with bated breath for Samuele's father to take up the conversation. An alarming twenty seconds elapsed before an uncouth voice broke the silence.

Ma tu, chi sei? [94]

---

[94] Who the hell are you? (The speaker disdainfully uses the familiar form of address)

Officer Emma Campione was looking petrified. But her next words were delivered in a tone of mocking jollity. Beppe was tempted to applaud her silently.

But, zio Salvo! How can you not know who I am? Your niece Violetta Alfieri - you know, the one who lives in Cimabianca near where *Zio*[95] Gianluca lives...

Wait a moment!

Beppe and his officers could hear a muted conversation. A woman's voice was predominant.

But Salvo – you should know who Violetta is...

The rest of the conversation was muffled but the wife of Salvatore Alfieri seemed to be going through a whole genealogical tree before the mafioso returned to the phone.

So...why are you phoning me? What do you want?

Two things really, *zio*. I'm so sorry to disturb you like this...

Just get to the point, will you!

Well, *zio* Salvo. It's like this. Gianluca seems to have disappeared. He's supposed to stay in that house and never leave it. I was just wondering if you knew anything about it. I'm very worried about him..."

---

[95] Zio - uncle

Gianluca and Monica are MY guests now. They are staying in a house I own just outside the city. Monica was getting fed up with being so far from her own family. Now what was the other matter you wanted to discuss?

Well, *zio,* it's a bit of a delicate issue…

Officer Campione had allowed her voice to become secretive, confidential – as if she had some delicate matter which she was reluctant to broach.

You see, Salvo, I work for a very important man called Fausto Gargiulo – he's from Caserta originally, I believe. He has a chain of private clinics dotted around Abruzzo and Molise. He's my boss and he keeps me on an impressively good salary… you know what I'm saying, *zio…*

There was a grunt from the Naples end of the line.

Well, he's got a big problem with getting rid of his medical waste. He's says if he keeps on going through the official channels, he won't be rich any more. He's heard from someone he knows that you operate a waste disposal service somewhere near a town called Pazzoli. I told my boss I know someone who might be able to solve his problem. Did I do the right thing, *zio?*

There was a protracted silence from the mafioso boss. Emma Campione was looking anxiously at Beppe. They hadn't rehearsed protracted silences. Beppe knew the mafia *boss* would be having an internal debate with himself – caution about a new situation would be vying with financial greed. Beppe put a finger to his lips. After ten seconds, he made gestures in sign language to his young officer to interrupt the silence with the words they had already rehearsed – without the long silence, however.

Zio Salvo – shall I send you my boss's number on *this* phone?

NO! Leave this to me.

Salvatore Alfieri – Totò u curtu – had cut off communications. Emma was looking at Beppe as if all her efforts had been in vain. She looked emotionally drained.
"You did brilliantly, *Agente* Campione – Emma."
"But he hasn't given us his number, *capo.* That was the one piece of information we needed," she said desperately.
"*Pazienza, mia cara!* Besides which, he never denied his involvement in all this. We've got him. We know who is responsible for Ginevra's death – and probably a host of other children dotted around Campania as well."
The group of four had fallen silent. Only Luigi Rocco looked serene. But he had the advantage of knowing how his chief's mind worked.
After ten long minutes, the tense silence was broken by a strange bee-like sound from the mobile phone which Beppe had placed on the table. The *commissario* was looking self-satisfied – he was in charge again! *Totò u curtu* had sent them a text message.
Beppe held up the phone triumphantly to show his colleagues the number on the screen.

"Got him!" said Beppe. "That was a truly professional piece of acting on your part, Emma. Congratulations! Not even Salvatore Alfiera thought to ask you how you got that phone number in the first place. *Brava davvero! Bravissima!*"

"I had an answer ready to that question if necessary, *capo,* but it wasn't all that convincing."

Beppe went up to Emma and planted a kiss on her forehead – and then one on Cristina's for good measure.

"Bravissimo, ragazze!" he said as he walked out of the room before their faces could register any reaction to his spontaneous, avuncular gesture. He nodded pleasantly at Officer Luigi Rocco.

"Keep up the good work, Luigi."

Commissario Stancato felt he was back at the helm.

***

He headed for his office and sat behind his desk for the first time since his return to Via Pesaro after his six-month period of enforced absence. He had had an informal chat with his friend, Pippo Cafarelli, on duty at the reception desk and filled him in on the morning's events – and told him to look out for Sonia round about midday.

"I shall be in my office if anybody wants to see me, Pippo."

"It's good to have you back, *capo,*" commented Pippo, "...back to normal, so to speak."

Beppe had a trickle of visitors throughout the morning – notably Officers Gino Martelli and Danilo Simone.

"We want to get involved with the Ginevra case, *capo*. Do you think you might find a role for us when things hot up?"

"I suspect there will be plenty of scope for you in a few days' time, *ragazzi*. Especially if you're happy to travel out towards Pazzoli."

Beppe could not have foreseen at that point just how involved these two officers would become in the 'Ginevra affair' – as everybody now seemed to refer to it.

He spent the time talking at length to Don Emanuele about how expertly his information had been exploited that morning by his two recruits.

"Those two girls already act like professionals. Now I need to go and see our *Questore* and put your offer of help to her. If you are serious about being involved in the investigation, then you could say a prayer or two for me while I am upstairs in her office."

"She won't put up any objections, Beppe. I bet you…"

"I didn't think archbishops were allowed to bet," Beppe said, filling the pause.

"Indeed, Beppe," said Don Emanuele, laughing. "I was just thinking I have nothing to bet with. Maybe a lifetime's supply of votive candles? What I *was* thinking, however, is that, if we set up a scam deal with *Totò u curtu,* we shall have to find a considerable sum of money to put upfront. I doubt whether that individual from Naples will do it for charity."

That's why I need to talk to Mariastella. Only she will have the authority to raise that kind of money – or at least the semblance of it. The DIA[96] will have to become involved."

"Good. I can cope with everything else except the financial aspect, Beppe."

---

[96] DIA = Direzione Investigativa Antimafia. The anti-mafia police

Beppe received a call from Officer Claudio Montano from Arturo Annunzio's farm, informing him in detail how to milk sheep.

"Me and Arturo are getting on like a house on fire, *commissario*. I think he's reassured by my presence. His wife certainly is. She's treating me like a son. Oh, and by the way, I can confirm that a couple with Neapolitan accents – a man and a woman – did do the rounds of many local farms some months ago. They claimed they were prospecting for land on which to build luxury chalets, or something of the sort. And, by the way, Arturo confirmed that he *was* contacted by the mafioso on that mobile number I gave you."

"Yes, that number has been put to good use, Claudio. I'll tell you all about it when I see you. You shouldn't have to wait too long before you get a call from the mafia boss. Right now, I have to go and see the *Questore. Bravo, Claudio.* You are making a valuable contribution."

"*Grazie, commissario.* But, it's just part of the job, you know."

* * *

The Archbishop had been correct in his analysis. Mariastella had listened to her second-in-command, taking in every detail of the morning's events with almost wide-eyed fascination. Her comment about Don Emanuele's involvement in setting up their very own version of *La Stangata*[97] was matter-of-fact.

---

[97] La Stangata = The Sting – that film!

"That's fine Beppe. I cannot see any objection to your idea. After all, Don Emanuele will only have to make an anonymous phone call."

Beppe must have been looking mildly suspicious at the ease with which she had been persuaded to go along with the deception.

She smiled sweetly at her *commissario* and said:

"On one condition, Beppe Stancato – the call takes place up here in my office. I want to be present this time – rather than always learning about your devious schemes second hand."

"With pleasure, Mariastella. Let me have a day to work out with Don Emanuele how we should set about the next phase."

"Yes, Sunday seems an ideal day in which to brief an archbishop!" said Mariastella with heavy sarcasm.

Beppe smiled sweetly back.

"Now I really must go out, Beppe. I have a lunch engagement which I cannot get out of. We'll see each other on Monday morning, *d'accordo?*"[98]

Beppe went downstairs. He saw Luigi Rocco heading purposefully towards the main door. He thought he could discern the return of that smug look on his broad features.

* * *

Beppe and Sonia arrived outside the seafront restaurant called *Da Pepé* – where their wedding reception had been held – at about one o'clock. There seemed to be a lot of people inside already eating. Sonia was peering

---

[98] D'accordo? – Agreed?

through the window to see if she could spot any free places. What she saw caused her to withdraw her glance in haste. She was suppressing a grin with great difficulty.

"Take a look, Beppe – cautiously though. Over towards the table on the far right!"

Beppe did more than grin. He broke into a peel of unrestrained laughter.

He had spotted an un-uniformed Luigi Rocco sitting at a table for two, opposite Mariastella Mancini. They were engaged in earnest conversation.

Beppe and Sonia walked arm-in-arm to the restaurant over the road – with an outdoor terrace overlooking the turquoise Adriatic Sea - which looked even more stunningly beautiful than usual.

Never had a sea-food pasta tasted so appetising, they agreed, sipping white wine from an equally outstanding bottle of Trebbiano.[99]

---

[99] Trebbiano – a grape variety native to Abruzzo

18: In which the commissario acts on his own initiative...

Mindful of the *Questore's* pointed comment about not devising complex plans with archbishops on a Sunday, Beppe decided he would go and see Don Emanuele that afternoon while Sonia was driving back home to Atri: "Seeing as we came in separate cars and can't be together, *amore*."

Sonia agreed on one condition: that they had a long and romantic walk along the seashore before going their separate ways.

"It will be the first intimate walk we have had since Veronica was born," she pointed out.

And so, the couple, silhouettes linked arm in arm as far as the rest of the world was concerned, strolled for one hour away from Pescara towards the shimmering horizon and then back again before they reluctantly took leave of each other.

"I'll be home before dark," Beppe said. "And, I promise to stay with you all day tomorrow."

"Even if I take the children to mass?" asked Sonia, knowing how Beppe found masses tediously repetitive – unless enlivened by an inspirational sermon; a rare event in their local church in Atri.

Beppe sighed and promised to go to mass if necessary. He would wait until the next day before he suggested taking the family to the mountains instead.

* * *

The mountains won. Sonia had shown little inclination to take a nappy-bound and grizzly Lorenzo to sit through an hour-long mass. She knew from experience that, whenever she suggested that they should observe the Catholic duties sworn to in the presence of none other than Don Emanuele himself, Beppe would propose an outing to any place which avoided going to the Church of the Immaculate Conception in Atri. Veronica looked quite put out by the announcement that they were not going to go and sing.

"She seems to have developed a liking for pageantry, candles and incense," explained Sonia.

"I hope that doesn't mean she'll end up becoming a nun," observed Beppe as they headed for the hills with a picnic in the boot.

"No worries on that score, *amore*. She always gets bored during the sermon."

Beppe had been surprised how early he had arrived home from Pescara the previous evening; it was still daylight and a great deal had been accomplished in a short space of time.

"Don Emanuele told me he never rehearsed any challenge such as this one beforehand – not even his sermons," explained Beppe on his arrival home well before seven o'clock the previous evening. "He told me he had to trust in the Holy Spirit to guide his steps through the wilderness ahead. He only wanted to know what his pseudonym would be, so he could get into the part, he told me."

"You can fill me in on the details just before we make the phone call, Beppe, he told me. Go home and be with your family."

Sonia had asked Beppe a question about an aspect of this risky venture that had been intriguing her for hours.

"Where are you going to get a supply of toxic waste from to make the operation look like the real thing, Beppe?"

"Oh, I think I've found the answer to that problem already," was all Beppe deigned to tell her.

The mountain scenery and fresh air was enough to dispel thoughts of what lay ahead. Even Veronica was aware of the breathless beauty that greeted them. She had stretched an arm out rigidly as if she wanted to touch the blue peeks of the Gran Sasso mountain range with her finger-tips.

"Do you see how that mountain top looks just like a woman lying down to sleep, Vero?"[100] Sonia said to her daughter. "We call her The Sleeping Beauty."

Veronica seemed spellbound, even if she might not have grasped the full meaning of her mother's words. But Beppe swore he had seen her nod.

"Che bello, mamma!" she managed to articulate.
Church candles and colourful vestments had nothing on this.

On arriving home later that afternoon, Sonia's mother and father greeted them with the words:

"Our old parish priest delivered the most rousing sermon I've ever heard him give at mass today," said Irene. "He told us all about the case you are working on, Beppe. He kept on talking about what happened to the little girl called Ginevra – whose soul still lives on..."

"We've been asked to help capture the people responsible for her death," continued Roberto. "We were each told to fill black plastic bags with anything we could

---

[100] 'Vero' – a diminutive form of 'Veronica'

find; old bandages, medicine bottles, empty tooth-paste tubes and tooth brushes – even used nappies and similar stuff!"

Roberto was looking meaningfully – almost accusingly - at his son-in-law.

Beppe was looking alarmed.

"I hope you were not told the reason why, Roberto."

"No, Father Tomaso himself did not seem to know what was going on. But he assured everybody that God would smile on their good deed. He seemed to be implying they could cut down their time in purgatory by cooperating..."

Beppe knew his father-in-law's tendency to be irreverent about Holy Mother Church and laughed at Roberto's turn of phrase.

Beppe inwardly sighed with relief that there had been no hint of the true purpose of this 'act of mercy' to be executed by the good citizens of Atri.

He had been to visit a private hospital a short distance away from Atri on the road to Teramo before coming home the previous evening. It was Don Emanuele who had phoned the parish priest, following instructions from Beppe.

When Sonia and he were on their own, Beppe explained in greater detail.

"It was an obvious place to go, *amore*," he explained. "But it became clear that the hospital would not be able to supply enough material to be convincing. It was just an idea I had to boost the limited amount of genuine medical waste we could hope to collect in the short time available. I didn't think you would want me to go into all the details."

"No wonder you didn't want to go to mass this morning, *mio caro!* That would *really* have constituted mixing business with pleasure."

Beppe laughed at the sarcasm of her comment – and kissed her on the forehead.

"You do that to *all* your female staff, I am told, Beppe Stancato."

He hugged her instead – trying not to be concerned as to how his recent departure from strict police etiquette had come to Sonia's notice so readily.

"You would have made an excellent *Questore, amore,*" he added, hoping to save some face.

"Who's to say I won't be one day, *commissario?*" replied Sonia.

Beppe sighed as Sonia led him towards the secrecy of their bedroom.

"*Agli ordini, signora!*"[101]

In the darkness, Sonia asked Beppe what she had been dying to ask for the last twenty-four hours.

"So, what do you make of Mariastella having an intimate lunch with Luigi Rocco, *tesoro?*"[102]

"Who knows, Sonia? Luigi is a dark one. He appears to create a sort of protection zone around him which some women are drawn to. Do you remember me telling you about the vanishing physicist's wife? She seemed to single out Luigi for comfort when her husband had been abducted by those two American agents. And then he knows this very attractive call-girl in Pescara who turns to him for consolation..."

---

[101] Agli ordinini, signora! Yes ma'am!
[102] Tesoro = treasure. A term of endearment.

"I told you Mariastella has a vulnerable side to her," said Sonia, who instantly understood the drift of Beppe's thoughts.

"I'm always astonished by the unpredictable manner in which we human beings are drawn to each other," commented Beppe. "Except in our case of course, *amore...*"

Sonia appeared to have fallen asleep in his arms.

* * *

Early Monday morning found the *Questore* and her highly inventive second-in-command in deep conversation on the upstairs level of the police headquarters.

Beppe had managed to work in the question which was uppermost in his mind early on in their discussion.

"How did your lunch appointment go on Saturday?" he asked with a look of total innocence on his face.

"Quite satisfactorily, thank you, *commissario*. It was purely a business lunch, you understand," replied Mariastella in a peremptory tone of voice which brooked no further discussion. "I understand you have been very busy indeed, Beppe, since we last met – displaying your inventive talents to great effect in your own home town."

Beppe was astounded at her words. How could she have possibly...?

"It is a sign of a competent chief of police to know what is going on in her domain apparently by the gift of being omnipresent, *Signora Questore. Congratulazioni!*"

"And is it equally a sign of a good second-in-command to take the initiative in an investigation without consulting the aforementioned chief of police first, Beppe?" she added sharply.

Beppe felt firmly put in his place.

"You are right, Mariastella. I should have consulted you first. I simply wanted to move things on a bit…"

"You do have my telephone number, do you not, Beppe? You are welcome to use it at any time of the day or night."

"May I ask how you knew…?"

"I spent ten minutes on the phone this morning with the editor of *Il Centro Pescarese*, who asked me if I knew anything about a parish priest in Atri, who has been exhorting his parishioners to collect and bag any vaguely medical waste products they could dig up to save the planet – and help capture the criminals responsible for the death of a child called Ginevra."

Beppe was feeling humiliated and deflated.

"I am sorry, Mariastella. I thought Atri was far enough away from Pescara …" he began feebly.

"I managed to persuade the editor not to print the story immediately with the promise that he would have exclusivity of the whole story within one week. But what did you think you were doing, Beppe? You might have wrecked the whole operation you were planning before it had even got under way."

Beppe looked so contrite that the *Questore* almost felt sorry for him.

"In future, short term or long term, you will undertake to keep me informed of *every* scheme you come up with – before, not after, you put it into practice. If it happens again, I shall dispatch you back to Calabria reduced to the rank of a mere foot-soldier. *Siamo chiari,*[103] *commissario?"*

Any moral superiority Beppe had been revelling in following his discovery of Mariastella's dalliance with the Mountain Bear was reduced to the level of sleezy muck-raking. This was a life-changing moment for him, he was gracious enough to admit to himself.

"I am truly sorry, Mariastella. You deserve to be treated with far greater trust and respect than I have shown you since your arrival…"

The lady *Questore* merely grunted her agreement with his statement whilst continuing to pierce his armour with a cold stare. She relented with the words:

"Now for heaven's sake, Beppe, let's put together some details about the rest of this investigation, which has already become so complex that it would leave even Albert Einstein's brain reeling. Don Emanuele is coming to the *Questura* at eleven o'clock. We need to be ready for him."

And that is precisely what they managed to do. Any rancour on the part of Mariastella Mancini had evaporated – she acted almost as if she approved of the strategic short cut he had taken. Beppe was even left with the impression that she wished she had thought of the tactic herself. But the severity of her threat of instant dismissal from the rank of *commissario,* coupled to exile in Calabria, echoed in his mind. This lady was a force to be reckoned with.

Beppe could never have imagined, at that moment in time, the extent to which his opinion of his new chief would be transformed by the end of the days ahead.

---

[103] Siamo chiari? Are we quite clear about that?

19: In which Don Emanuele becomes embroiled in non-ecclesiastical matters...

"*Pronto,* Don Emanuele?" asked Mariastella.

To the astonishment of the *Questore* and Beppe, the Archbishop had arrived in civvies, less than an hour ago.

"You seem to have forgotten that my name is Fausto Cargiulo, *signori,*" he had told them.

Beppe had been on the point of going through his precise set of instructions for a second time. The tall business man that the archbishop had been transformed into held up a hand to stop Beppe from repeating words unnecessarily.

And so began their unrehearsed routine. Beppe's heart was in his mouth.

'Fausto Cargiulo' dialled the mafioso's number on the smartphone which Beppe had supplied him with. As he had been instructed, the archbishop let the phone ring until it was answered by the gruff, hostile voice of Don Salvatore Alfieri. Don Emanuele cut off the call without saying a word, counted up to fifteen and then re-dialled the number.

"We needed to make sure that the right person would answer," Beppe had explained.

The irritation in the mafioso's voice the second time he answered was apparent.

As the conversation got under way, Mariastella looked in amazement at her colleague. Beppe was looking smug again. Mariastella was visibly impressed by the fluent Neapolitan dialect that was issuing from the archbishop's lips.

Beppe nodded knowingly. He had encountered the phenomenon once before.

Who are you? Was it you who phoned me a few seconds ago?

Yes, Don[104] Salvatore. I had to close my office door. I didn't want anyone listening in on what I am about to say to you.

So, I repeat, who the hell are you?

My name is Fausto Cargiulo. I employ your granddaughter, *Signorina* Violetta Alfieri, Don Salvatore..."

Niece!

Ah, indeed! Whatever her relationship is to you, she always speaks very highly of you. I am sure she has already spoken to you and outlined the purpose of my call. I understand you can help me with a waste disposal problem that I have. Is that true?

(Don Salvatore Alfieri utters a grunting sound which might have been an affirmative.)

I hope I am not wasting my time talking to you, Don Salvatore. I have three private clinics to run in Abruzzo. So, are you able to help me or not?

We offer such services to our tried and trusted clients, Signor Cargiulo, yes.

---

[104] Don – a title attached to mafia bosses as well as to priests!

Well, Don Salvatore, there needs to be one occasion at least – or so it seems to me – when you need to put a new client's good faith to the test. Now is such an occasion. After that, I am sure we shall be able to establish a working relationship on a more permanent basis. What do you say, *Totò u curtu?*"

Beppe had drawn in his breath sharply at the Archbishop's sheer audacity. But, staggeringly, the mafioso seemed to find the use of his sobriquet flattering – or reassuring. But the mafioso's next words sent a chill down Beppe's spine. His minute planning of this first encounter was shattered by Don Salvatore's next words.

You will come to Napoli, Signor Cargiulo. We shall meet at my house. You can bring the cash with you – thirty thousand euros. That way, I might feel able to trust you.

Whereas the *Commissario* and the *Questore* were looking at each other in alarm at the prospect of their scam collapsing, 'Fausto Cargiulo' let out an unrestrained guffaw.

I don't think you seriously imagine that I am going to travel all the way to Naples carrying that amount of cash, do you Don Salvatore? I shall bring my electronic device and pay whatever sum we finally agree upon via electronic transfer. I shall then enjoy your hospitality until such time as the transaction is complete. That's the way business is done in *my* world. How does *that* sound to you, Don Salvatore?

The rest of the phone call had, of necessity, involved a lengthy logistical discussion about the eventual operation, during which Fausto Cargiulo had laid down his 'very reasonable' arrangements for the collection and disposal of the 'toxic waste'.

"Atri is not so far away from the place where, I am told, you have a well-hidden dumping site…"

Fausto Cargiulo had held his breath, in anticipation of some objection from Salvatore Alfieri, but none was forthcoming.

This told Beppe that it was unlikely that the mafia boss had another dumping site in Abruzzo – the only potentially weak point in his elaborate scheme.

* * *

"I expected him to say I would have to meet him in person," explained Don Emanuele, after he had been showered with unrestrained praise by both the police officers for his adept handling of the mafioso boss.

"As for him demanding to be paid in cash, that was just the usual 'mafia language' to indicate the amount he was hoping to be paid…"

"*Trattabile,*"[105] added Beppe, who had temporarily forgotten how the mafioso mind usually worked.

"Of course," replied Don Emanuele. "I should be able to get that amount down to €25 000."

"You made the right move to suggest you couldn't go to Naples before Thursday," said Beppe. "We shall have a lot of ground to cover in the next three days. That means we should expect the arrival of the waste at Arturo Annunzio's farm early next week."

---

[105] Trattabile = negociable

Mariastella was looking anxious. She had convinced herself that the whole manoeuvre could be arranged over the telephone. Leaving Don Emanuele to visit the mafioso face to face was an alarming prospect.

The Archbishop understood what was going through her mind.

"I was expecting this complication, Mariastella," he repeated. "Don't be concerned. It is entirely my choice to make this trip to Naples. It needn't involve anybody else – and I shall come away unscathed. Have no fears on my account."

The *Questore* had reassumed her habitual air of authority. She had already made up her mind and bowed to the inevitable.

"There is no way you are going to that man's house without an escort, Don Emanuele – even if you do believe a whole cohort of guardian angels will be accompanying you. Beppe and I will arrange an escort for you – and the means of transport."

She had spoken so decisively that neither Don Emanuele nor her second-in-command had demurred.

"Come back on Wednesday, Don Emanuele. I shall have arranged an escort – and a bank account for you by then. Then we can finalise the details."

Don Emanuele took his dignified leave. He had an unaccustomed gleam of excitement in his eyes.

Mariastella ordered Beppe to remain where he was. He was taken aback by her next words. He had been expecting a remonstration for his lack of foresight – or an accusation that he had failed to convey to her the likelihood that the Archbishop would be forced to confront the mafioso in person. Her words took him completely off his guard. She was looking at him in a kindly manner and smiling.

"Please do not take what I am about to say the wrong way, Beppe. From this Thursday, I am reinstating your period of unpaid leave for the remaining two weeks that you should have been in exile. You do understand what I am saying, don't you *commissario?*"

Beppe merely stared in disbelief at his new leader with mingled admiration and gratitude on his face.

She was giving him a free hand.

* * *

The short time that Beppe had left to organise the execution of this complex operation took up every waking hour of the two whole days that remained. On the Wednesday evening, he headed back to Pazzoli with his family. He had tried to dissuade Sonia from coming too on the grounds that his whereabouts might be unpredictable. Sonia had insisted that he maintain his promise.

"There's no way I want to be stuck in Atri while there is a risk you may be gallivanting around central Italy doing heaven knows what...*commissario,*" she said adding his title for good measure.

"I'm glad you'll be nearby, *amore,*" he admitted.

He had visited the private clinic in Atri and warned the *padrone*[106] that he might receive a phone call from one Don Alfieri.

"Just remember you must tell him that Fausto Cargiulo – the owner of this clinic and another two in

---

[106] Padrone - proprietor

Abruzzo – is away on business. Tell him, yes, the consignment is ready to pick up. Be very wary, *signore,* you may be talking to a dangerous mafia boss – or more likely one of his faithful sidekicks."

Beppe was impressed by the considerable amount of black sacks that the worthy citizens of Atri had managed to collect – cajoled by Sonia and her parents. Each bag had a yellow sticker with a skull and crossbones label stuck on – accompanied by the word PERICOLO[107] in black letters; the work of the *commissario.*

"I'll phone you to let you know when the mafia gangsters will be arriving. They'll just be small-fry – and anxious to get away quickly. Just leave everything where we agreed and make sure you are well out of the way. Warn your night-duty staff at the last minute…"

The owner of the clinic was looking aghast at every word the *commissario* was uttering.

"Don't worry, Alberto, I'll explain everything to you when it's all over," said Beppe.

"I understand it's something to do with the death of that little girl…" began the owner of the clinic.

"*Acqua in bocca,*[108] Alberto!" said Beppe as he left the clinic with a warning finger waved in the owner's direction.

Beppe had spoken at length to Officer Claudio Montano, now fully versed in the skills of milking sheep and lugging full milk churns from milking shed to departure point. He had, out of sheer necessity, developed a taste for Pecorino cheese and mutton, he informed his chief.

"You should warn Arturo Annunzio that he will be getting a phone call from Don-Alfieri-the-Second over the

---

[107] Pericolo - danger
[108] Acqua in bocca – Mum's the word (Lit: Water in the mouth)

next few days. You might like to help him dig a nice deep hole – for the last time…"

"We've already discussed that, *capo*," stated *Agente* Montano.

"I shall be phoning your Inspector De Sanctis in a moment. I'll get him to send someone over to Pazzoli to give you a break if you like, Claudio – or simply to keep you company."

"Thank you, *commissario*. But I'm quite happy just…"

But he noticed that the *commissario* had already hung up. He shrugged his shoulders. Either way would be good, especially if it happened to be Valentina Ianni who turned up.

* * *

Beppe was not present when Don Emanuele set off from the *Questura* in Pescara late on Wednesday evening, in an unmarked police car. His escorts were Officers Danilo Simone and Gino Martelli – pleased that, after years of being considered the *novellini* of the Via Pesaro team, they had been entrusted with a 'real' task. They were dressed in casual but smart, clothes – having been forbidden, for obvious reasons, to wear uniforms. Harder to bear had been the strict injunction from the *Questore* herself that they were not to carry arms.

"Believe you me, where you are going, you will be safer off without your weapons. This is *real* undercover police work, *ragazzi!*" a uniformed Mariastella had assured them. "You have only your wits to defend you. Take care of Don Emanuele and *in bocca al lupo* to all three of you!"

At round about the same time, Beppe and his family were setting off for Pazzoli, heading for the home of the mayoress, Eugenia Mancini, who had been overjoyed at the prospect of becoming a true hostess once again.

"I've already made up the beds, Beppe. I can't wait to meet your family. Alice is trying to make your arrival an excuse not to go to school – but of course, I said 'no' – very firmly, I might add!"

It felt to Beppe as if they were heading off for a family holiday. But one part of his brain was warning him that the way ahead would be fraught with unforeseen problems.

Sonia was thinking along the same lines – but kept the lurking dread entirely to herself. From past experience, she knew that her husband – and father of their children - would be unable to resist the desire to become personally involved in every twist and turn of the events which were about to unfold.

She sighed in resignation and said a silent prayer. At least she would be by his side some of the time.

20:   'Totò u curtu' shows his true colours...

Apart from being large and set in spacious grounds, the house of the mafioso looked unremarkable viewed from the outside. Don Emanuele had spent the night as the guest of his old friend, Don Alfonso, the local parish priest. His escorts had found an anonymous-looking bed and breakfast nearby. The three of them had arrived outside the mafioso's stronghold on foot.

"This is it, *ragazzi!*" stated Don Emanuele tersely. "Here, I want one of you to look after this."

To Gino and Danilo's discomfort, he handed over the mobile phone he had been supplied with by the *commissario*.

"Keep it somewhere on your person where it can't be readily found if you're searched," ordered Don Emanuele.

"But you might need to call us for help, Don Emanuele," began Gino.

"It's the first thing they are likely to confiscate and they'll use it to check it out to see if I am who I say I am. If they find nobody's name on it, they'll be a hundred times more suspicious. Trust me, *ragazzi!* I know how they operate."

The imposing, bald-headed businessman walked unhesitatingly up to the security gate and announced his presence into the elaborate *citofono*,[109] in a language quite unfamiliar to the two police officers.

"Fausto Cargiulo to see Don Salvatore Alfieri. We have an appointment."

It was Don Salvatore himself who answered the summons after a deliberate delay. Don Emanuele turned to

---

[109] Citòfono - entryphone

the two officers with a broad grin and a shrug of his shoulders – as if to say this was all part of the game.

"*Benvenuto, Signor Cargiulo.* Please come in. Tell your bodyguards to step inside. But I won't have them in the house. They can stay in the forecourt."

Danilo and Gino looked petrified. Gino had instinctively put his hand to where his holster should have been, feeling its absence as if he had just discovered he was standing stark naked in an unfamiliar street.

The wrought iron security gate slid with a soft humming noise into the cavity between a double wall. The three of them were committed to a course of action that could no longer be reversed.

Gino could feel his knees shaking, he confessed to his friend later on. The group was greeted by a couple of rough-looking hoodlums who towered above the two policemen and looked scornfully at these miniature bodyguards. Gino and Danilo were patted in a superficial manner in places where they were likely to have carried guns. They then subjected Don Emanuele to a more thorough search, opening his briefcase to check its contents.

"*Va bene!* You two wait here where we can see you. Signor Cargiulo, come this way please. 'Signor Cargiulo' had managed to maintain a cynical smile on his face throughout the brief but humiliating procedure the trio had been subjected to.

"See you in a couple of minutes, *ragazzi,*" said Don Emanuele cheerfully as he detached himself from the grip of one of the hoodlums, uttering a few well-chosen words to his escort, implying he was here of his own free will.

Don Emanuele was surprised on seeing *Totò u curtu.* The mafia boss was indeed 'short' as his nickname implied.

He had been expecting a greater family resemblance to the other Alfieri he knew, Gianluca – the 'repentant' ex-mafia boss whose confession he had extracted a couple of years previously. Gianluca was overweight and walked with a pronounced waddle. Salvatore Alfieri was wiry and moved like a snake. He was looking at the new arrival with suspicious, appraising grey eyes.

Salvatore pointed to an upright chair – one of many set out round a large oval table – and indicated to this lofty man that he should sit down. Salvatore remained standing, looking disdainfully at his visitor. Even standing up, Don Salvatore Alfieri was barely taller than his seated visitor. He continued to stare at his adversary – in an attempt to unnerve him.

"Well, Don Salvatore," snapped Don Emanuele, "can we get started? I'm sure you have had time to register my presence in your house by now. I suggest we get things moving."

If the mafioso *boss* was disconcerted by his new client's forthright manner, he did not show any signs of being intimidated by it.

Do you accept the price we agreed during our phone conversation, Signor Cargiulo?

I do not recall agreeing to anything, Don Salvatore. In fact, €30 000 is almost as much as I would have to cough up to have the waste disposed of through official channels. I was thinking more along the lines of €20 000.

The burst of laughter emanating from the mafioso's mouth was mocking and humourless. But Don Emanuele's smile never wavered.

You are living in an imaginary world, Signor Cargiulo. You have no idea what is involved in the correct disposal of toxic waste.

Ah, you intend to dispose of my load of black bags legitimately, do you, Don Salvatore? I was under the impression you had found a place to dump this stuff, euh, unofficially, should we say? A place in the mountains called Pazzoli, so I was told...

The first sign of irritation crossed the mafioso's face. How did this imposing looking man know so much?

I got in contact with you – rather than anyone else, Don Salvatore – indirectly via your niece – because you would not have so far to transport my accumulated store of medical waste, compared to going through official channels, which would have involved it having to be transported to some incinerator in the North. I hope I am not going to be disappointed by this visit?

Beppe had implored the Archbishop to attempt the difficult task of ensuring that the mafia clan would use the same site as before – at the Annunzio farm.

Because this is the first time you are doing business with me, signore, I will do the job for €24 000 – paid in full, up-front. That is to say, immediately!

It was Signor Cargiulo's turn to let out a guffaw of disbelieving mirth. Don Emanuele was now going contrary to Beppe Stancato's strict instructions. But Don Emanuele had his own idea as to how the monumental task ahead of them would be best achieved. He would make doubly sure that the death of Ginevra – and so many other children – would be properly avenged. He wanted no loop-hole for evasion left open to this man. He was painfully aware that he was going one risky step beyond what his friend the *commissario* had been intending. *Abbiamo fatto trenta, facciamo trentuno!*[110] reckoned Don Emanuele.

€12 000 now and the balance on completion of the job on my terms, Don Salvatore. Take it or leave it.

    The twisted, sadistic smile on *Totò u curtu's* face told the Archbishop that the bait had been taken. The arrangements for the pick-up and disposal of the special consignment of toxic waste was agreed. Signor Cargiulo took out his iPad and the transaction – which he had practised a hundred times with Beppe – was completed successfully.
    Don Salvatore Alfieri had sent a covert signal to his two henchmen. As Don Emanuele replaced his computer in its case, he was aware of the movement – and the smell of the gangsters right behind him. The hood that was placed over his head and tied roughly round his neck came as no surprise. It was so predictable that he had to force himself to shout his angry but muffled protestations to the world around him.
    "Don't be alarmed, Signor Cargiulo," sneered the mafioso *boss,* "This is just a precaution. You will remain my guest until this job is complete. Then you can pay me the

---

[110] In for a penny, in for a pound. (Lit: We've done 30, let's do 31)

rest and we shall send you happily on your way. It will all be over in a few days' time."

"You *bastardo!* You crook!"

Don Emanuele continued to use language – in dialect – that he had learnt in the streets of Naples during his childhood. He only stopped when the two hoodlums yanked him to his feet and led him out through the back of the house and shoved him unceremoniously into the back seat of a SUV that smelt of...sin, Don Emanuele decided.

* * *

Outside the house in the front courtyard, *Agenti* Danilo Simone and Gino Martelli were shocked to the core to see the hooded figure of a tall man being driven at speed out of the courtyard towards the main gate. They were sure that the hooded figure had raised a hand in a farewell wave.

Another hoodlum, armed with what looked like a Rottweiler on a massive leather lead was emerging from the house and heading in their direction.

Danilo grabbed his friend, shouting: "No time for heroics!" as they ran for the main entrance just as the massive gate began to close.

They instinctively took refuge in the back-street bed-and-breakfast hostel where they had slept. They both looked downcast. Yet again, they had let their chief, *Commissario* Stancato, down badly.[111]

They would have to phone him immediately and face his wrath at their sheer incompetence.

---

[111] A reference to an incident in 'The Case of the Sleeping Beauty"

The Archbishop's phone had been retrieved from its hiding place tucked behind Gino's broad leather belt.

Without thinking, Gino had switched on the phone. To his astonishment, he discovered that there was a message on the screen – apparently left for them to see.

It read: *Ciao ragazzi! They have probably taken me to Totò u curtu's country house in a hamlet in the hills just outside Naples. It's called Civitella della Torre. The parish priest knows where it is. Forgive me for this departure from our plan! I know it's for the best. See you all soon. Pregate per me.*[112] *D.E.*

Gino showed the message to Danilo.

"But that means..." began Danilo.

"...that he *knew* he was going to be taken as a hostage." Gino completed the sentence.

"Or that he had planned it in advance without telling the chief what he was intending to do. That would explain why he left the phone with us, Gino."

The discovery made both of the officers feel a degree less guilty. But there was no putting off the moment when they would have to phone the *commissario* with a piece of news which was sure to complicate his life. They tossed a coin to decide who would break the news to their *capo*.

---

[112] Pregate per me – Pray for me

21: *La trappola è tesa...* *(The Trap is Set)*

The warmth of the greeting that the Stancato family received from the mayoress of Pazzoli – and her daughter Alice - was overwhelming. It became instantly apparent that Sonia and Eugenia Mancini would bond like sisters.

For Beppe, the extended family atmosphere which was created by the simple act of being seated round Eugenia's kitchen table with the smell of food wafting round them was marred by the phone call he received after only a couple of mouthfuls of her *melanzane alla parmigiana.*[113]

Beppe excused himself and took Gino's phone call out in the garden. The tone of his young colleague's voice had instantly alerted him that something had gone wrong with the plan.

Gino spoke without drawing a breath, it seemed. He was anxious to get what he had to say off his chest.

"Alright, Gino. It was inevitable that something like this would happen. No harm will come to him as long as he stuck to my strict instructions only to pay half the sum of money upfront and the rest on completion. There is no point in you two hanging about in Naples. I shall need you here at Arturo Annunzio's farm. Make your way to Pazzoli, please."

"D'accordo, capo. We are on our way."

The feared lambasting had not occurred.

"No chance you've picked up some hint as to where they have taken him by any chance, is there Gino?"

"Yes, *capo*, it seems that the mafioso boss has a country house in a hamlet called Civitella della Torre, about fifteen kilometres out of Naples."

---

[113] Melanzane alla ... - A dish made with aubergines, tomatoes, and Mozzarella, originally from the city of Parma

Gino explained to Beppe the text message he had found on the Archbishop's phone.

"It seems that the parish priest where Don Emanuele was staying knows all about their local Mafia *boss*. We get the impression that Don Emanuele was preparing himself for the possibility that he might be held hostage," concluded Gino.

"Or that he was intending it should happen," said Beppe as if he was thinking out loud.

"*Appunto, capo.*"[114]

"*Bravi, ragazzi.* You couldn't have done any better. Your presence at the mobster's house will have helped to make the whole scenario seem authentic to Salvatore Alfieri. That was the essential thing."

Beppe returned to the lunch table, where the first course plates were being mopped up with pieces of fresh bread.

Beppe made a supreme effort to sound cheerful throughout the rest of the lunch. He did not want Sonia's first few hours with their hostess marred by the worrying news of Don Emanuele's fate.

Only Sonia looked knowingly at her husband. She knew him too intimately not to detect the signs of anxiety through his exaggerated pretence that all was well. Eugenia Mancini continued to chat in her own characteristically inconsequential manner about life in general.

But to Beppe's amazement, it was Eugenia who, as soon as the dessert had been eaten and coffees appeared on the table, turned to him and said:

---

[114] Appunto, capo – precisely, chief

"What is it you are not telling us, Beppe? I could tell by the way you were cutting up your chicken that you were worried about something. We ladies are not blind, you know!"

Sonia had laughed at Eugenia's unusual turn of phrase. Her laughter turned to an expression of suppressed despair when Beppe told them.

"Don Emanuele has been kidnapped by the mafia boss."

Eugenia let out a cry which sounded like one of pain.

"*Mamma* will be talking in her sleep tonight, I should warn you all," piped up Alice. "She's in love with Don Emanuele, aren't you, *mamma*?"

Alice's unrestrained comment produced universal laughter. Even Veronica appeared to find the situation amusing as she clapped her hands together as if in applause. Lorenzo joined in by throwing his plastic feeding spoon on the floor.

"What silly things you do come out with these days, Alice!" said Eugenia in scolding tones.

But the blush which suffused her cheeks could not be concealed. Eugenia was fanning her cheeks rapidly with both hands.

"I've never heard anything so silly in all my life!" proclaimed Eugenia. "Whatever will you come out with next, *figlia mia?*[115] You'll be telling them all I'm The Blessed Virgin Mary come back to Earth in disguise – or something equally outlandish."

***

---

[115] Figlia mia – O daughter of mine! A rhetorical form of address, as befits Eugenia Mancini's character!

Beppe, unable to sit around idle when a dilemma presented itself, did the only thing he could think of. He excused himself for the afternoon, kissed Sonia and his children and headed for Arturo Annunzio's farm.

"I'll be back in time for supper, Eugenia," he promised.

"He's always like this when he's in the middle of an investigation, Eugenia – restless and preoccupied," explained Sonia.

"Would you folk mind accompanying me and Alice back to afternoon school, Sonia? I can show you round the town. Not that there's much to see, but it will take our minds off Don Emanuele, won't it?"

"I wouldn't worry too much about Don Emanuele, Eugenia. He has a remarkable instinct for survival."

"I'm sure you're right, Sonia. But I had the impression he is very fed up with 'churchy' things when he came to Pazzoli. He's at the age when he needs an adventure – almost as if he wants to put the Holy Spirit to the test. And I am not in love with him, you know, Sonia. But I do care what happens to him," Eugenia added in her earnest, 'let's-get-things-into-perspective' tone of voice.

"I never thought otherwise, Eugenia. But Alice's interpretation was very touching, you have to admit."

"*Out of the mouths of babes and sucklings,* and all that sort of thing," quoted Eugenia, as if Sonia had not said a word.

Sonia was beginning to get used to her hostess's elaborate linguistic idiosyncrasies – and loved them.

Alice gave her mother a hard, knowing look which clearly stated that *she* was not as easily fooled as their very *simpatica* guest.

*　*　*

Before even getting out of his car at the farmhouse, Beppe made a phone call to Mariastella Martellini, heart in mouth. He was sure the *Questore* would take this setback personally – as a failure on her part for allowing her second-in-command's extravagant plan to go ahead. She would no doubt have words to say to him, making sure he shared the moral blame.

Thus, her opening words came as a great surprise.

"Before you say anything, Beppe, I already know. Danilo phoned me about the same time as Gino called you, I imagine. I just want to say to you that you mustn't take it too hard. It's not your fault. Don Emanuele told me in private some days ago that he might end up as a kind of hostage to fortune. He didn't want you to be worried about him."

There was a silence from the *commissario* which lasted a long time. It was broken by a trill of laughter from Mariastella Mancini.

"You thought I was going to blame *you,* didn't you Beppe? It probably took you quite some time before you picked up the phone to tell me the bad news. That's really sweet of you," she concluded.

The conflicting thoughts going through Beppe's mind were waging an internal battle to gain supremacy one over the other. As a result, he continued to be lost for words.

"Shall I ring off now, *commissario,*" asked Mariastella gaily.

In the end, Beppe managed a few words:

"I am grateful to you, Mariastella. You are not the person I feared you were going to be. *Grazie mille.*
I need to set up the trap at Arturo Annunzio's farm. My guess is that the mob will arrive on Monday night – Tuesday at the latest. After that, I need to talk to Sonia before I set off to Naples. I can't just hope that Don Emanuele alone – even with God on his side – will be able to escape unharmed. Do I have your permission to go to Naples, Mariastella?"

"You have *carte blanche,* Beppe. Remember from now on you are on leave – and out of my jurisdiction."

"You foresaw all this happening, didn't you?" said the *commissario,* unable to keep the note of admiration out of his voice.

"No, honestly, I didn't. But knowing you, I suspected you would want to mount a private rescue attempt of Don Emanuele if things did not go quite to plan. And I have to respect *you* for that."

"I want to set up a foolproof trap for the mobsters before I do anything else. And put Sonia's mind at rest. She came with me to Pazzoli, by the way. With the kids. We are staying with…"

Mariastella laughed.

"I knew that too, Beppe."

"Congratulations, *Signora Questore.* You are as well-informed as your predecessor," said Beppe ironically, "if not more so."

"I shall take that as a compliment, *commissario!*"

"I was thinking," continued Beppe, "of asking *Ispettore* De Sanctis to lend me some officers to be present when the mobsters turn up at the farm. With your permission, I was wondering if you could spare me Officer

Luigi Rocco? He is always brilliant when it comes to putting the fear of God into the mob – just because of his imposing presence…"

"Ah, *commissario,* I fear I shall have to say 'no' to that request. *Agente* Rocco has been assigned to another operation. I cannot tell you what that is just yet. I was going to suggest Officers Danilo Simone and Gino Martelli – seeing as they will be with you soon anyway. I think they would like the opportunity to get their own back on the mafia."

Eaten up by curiosity as to what Mariastella had in store for Luigi Rocco, Beppe had a sense that the new *Questore* was firmly in charge, He could only mutter the words:

"*Come vuole Lei,* Mariastella.[116]"

"I think we can dispense with formalities at this stage, don't you? *Tienimi aggiornata,*[117] Beppe. *E in bocca al lupo!*"

Mariastella hung up.

Grudgingly, Beppe had to admit to himself that he and his team had acquired an exceptional new leader. He sighed and got out of his car to greet *Agente* Claudio Montano – who looked far more like a sheep farmer than a police officer in the space of just a few days.

"Maybe you would like to consider a change in profession, Claudio?" Beppe had suggested to Officer Montano.

"Not just yet, *commissario.* In fact, now I know that this operation should be over by next week, I'm quite

---

[116] Come vuole Lei – as you wish. Beppe uses the formal 'Lei' for 'you'
[117] Tienimi aggiornata – keep me posted. She uses the familiar 'tu' form of the verb. A subtle distinction now lost from the English language since the disappearance of the word 'thou'.

relieved. But it has been enjoyable – probably just because I knew there was a term to it."

"I'm not sure what the sheep think of you but Arturo Annunzio seems to be a changed man, Claudio. You have worked wonders with him."

"I think he misses not having a son or a daughter on the farm to help him, *capo*. He was telling me a tragic story of a baby daughter who died only a few months after birth."

Arturo Annunzio's look of fear returned as soon as Beppe explained to him that he should expect a call from the mafia boss within the next couple of days.

"You and Claudio should dig a big hole this weekend. But don't be scared, *Signor* Arturo," Beppe had reassured the farmer. "This visit really will be the last. We know the identity of the man who is responsible for doing this. He will be behind bars very soon. All you have to do is play your part one more time. You must act scared – just like the other times. Whatever happens, they must be convinced that this visit is just like the others. Don't worry. We will be here to protect you – out of sight."

"What if they don't pay me, *commissario?* What shall I say? One of them taunted me last time that if I made a fuss or told anybody, I would have to carry on doing it for nothing."

"If they don't pay you, you whinge and whine like hell! You'll manage alright, Arturo. And when the phone call comes, make sure Officer Montano is with you. But it must be you who takes the call. The mafia boss must not have *any* suspicion that things have changed. Another man's life is at stake – one of our men," concluded Beppe, stretching the truth a little.

Beppe waited until Gino Martelli and Dino Simone had arrived at Pazzoli. They had phoned him from the village, having no idea where the farm was out in the countryside.

"Come and meet Officer Claudio Montano. You must remember seeing him on the day of his interview at *Via Pesaro*. After that, you can go home to Pescara, if you want, *ragazzi*. You'll need to come back at short notice – but in any case, come back in uniform and armed this time."

"We'll be back on Monday morning, *capo*. We can't wait to get our hands on Don Salvatore Alfieri's mob," said Gino.

"They treated us with complete disdain back there in Naples," added Danilo.

"You'll get your chance for revenge, *ragazzi*," said Beppe.

But Beppe's thoughts had automatically come back to the new problem that faced him. He did not point out to Gino and Simone that the abduction of Don Emanuele might well force him to radically revise his meticulously conceived plans.

* * *

"Oriana has had a baby girl, *amore*," announced Sonia as soon as he set foot in the house some ten minutes later, well in time for supper. "She phoned me about twenty minutes ago."

"I thought we would open a bottle of wine to celebrate," said Eugenia. "I gather that this is quite an event in the life of your team, Beppe. I'm right, aren't I?"

"So, you've met Oriana, have you?" asked Sonia.

"Yes, she arrived with the 'first wave' of police officers, so to speak. A very forthright young lady indeed, Sonia. I liked her."

"Has she given her a name, yet? I bet Giovanni is pleased," said Beppe.

"Oriana is upset because she was convinced it was going to be a boy. She is threatening to give the baby a boy's name anyway. She wanted to call it Beppe and make sure it was the diminutive form which would be his given name. Giving birth to a baby girl has really upset her outlook on life. She says that having a girl is too big a risk! Because a girl will turn out to be just as difficult as she is. And a baby girl will interfere with her police work, or so she claims."

Beppe found Oriana's reaction comical, knowing full well that underneath the surface, she would be in her seventh heaven.

"If she had had a boy, I bet she would have shown the same reaction and wanted it to be a girl."

Sonia laughed at this interpretation of Oriana's capricious nature.

"She is threatening to give the baby away for adoption. She is even blaming Giovanni for giving her a daughter, she told me. Apparently, she told him that she was regretting running the risk of deforming her figure for the sake of bringing a child into the world who will turn out to be a copy of herself. And I could hear her putting one of the nurses in her place as she was breaking off the call to me. She has obviously taken giving birth in her stride – as with everything else she does."

Beppe and Eugenia laughed at the images of their feisty colleague, conjured up by Sonia's words.

"She sounds as if she's survived the ordeal in style," added Eugenia, popping the cork of a bottle of Prosecco.

Alice looked sternly at her mother and held out an empty glass, daring her to exclude her own daughter from the celebration. Eugenia looked quizzically at Beppe.

"It's illegal at her age, isn't it, *commissario?*" she asked hopefully.

"I think Alice might deserve a half glass for being such a charming junior hostess, Eugenia."

His words earned him a look of gratitude from Alice.

The extended family broke into laughter as Veronica held out her plastic beaker pouting furiously at the social omission committed before her very eyes.

"You can have some of mummy's, *tesoro*," said Sonia. The liquid was spat out indelicately from her mouth as soon as she tasted it.

"*Non mi piace,*" [118] she pronounced in disgust, deciding that older people had a decidedly peculiar sense of taste.

* * *

Sonia and Beppe lay together in comfortable intimacy later on that night. It was Sonia who softly broke the silence.

"I know you're planning to go to Naples to rescue Don Emanuele, *amore*. You don't have to keep it a secret from me, you know."

Beppe held her tightly to him.

"I promise I won't go on my own. I was thinking of taking Gino and Danilo with me. I shall talk to Mariastella

---

[118] Non mi piace – I don't like it

tomorrow. I'm certain she will contact the local police force in Secondigliano and get the local police mobilised."

"I would guess that Don Emanuele being kidnapped will completely alter the rubbish dumping scam up at the Annunzio farm, won't it?" hazarded Sonia.

"Yes, that has been worrying me. I was going to simply arrest the convoy that arrives to dump the waste material we've collected. But because of Don Emanuele's rash action..."

"Very courageous, would be more accurate, Beppe."

"Yes, I am sure he knew that his being held hostage was inevitable. But it means we shall just have to remain hidden in the darkness while the mob dump the waste in the hole. They will certainly have to report back to Salvatore Alfieri – and we can't risk arresting them in case it gives one of the mobsters the chance to send a signal to him before we can stop him."

"It wouldn't even matter if they took the waste away and dumped it somewhere else, would it?" stated Sonia.

"Exactly, *amore*. But I suspect they will keep to that plan. I hope so, because it's my only way of being sure that the scam has worked. If they go and dump it elsewhere, it might mean they've cottoned on to the fact that it's a set-up. That's the worrying aspect of my crazy idea."

"Beppe, your instincts are always right. Don't worry. But you swear to me now that you won't act on your own when you shoot off to Naples."

"*Te lo giuro,*[119] Sonia," said Beppe – and he meant it. "By the way, I did ask our *Questore* if I could take Luigi Rocco with me to Naples, but she told me that she had assigned

---

[119] Te lo giuro – I swear it to you

him to another operation. I just wonder what that might be that it can't be revealed."

"Maybe there's a genuine reason – I mean an official reason – why she wants him to remain in Pescara, *amore*. You shouldn't underestimate that woman, you know."

"I don't anymore, Sonia. I am actually beginning to respect and like her – despite my best efforts not to."

They talked sleepily about the delightful character of their hostess, before falling asleep. Thus, they did not hear, wafting up from the floor below, the echoes of Alice's prediction about her mother's unconscious re-enactment of Don Emanuele's kidnap.

Alice regaled them with an account of her mother's dream sitting round the breakfast table the following morning.

"*Mamma* told him off for being reckless in the face of danger and said he couldn't go on being like that when they were together," Alice claimed maliciously.

"You are far too inventive a child for your age, *tesoro!*" stated Eugenia, scolding her daughter unconvincingly. But her fingers were busy fanning the flushed cheeks again. "Don't listen to my daughter – she has an over-active imagination, Sonia, Beppe," she protested – but with the hint of a complicit grin on her face.

22:   Arturo Annunzio surprises himself...

It was not until late on Sunday evening that Beppe received the call from *Agente* Claudio Montano, to tell him the mobsters would be arriving on Monday night – or more likely after midnight on Tuesday.

"It's GO GO GO, *commissario* – as the Americans always relish saying during their movies."

Beppe chuckled at his young officer's sardonic humour.

"Yes, they do get overexcited on these occasions, don't they, Claudio – charging in with all guns blazing. I'm sorry to say we may well not be firing a single shot."

"What a shame, *commissario!* Ah well, firing the first shot of my career will just have to wait, I suppose," he said with mock regret.

"Remind me to tell you the story of Officer Remo Mastrodicasa one day, Claudio. He only fired one shot in his whole career[120] and then went off to run an *agriturismo* just outside L'Aquila, called *La Bella Addormentata.*"[121]

"Everybody talks about that place in L'Aquila, *commissario.*"

"That is where you should go on your first date, Claudio. I'm sure Valentina Ianni would love it!" said Beppe mischievously.

"How the hell did he...?" thought Claudio but decided to play it cool.

"I'm sure Valentina Ianni must have been there many times before, *commissario*. And we are certainly not at that stage at the present time."

---
[120] A reference to "The Case of the Sleeping Beauty"
[121] La bella addormentata – The Sleeping Beauty

"Sorry, Claudio, it's none of my business."

"You are right, as ever, *capo*," replied the young officer with cutting aplomb.

"*Bravo,* Claudio."

But, rather than embarrassment, Beppe's uppermost feeling was one of utter relief that the raid was to go ahead. He had read the situation accurately. Barring the unforeseen, they could simply let the mobsters unload the fake toxic material and drive off unmolested. He would not even need to be present. He could be on his way to Naples in the company of Gino Martelli and Danilo Simone on their mission of rescue – which, his inner brain told him, would undoubtedly prove to be far more fraught with obstacles.

"The only tricky aspect of your job, Claudio, is that it would be very helpful if you could arrange to take pictures of the number plates of the mobsters' vans – without them knowing, obviously. We want to be able to present hard evidence to any court of law later on."

Claudio Montano was inwardly astonished at the way his chief's mind seemed to think of tiny details that others in his position may never have thought of so far in advance. This was what it meant to be a 'professional' considered Officer Montano.

"Leave that to me, *commissario,* I have a night time lens on my camera. But I shall need to go back to L'Aquila to pick it up."

"Go now, Claudio. I shall stand in for you. Leave your tent where it is. I want you to be visibly present when the mobsters arrive. You can pose as Arturo's nephew or something. It will make it much easier for you to take a couple of pictures if your presence is not questioned. The other officers with you must stay out of sight at all costs. They will be vital witnesses to proceedings – *e basta"!*[122]

"You sound as if you don't intend to be here, *capo*," said Claudio.

"No, your *Ispettore* Fabrizio De Sanctis will be the senior officer present. But this is *your* show, Officer Montano. You are quite able to cope with a few minor gangsters, I am sure. I shall be on my way to Naples with Officers Gino and Danilo by then."

Claudio Montano was inwardly shocked that he would be the front man in this operation. He had only arrived at the *Questura* a few days previously, it seemed. A baptism of fire, or at least, its burning embers.

"By the way, Claudio, how did Arturo Annunzio cope with the phone call from the mafia boss, Salvatore Alfieri?"

"He was brilliant, *commissario*. We had rehearsed the conversation beforehand. He even managed to sound aggressive when he demanded a pay rise. Or, so he threatened, he would pull out."

"Was that *his* idea, Claudio?"

"No, it was mine, but he executed it beautifully."

"What was your reasoning behind such a risky tactic, may I ask, Claudio?" asked Beppe with a hint of severity in his voice.

Claudio Montano feared that he had miscalculated. His chief was about to berate him for a clumsy, self-indulgent attempt at showing how clever he was.

"I thought it might make the mafia boss more aggressive and hostile – you know, he would want to

---

[122] E basta! – And that's all. 'Basta' = enough

exercise his sadistic power a bit more. That way, he would be far less likely to think it was all a scam and pull out..."

There was a lengthy silence from the other end of the line. The new recruit was quaking in his boots.

"Congratulations, Officer Montano. You will go a long way in our police force. You even seem to understand how the mafioso mind works – without having met one, I assume. Now, go home and get your camera, and take your time coming back. You tell Arturo Annunzio I'll be with him in about two hours' time. And tell him to dig a big hole while you're away..."

"The pit has already been dug, *commissario*. We did it earlier on – just in case they arrived unexpectedly."

* * *

Beppe was cursing himself for forgetting to tell Claudio Montano to wear something very dark the following night so he could take the photos without being too visible. But he had an image in his mind of Mariastella Mancini telling him to stop treating his young officers like a Sunday School teacher would. "Leave them some space to use their initiative, Beppe," she was saying. He picked up his smartphone and called the lady in question to arrange a police escort for himself and Officers Martelli and Simone when they arrived in Naples.

"Don't worry Beppe, I'll phone the local *Questura* in Secondigliano and get back to you later this morning. With any luck, we shall be celebrating the completion of our first major investigation together in a few days' time. What do you say, *commissario?*"

Beppe chose his words carefully before replying:

"That will be a good feeling, *Signora Questore*."

An ignoble thought flashed through Beppe's mind – quickly rejected. Would she bathe in the limelight of their supposed success – or shift the blame for failure on to *him*?

* * *

Tension was palpable at the sheep farm as midnight approached. Officer Claudio Montano was present with his own commanding officer, *Ispettore* De Sanctis, Simona Gambino and Valentina Ianni. Officer Giovanni Palena was excused – against his will – as he was more needed at home with his wife, Oriana Salvati, and their newborn child.

Two additional officers from Pescara had volunteered to make the journey to Pazzoli that afternoon to bolster the numbers – Giacomo D'Amico, for whom retirement was beckoning, and Officer Pippo Cafarelli.

These two had driven together from Pescara earlier in the afternoon from a strangely deserted *Questura*.

Mariastella Mancini, who was always nearby to offer her encouragement and blessing, had excused herself earlier on that morning. Of *Agente* Luigi Rocco, there had been no sign at all that afternoon. He had driven off by himself, in full uniform, in his own car, saying he was 'going up north' on police business.

Beppe had arranged for the owner of the private clinic in Atri to send out a multiple text message as soon as the mobsters had left with the two large white vans, each carrying two of the mobsters from Naples and loaded to bursting point with black bags containing all the refuse so diligently collected by the townsfolk of Atri.

"Six of you should be enough to cope with the mobsters if anything goes wrong, *ragazzi*," Beppe had told them that afternoon, as he, Gino Martelli and Danilo Simone had headed off towards Naples, with the sole purpose of saving Don Emanuele and being present when *Totò u curtu* was arrested.

Beppe had insisted that the *Questore* should request that he should be the one to speak those magic words when the moment arrived: *'Salvatore Alfieri, io La dichiaro in arresto.'*[123]

* * *

As soon as the sun had dipped below the mountain tops, the atmosphere at the farmhouse grew more strained. Maria Pia Farina, the farmer's wife, had prepared a meal copious enough to feed an invading army. Inevitably, it was a variation on the ubiquitous lamb stew theme. But it did not match up to the pungent, anti-environmental strength of the stew which had so repelled Oriana Salvati on the previous visit of the L'Aquila team. Eating the food put in front of them was almost pleasurable and the officers seated round the oblong wooden table managed to express their admiration for the cook's skills with a reasonable degree of sincerity. Some of the male team, notably Giacomo D'Amico even accepted second helpings – despite covert signals from Officer Claudio Montano that their constitutions might suffer at a later stage of that crucial night.

There were copious amounts of red wine on the table, looking innocently young and fresh in two tall unlabelled

---

[123] Io La dichiaro... You are under arrest.   Lit: 'I you declare in arrest'

litre bottles standing on the table. But since the police officers all declined to a man to touch even a drop of the liquid, it was left to Arturo Annunzio to drink most of the contents of one bottle all by himself.

Maria Pia surreptitiously removed the second bottle well before her husband had emptied the first one.

To the surprise of the officers who had previously visited the farmhouse, Arturo Annunzio smiled kindly at his wife and said:

"*Grazie, Maria Pia.* I have had just enough to feel able to stand up to those crooks when they arrive."

Claudio was looking meaningfully at his colleagues as if to say:

"See how things have changed since I arrived."

The change was indeed palpable in Arturo's voice and body-language. It was as if he had accepted his life-style with reluctant good grace.

Inspector Fabrizio De Sanctis dispatched Claudio Montano off to the neighbouring farm.

"You had better go and warn them not to phone the police when they are inevitably woken up during the course of tonight," suggested the Inspector.

"Anybody want to come with me?" asked Claudio.

It was Valentina Ianni who leapt to her feet with the words.

"*Io vengo con te,*[124] Claudio. I need to walk off that meal."

It was what Claudio had been hoping would happen.

"No dawdling on the way back, *ragazzi*," added the Inspector.

---

[124] Io vengo con te – I'm coming with you

The other officers went outside and sat round the wooden picnic table whilst Maria Pia prepared copious amounts of coffee. Only Giacomo pulled out a box of cigars and smoked one. The aromatic smoke drifted round the courtyard in the light evening breeze. A crescent moon appeared low down in the evening sky. A packet of playing cards appeared from nowhere as some of the officers began a game of *Briscola*[125] - at which Simona Gambino excelled, to the good-natured irritation of the male contingent.

By eleven o'clock, the inevitable lethargy hung over the group at the prospect of a long evening's vigil. Maria Pia had taken herself off to bed.

"Sweet dreams, *amore*," Arturo had said kindly to his wife. "When you wake up, all this will be over for ever."

Arturo and Claudio Montano had then busied themselves rounding up the flock of a hundred or so sheep and hoarded them into the vast milking shed. The animals protested noisily, failing to understand why they were not being allowed to continue grazing on the hillside. Arturo was not going to risk a repeat performance of the mafia's previous visit.

The text message from the owner of the clinic arrived just after one o'clock, startling the sleepy officers into a state of sudden alertness. The jangling noise of the landline rang out on the early morning air. Claudio ran indoors to take the call.

"Just checking that you're all awake, Claudio!" said the cheerful voice of Beppe Stancato. "Best of luck to you all. The mob should be with you within one hour."

---

[125] Briscola – a card game resembling whist, where the trump card is the suit indictated by the upturned card.

"Thank you for your thoughtfulness, *commissario*," replied Claudio Montano, with as much sarcasm in his voice as he could muster.

He heard a suppressed laugh and a brief word of apology from Beppe before the line went dead.

As on previous occasions, the white vans arrived with engines revving unnecessarily loudly and reversed up to the edge of the hole. The brakes were slammed on noisily just before the men leapt out and looked around menacingly. There were only three of them. The second van was manned by a single individual. The mobster with tattoos all over his body approached Arturo. Officer Claudio Montano was standing by his side – looking nervous and cowed. This was not difficult to simulate. It was Claudio's first face-to-face encounter with his beloved country's low-life. The gang leader gave off a sense of evil like some powerful force which could be physically felt.

"*Che cazzo! Chi è questo?*"[126] spat out the tattooed gangster.

"He's my nephew. And he's here to help ME on the farm."

The mobster looked disdainfully at Claudio and then leered at him.

"Good. He can help us unload. We're one man down tonight."

Claudio did not know what to do in the face of this threat. He would just have to comply – and then he would not be able to take the photos which the *commissario* considered to be so important.

---

[126] Che cazzo... Who the f..k is this?

"Do your own dirty work, mate! Leave my family out of this! It's up to you if you are happy handling toxic stuff. My nephew won't touch it."

The anger in Arturo's voice was unfeigned. It was as if he needed to vent his frustration and anger for all the past humiliations in one final desperate bid to assert himself. Thank God they hadn't stopped him drinking all that red wine, Claudio thought.

The man with the tattoos looked shocked. Nobody had ever stood up to him like that in his whole life. Claudio had to make a supreme effort to remain unmoved.

"You heard my uncle," he managed to say. "Get the job done and clear out."

He had, without thinking, placed his right hand on Arturo's shoulder. Claudio was sure he would not have had the courage to stand up to the mobster had he not known that his colleagues were well within firing distance. That, plus his admiration for Arturo's new found pluckiness.

Shouts from the other two men telling their leader that there was too much to unload without his help finally broke the gangster's resolve.

"You just wait until this job is done, you two. Then I'll have time for you," he threatened as he shuffled off to help his mates. "Maybe we'll go and kill a couple more sheep!"

There was no time to lose. Claudio rescued his already primed camera concealed under an upturned flower pot and, within twenty seconds, had taken a close up shot of the two front number plates. When he returned to his spot near the farm door, Arturo was nowhere to be seen. Strange! He hoped that the farmer hadn't lost his nerve.

The team of hidden police officers had been observing the scene unfolding before their eyes from behind the milking shed. Giacomo D'Amico had a pair of night binoculars trained on the little group by the farmhouse. He was doing a running commentary which only Pippo could hear. The noise that the imprisoned sheep were making from inside the echoing shed made Giacomo's words hard to distinguish.

"Be prepared, *ragazzi.* We may well have to intervene after all," Giacomo warned them.

It was a crisis. Giacomo understood perfectly well what was at stake, since Beppe had explained why they could not just capture the mobsters. He kept on peering through the binoculars and became even more alarmed at what he saw.

The mafia gangsters had finished unloading the vans, flinging the skull-and-crossbones marked waste bags carelessly into the pit. One of them appeared to be staring at the job they had just done.

The tattooed mobster had walked menacingly over to the farmer and his colleague. The other two had got back into the vans so that they were ready to depart, engines revving noisily.

Arturo was arguing with the leading gangster. His angry voice was audible even if the individual words were lost. The gangster appeared to be laughing in the farmer's face. Suddenly, from out of the blue, Arturo was wielding a shotgun and pointing it directly at tattoo-man's chest. He was taking a menacing step towards the unprepared gangster. Inspector De Sanctis broke free of the group and ran up the hill, pistol drawn. The others began to follow him. Giacomo was afraid they would all be spotted in the moonlight.

In the end, Fabrizio De Sanctis came to a halt, having covered half the distance between the two contingent groups. He held out an arm signalling to the officers behind him to stay where they were.

The gangster had thrown a package down on the ground in front of the farmer – presumably he had been intending to take the farmer's share of the money for himself.

The gangster's mates were edging the vans forward, debating whether to leave their boss to face the music on his own. He obviously thought better of it and ran towards the departing vans. Over his shoulder he shouted:

"Just you wait until next time you spineless old fool. You're dead meat!"

* * *

The whole team acted in unspoken unity. The bulky form of Arturo Annunzio was hoisted up on to male shoulders and carried victorious into the farmhouse. He was holding the shotgun in the air.

"It wasn't even loaded!" he exclaimed as he pulled the trigger. The explosion from the barrel echoed round the countryside. The lights in the neighbouring farm came on. The policemen dropped their burden back onto his feet in shock.

Nobody was sure who began to laugh first. But it was catching. Arturo walked into the house and had to be supported by Maria Pia, who had been watching her husband from an upstairs window. She headed for the kitchen table and sat Arturo down heavily.

It was Claudio who looked quizzically at Maria Pia. She nodded. Claudio rescued a bottle of Grappa and glasses from a cupboard. Nobody declined the little glass which was handed to them, full of the fiery liquid.

"*Un brindisi*[127] to Arturo – today's absolute hero!" proposed Pippo Cafarelli. "Without his courage – even if it was partly generated by his own red wine - this evening would have been a disaster."

There was general laughter, which Arturo had the grace to acknowledge.

"Well, *ragazzi,* it had to be me alone who did it. Otherwise, what might have happened to Don Emanuele?"

Agente Claudio Montano was looking smug.

"A good job Beppe and I told Arturo the full story behind this evening's charade!" he told himself.

Pippo Cafarelli went outside to make a phone call to Beppe to say the raid had been successful.

"No secrets out of the bag so-to-speak, *commissario,*" he told his chief.

* * *

Somebody else was making a phone call to *Totò u curtu* at roughly the same time.

"Just one strange thing, *capo.* One of the younger guys unloading the rubbish noticed a bag had split open."

"So what?" snapped Salvatore Alfieri. "As long as it got buried."

"But all he could see was an empty tube of toothpaste, Don Alfieri…"

---

[127] Un brindisi – a toast

23: *Don Emanuele's unusual dilemma...*

Don Emanuele was attempting to analyse why he wasn't feeling afraid. The mask over his head was stuffy and uncomfortable, admittedly, but he had no apprehension for his own life. Perhaps, quite simply, because this was by no means the worst thing that had happened to him during his fifty years of life. Also, he realised, any fear was lessened by the knowledge that he already *knew* where he was heading – or so he assumed – and had been able to warn Gino Martelli and Danilo Simone of the existence of Don Salvatore's isolated property somewhere up in the hills near Naples.

The other half of the payment owed to the self-styled psychopath, *Totò u curtu* – why was it that this sobriquet sounded so much more sinister just because it was in dialect? – was a guarantee that he would be kept alive for another few days. After that, he might have to find ways to evade his captors.

He smiled at the memory of himself as an eleven-year-old boy in the backstreets of another notorious district of the city. A local gang of aspiring teenage hoodlums had decided to practise the arts of sadism on him and had kidnapped him on his way back from school one afternoon. His academic ability, even at that age, had marked him out as 'different' in the eyes of the local low-life. And so, he had had to suffer one whole evening of imprisonment in the filthy basement of a neighbouring tenement block. They had force-fed him a packet of crisps and a bottle of warm fizzy mineral water just for the pleasure of seeing the terror in his eyes and hear him begging them to stop.

This episode in his life had taught him about the dark side of the human soul and its propensity to inflict gratuitous suffering on those weak enough to be unable to resist. It had been his screams of terror necessitating a gag being put into his mouth, in addition to his involuntary soiling of himself that had made them grow tired of their game.

His formidable, but not very tall father, a long-distance lorry driver, had, on his son's tearful return home, propelled himself out into the neighbourhood to seek out the perpetrators of this cowardly act on his son – the youngest of four children. Retribution had been swift, wordless and effective.

After that, as if by some auto-generated genetic modification, the young man who was to become the Archbishop of Pescara had magically grown head-and-shoulders taller than everybody else in his year group – and become adept at defending himself on the rare occasions when it became necessary. It became his tireless mission in his adolescent life to protect the vulnerable members of his neighbourhood from bullying and intimidation. He had been nicknamed *Holy Jo* by his peers.

As to his stint as an army chaplain during the Iraqi conflict, he preferred not to evoke the images and memories of that atrocity, which still disturbed his hours of slumber.

Despite taking his fears of the past into the reckoning of his present dilemma, the Archbishop was nevertheless relieved when, after only fifteen minutes or so had elapsed, he felt the car trundling over an unmade road and pull up a few seconds later on a gravelly drive. He must have been correct in his assumption as to his destination.

Don Emanuele had no delusions about the two mobsters who tried to manhandle him out of the car. They would enjoy eliminating him when ordered to do so. All the more reason for him not to display fear. He refused to get out of the car – knowing that the confined space would make it difficult for them both to get a firm grip on him.

"Get this bloody contraption off my head. I can't breathe," he shouted at his captures in backstreet dialect, to the astonishment of his escorts.

He could imagine them shrugging their shoulders as if to say 'What difference will it make now?' before removing the bag-shaped hood with which they had smothered him. Don Emanuele drew in deep breaths of unpolluted country air, given off by the forest which surrounded them on three sides.

Gangsters of the lowest order they might be - but they would be in mortal fear of their *capo* and under orders not to harm their prisoner until he had signed off the remaining 12 000 euros.

He was escorted to a stable abutting the house – which, he noted, was inhabited. The front door was wide open and there were lights on in the room. He thought he knew who the 'guests' might be. The next few days should prove to be very revealing.

"You make a noise in here, *Signor* Cargiulo, and we shall chain you to the walls and gag you. Don Salvatore has two family members staying with him in the house. They don't want to be disturbed by you."

The mobsters failed totally to understand why their words produced a secret smile on their captor's face. Indeed, this tall man's apparent lack of any fear was unusually disconcerting.

* * *

Don Emanuele took one look round his prison. To say the least, it was no better than a cow shed. No washing facilities, a kind of manger filled with old straw was the nearest thing to a bed – and nothing resembling a toilet. He strode over to the door where some sunlight managed to find a way through some ill-fitting wooden slats. He shook the door in frustration. He guessed the door was held shut with a wooden beam hooked across the doorway. Nothing more substantial than that. He was aware that, even if he got out, the circumstances would not allow him to escape until Don Salvatore Alfieri deigned to reappear with the confiscated computer. At least, the mafioso would never work out the access code, thought the Archbishop, smiling to himself. He held the trump card – at least until the second half of the payment had been made. He reasoned that greed would play its part – at least for a couple of days longer.

There was nowhere to kneel and pray – as instinct dictated. Instead he walked steadily round in a circle. As usual, his unworldly spirits seemed strangely silent. After several prayer circuits, he was astonished and moved by an image, which he swore later on was external to himself, of a little girl called Ginevra standing in a dark corner, smiling at him with radiant joy. The vision, of course, collapsed as soon as he registered it with his conscious mind. What puzzled Don Emanuele was the fact that he had never seen the child in the flesh, but only the photograph that had adorned her grave at the time of the funeral.

But it was more than enough to bring a sense of solace and purpose back to his soul. He made the sign of the cross and made himself as comfortable as possible in the manger. He felt pleasantly weary. It must have been decades since the ground level stall had been occupied by animals, but he could swear that the reassuringly warm smell of cattle still lingered in the straw – a childhood memory that returned vividly and unbidden to his mind.

"*Grazie mio Dio!*" he said out loud.

His encroaching desire to sleep was kept at bay by an outburst of an angry altercation from the house. The stone wall was too thick for individual words to penetrate, but he could hear the raised voices of three or four different people. After ten or so minutes, Don Emanuele heard a car being driven off angrily. The gangsters had left. So only the 'house guests' remained. There had been no other car visible in the yard in front of the house.

That made sense if his surmise had been correct.

It was growing dark when the sound of the stable door being opened woke him up from his slumbers.

A striking-looking lady in her fifties presented herself in front of his manger. Comically, she had been walking round calling out a name which, in his sleepy state, he had not recognised.

"Signor Cargiulo? Signor Cargiulo, are you here?"

The lady had been so astonished, as the figure of an exceptionally tall man arose from the stall, that she took several steps backwards in alarm.

"Stop!" said the commanding voice of the beautiful man who had risen up before her very eyes. "You are about to trip over a milking stool!"

Don Emanuele was disappointed to see that the lady was not carrying the hoped-for *panino* – nor even a glass of water.

"*Grazie, Signor Cargiulo.* Would you like to come into the house and join myself and my husband? Apparently, you are to be our guest for a day or so."

"It will be a pleasure, *signora*," replied Don Emanuele. "*Ciao, Ginevra!*" he said out loud.

"Who...?" began the woman.

"Just a small ghost, *signora!* No cause for alarm."

He must be half deranged already, thought the lady as she preceded him into the main house. The door led straight into the kitchen area.

The husband, a short, stocky man, was raising a glass of red wine to his lips. He was sitting at the long wooden table with his back to the approaching figures.

"*Caro...*" began the lady, to attract her husband's attention.

"Good evening, Gianluca. I thought I would find you here," said Don Emanuele.

The former mafia boss swung round in alarm at the sound of the familiar voice in a context where it was quite impossible for that voice to have been. Inevitably, he had upset his glass of wine. The red liquid had splashed out across the surface of the table.

He stood up to face the man who occupied the unique position on Planet Earth of being the only human being who had made him see the error of his ways. He stared disbelievingly at the lofty figure before him, inexplicably wearing crumpled civilian clothes. Gianluca's mouth was still open in shock. His instinctive reaction was to make the sign of the cross.

Don Emanuele laughed pleasantly at Gianluca's gesture.

"I hope you do not consider you need the Good Lord's protection from *me*, Gianluca."

It was Gianluca's wife, who had instinctively gone to the sink to fetch a cloth to mop up the spilt wine, who spoke first.

"*Grazie a Dio,* Don Emanuele. Have you come to rescue us from this place?" she asked with a sort of guileless innocence which Don Emanuele found touching.

"That was not the purpose of my involvement in the life of your relative, Salvatore, *signora.* But it might well be a consequence – God being willing. I am sorry, *signora,* I don't even know your first name."

"Isobella," she said simply.

Gianluca had covered the distance between the table and the Archbishop and had put his arms round the astonished clergyman in an awkward hug. The ex-mafioso's head still came to below the level of Don Emanuele's shoulders.

Eventually, Gianluca found his voice.

"But how the hell did you end up in this awful place, father?" he asked.

"That is a very long story, Gianluca. But before I begin, I would very much like to see the inside of a bathroom..."

"Of course, Don Emanuele. *That man* has instructed us – via those two mobsters who brought you here – to supply you with a room upstairs. I'll take you there now – and find you something more comfortable to wear. Then I shall prepare us something to eat. Salvatore Alfieri has left us with just about enough freedom to eat fairly decent food," Isobella added bitterly.

* * *

The unlikely trio sat around the kitchen table until it was dark outside. Don Emanuele had spent well over an hour relating everything that had led up to his capture by Don Salvatore Alfieri.

"I was supposed to be the bait, you see," concluded the Archbishop.

The couple had remained spellbound by his account of the toxic waste dumping – and by the death and 'resurrection' of a little girl called Ginevra.

"Ginevra was the name you called out earlier on in the stable, wasn't it, Don Emanuele?" asked Isabella, puzzled.

"Yes, it was. She was there for a split second," replied Don Emanuele simply.

His two hosts did not think to question his words.

The only event which interrupted the non-stop exchange of words was a power cut round about half past ten. Isobella had already lit candles on the table in anticipation of the electricity being cut off.

"It happens every night, Don Emanuele. We are convinced that Salvatore, or *Totò u curtu,* as he likes to call himself, has the electricity on a timer to make sure we're in bed by ten-thirty. The man's a tyrant," she added in a tone of desperation.

"We never wanted to come here, you know, Don Emanuele," stated Gianluca. "We were content to live out our lives in the house we had been allocated in that small community in Abruzzo. I accepted the constraints of being a prisoner there as a just punishment for my way of life. My niece, Violetta, came and visited us regularly – as you know."

"*I* was free to go out shopping unrestrained, of course," explained Isobella. "The people there were charming and talkative. They never really questioned why a couple from Naples had ended up in their remote village up in the mountains."

"So why did Don Salvatore take you away from there?" asked Don Emanuele, puzzled.

"It was something I once said to Violetta about missing my friends and family in Naples," explained Isobella, bitterly. "He just decided he would kidnap us – absolutely against our wishes, telling us he had just the place where we could be safe and free for the rest of our lives. The man's a control freak, as we rapidly discovered. We are his prisoners – whereas before, we were quite content to be prisoners of the State."

"And now I'm an illegal *latitante*[128], Don Emanuele. If they find me, I shall be put in prison and never be able to live out my wretched life with Isobella in relative peace. I know I shall have to spend a century in purgatory when I die. I accept that..."

Don Emanuele had never seen – or dreamt he would witness – the ex-mafioso boss in tears. He felt simply moved to get up and put an arm around Gianluca's shoulder in comfort.

"Leave it with me, Gianluca. As soon as we are out of this situation, I shall make sure you are never blamed by the police for the plight you are in now. We shall have *Commissario* Stancato on our side – plus their amazing new lady *Questore*. Justice will be done, you will see!"

It was as if Gianluca had suddenly become aware of his own vulnerability. He almost shook the Archbishop's arm away from his shoulder – even apologising for his moment of weakness.

---

[128] Latitante – a mafioso in hiding from the law.

"I was a very bad man in my life, Don Emanuele. I admit it freely. But in truth, I hated the necessity of being the *boss* of the Alfieri clan. I just felt it was incumbent on me to fulfil the role – out of duty to the clan."

The Archbishop went back to his place on the opposite side of the table, facing Gianluca.

"I understand, Gianluca, that you are truly repentant now. God has forgiven you - I am certain of that."

Gianluca looked as if he was going to cry again.

"I believe you, Don Emanuele. The problem really is that I cannot forgive myself."

Isobella came to his rescue before he really wept out loud.

"You must understand, Don Emanuele, Gianluca was a very bad man who never really wanted to be bad. His nephew, Salvatore, is a different kettle of fish altogether. He knows he is evil and he revels in it – every minute of the day and night. We must spend the next couple of days before he returns working out how we can keep you alive. Because if he even suspects that you have double-crossed him, he will have you eliminated without any compunction whatsoever by those two soulless thugs he employs."

"Do not fear for me, *cara* Isobella. We shall be rescued by the police – and I know that The Holy Spirit will look after me – and you too. But it would help if I could use a phone to contact the *commissario*..."

"Dear uncle Salvatore has recently confiscated our mobile phones, Don Emanuele. As I said, he is a control freak. We shall only have our own wits on our side."

On that sombre note, the three of them headed upstairs, each one clutching an almost burnt down candlestick, whose flames threatened being extinguished before they reached the upper landing.

Don Emanuele lay awake thinking for hours, listening to the sound of owls in the darkling forest – a sound he had not heard since his childhood.

He was struck by the fact that by putting his own life at risk, he had inadvertently involved two other souls who would need saving too. For once, Don Emanuele was quite unable to foresee how the future would unfurl. His faith was about to be severely tested, he intuited.

"*Era ora!*"[129] he sighed and fell into a deep sleep.

---

[129] Era ora – It was high time

24: How it's done in Naples...

Beppe and his two uniformed officers, Danilo Simone and Gino Martelli, arrived at the local police headquarters on the Monday as the first hint of dusk was descending over Secondigliano.

As it was Beppe's first visit ever to this outpost of Naples, he could not help being struck by the incongruous mixture of Old and New in this suburb. The old town of Secondigliano looked like so many traditional villages, with its picturesque piazza and its main church dedicated to two saints – Cosma and Damiano.

"Was Cosma a man or a woman?" asked Gino.

"Maybe they were gay saints," suggested Danilo irreverently.

"I suggest you both do some proper research on that. Or ask the parish priest when we meet up with him," suggested Beppe tersely, not being in the mood for their flippancy.

The rest of the town looked precisely what it was – a sprawling suburb of Naples with endless rows of cheap housing and clothes factories where most of the counterfeit 'brand names' were churned out *en masse* by the mafia clans.

As if to emphasise the remoteness of the historic town centre from its origins, the non-stop roar of jet planes passing overhead had their landing gear lowered in preparation for their descent to Naples' main airport just to the north.

"Poor old Secondigliano!" commented Gino.

There was no visible reaction to his heartfelt comment from his companions.

Beppe was reaching that stage in the investigation when his anxieties and a fear of failure were looming. What if he had completely miscalculated the whole of the devious plot he had initiated? Why had he not just waited a few more weeks until Arturo Annunzio's farm had been raided by the mafia gang – as would have surely happened in the course of time?

His misgivings were aggravated immeasurably when, on presenting themselves at the reception desk of the *commissariato,* a young male officer looked blankly at Beppe, as soon as he had introduced himself.

"We are expected, *agente.* I am *Commissario* Stancato from Pescara. We have an appointment to meet your *Commissario* Gennaro Coppola at 19.00 hours. We are just ten minutes early."

The officer on duty was not defensive or aggressive. He looked genuinely embarrassed that he knew nothing of their arrival.

"Our *Questore* set up the meeting with your *commissario* only a few hours ago, *agente.* We are down here on very important business. A man's life is at stake. I would suggest you phone your..."

A nondescript but smiling figure, casually dressed in jeans and a leather jacket wandered over towards the desk. The junior officer looked relieved but did not salute the new arrival – who managed to look more like an amiable mafioso than a member of the forces of law and order.

"Sorry, *Agente* Russo," he said to the officer on duty, "I meant to come down earlier to warn you that three colleagues should be arriving at seven o'clock from somewhere remote. Ah yes, Pescara, that's right! Keep an eye out for them, will you? They are important visitors and will have travelled a long way."

The officer coughed politely and indicated the visitors.

"I think they have already arrived, *capo.*"

The *commissario* from Naples looked in amazement at the group. A genial smile lit up his face in an instant as he held out a hand in greeting.

"I'm so sorry, *Commissario*. This is Naples, you must understand. Nobody ever arrives on time – let alone ten minutes early. I'm *Commissario* Gennaro Coppola. I spoke to your lady *Questore* earlier on."

As if the gesture of greeting was a natural reaction to strangers, he shook the hands of Danilo and Gino with equal warmth. He seemed to find their early arrival greatly entertaining.

"Come on upstairs, *ragazzi*. Officer Russo – please ask one of the ladies to bring us up four coffees, will you? Or something a bit stronger if you prefer?"

Beppe was tempted to accept the offer of 'something stronger' but shook his head regretfully.

Up in his office, Gennaro Coppola indicated three upright chairs which were standing higgledy-piggledy at unequal distances from a desk littered with a plethora of files all wide open, as if the *commissario* was attempting to take them all in with one single glance.

"Sit yourselves down, *ragazzi*. Make yourselves at home – as far as that's possible in my office."

He himself shoved a few files into the middle section of the desk and perched himself on the edge of it.

"I understand from your *Questore* that someone important – not a member of the police force – has been abducted by our local *boss, Totò u curtu,* and is being held hostage in this gentleman's country residence. Poor sod! What is she like by the way?"

Gino and Danilo were looking incredulously at the *commissario* from Naples.

"It's a man who is being held prisoner, *commissario*," blurted out Gino, almost angrily.

"He's the archbishop of Pescara, disguised as a businessman," added Danilo.

Beppe was smiling broadly at this unconventional *commissario* from Naples. He had instantly taken a liking to the man for reasons he had not bothered to analyse.

"I think *Commissario* Coppola is curious to know something about our lady *Questore,* Gino…Danilo."

The two younger officers sniggered in embarrassment at their own gaffe.

"She's smart," said Gino.

"And quite sexy, I suppose," added Danilo.

"That's the impression I got too," said *Commissario* Coppola. "What's it like having a woman in charge?"

He had asked the question as if he was genuinely motivated by curiosity at such a novel idea.

"We are still waiting for such an event to happen here in Napoli, *ragazzi,*" he continued. "I'm sure you've heard what a load of sexist retards we are on this side of our peninsula. I can think of a couple of ladies who have just about made it to the rank of *ispettore.* You see, we haven't even thought of inventing the title of *ispettoressa*[130] as yet!"

"In answer to your question, *commissario*…"

"Call me Gennaro, for heaven's sake…"

---

[130] Ispettoressa – this would be the feminine form of *ispettore* - if it existed!

"It's early days yet, Gennaro, but there are very positive signs."

The ice was broken. How would it be possible not to take to this roguish policeman from Naples, thought Beppe.

A young lady officer arrived carrying a tray of coffees and sweet biscuits which she offered to the visitors individually.

"Sorry to interrupt, *ragazzi*," she explained informally. "There's never any room for a tray of coffee on our *commissario's* desk."

"Thank you Iolanda," said Gennaro Coppola. "You see before you one of our treasured young female officers – and I reduce her to the rank of a waitress! We Neapolitans are past praying for. See you all at the briefing meeting in about one hour," he said addressing the lady officer. "Is that alright with you, Beppe? Not too late for our purposes?"

Beppe looked at his newly-acquired colleague and said:

"That will be good, Gennaro. And thank you for our unique welcome to this part of the world."

"On the contrary, Beppe. It is I who should be thanking you three for coming all this way to Secondigliano – and giving us the chance to nail that bastard with something that will hold up in a court of law – without any interference from the *Carabinieri*, furthermore. Now, before we go to this briefing meeting, would you be so kind as to tell me how the devil an archbishop got involved in your investigation?"

* * *

Beppe had always prided himself on his relaxed attitude to all his staff. But by comparison with his new Neapolitan colleague, he would have come across as a rigid disciplinarian.

The meeting room was full of police officers – predominantly male – who, on the arrival of their *commissario* accompanied by the three 'strangers' from Pescara, made no sign of stopping their animated conversations with their neighbours or even calling out lively banter to officers on the other side of the room. It sounded and looked like chaos.

Commissario Gennaro Coppola seemed completely unperturbed by the noise.

"They're very keen to meet you, Beppe," he said smiling broadly at the three nonplussed visitors.

The tumult died down amidst the more observant members of the team uttering loud *Ssshhushing* noises.

"Ladies and gentlemen, may I introduce you to *Commissario* Stancato and two of his colleagues, Danilo Simone and Gino Martelli from the *Questura* in Pescara..." began their *commissario* when the assembly had finally fallen silent.

The room then broke into noisy applause, with one of the officers calling out: "Pescara? Where's that on the planet?" This produced an outburst of laughter.

"I'm going to ask our friend *Commissario* Stancato to tell you briefly what has brought him to our neck of the woods, seeking our help. You are going to find it a fascinating account. *Commissario* – they are all ears!"

Something resembling a respectful silence fell as Beppe outlined the details of their investigation and the problem which they faced. Beppe managed to reduce his account to no more than ten minutes, at the end of which he was applauded respectfully.

"Now, *ragazzi,* we need a few volunteers to drive out to Civitella della Torre some time tomorrow and, once there, we are going to nail *Totò u curtu* and put him behind bars for a number of years."

Every officer present – not far off twenty of them – instantly raised a hand to volunteer. One of the girls even raised both hands.

Commissario Coppola pretended to look overwhelmed by their generosity. But within half a minute he had selected two ladies and four men to join Danilo Simone and Gino Martelli for the raiding party. He had organised the others to take it in turns to keep constant watch over the Alfieri residence and report back any movement.

"Don Alfieri doesn't go out these days unless he has to," explained Gennaro Coppola to Beppe. "He's become a night owl."

"All of you will have to be ready to go anytime in the next twenty-four hours, *ragazzi.* But this is the best chance we've had for years. Don't mess it up!"

The Naples *commissario* dismissed all the officers apart from his six volunteers plus Danilo and Gino. It took a few minutes for the Pescara team to mingle in with their colleagues from Naples, before Beppe began to brief them.

"It might well be Tuesday night before Don Salvatore Alfieri makes a move. I'm waiting for a call from my team at the Annunzio sheep farm to tell me the waste has been dumped," explained Beppe.

"Any questions at this stage, *ragazzi?*" asked *Commissario* Coppola. "Yes, *Agente* Davide?"

"Should I bring *Bella* along tomorrow, *capo?*"

Beppe was looking quizzically at his colleague.

"*Bella* is her pet Labrador," explained Gennaro Coppola with a conspiratorial smile. "She has the knack of getting herself involved in our excursions into the world of crime like no other dog has ever managed before. I would seriously recommend that she comes too, Beppe."

Beppe merely smiled and shrugged his shoulders in assent. He had just wholeheartedly resigned himself to the fact that this escapade would be played out according to Neapolitan rules.

"Now I'm going to treat you guys to a *real* pizza!" announced Gennaro Coppola proudly.

* * *

It was eleven o'clock before *Commissario* Coppola deposited Gino and Danilo at the bed-and-breakfast hostel where they had stayed a few days previously. Beppe was staying nearby with Father Alfonso – the parish priest and friend of Don Emanuele.

Father Alfonso had been alarmed by the non-appearance of his friend the archbishop. He hardly felt reassured by what Beppe told him.

During the course of their conversation, Beppe learnt from Don Alfonso that the church of Santi Cosima e Damiano was dedicated to two male Arabic physicians, who had become early Christian martyrs.

"I don't have any reason to think they were gay, Beppe. But we should keep an open mind, I suppose," said Father Alfonso ironically before they retired to their beds at past midnight.

Beppe's last conscious act was to phone Sonia in far off Pazzoli. He then fell into a deep sleep until he was woken up at four in the morning by a phone call from *Ispettore* De Sanctis – telling him that the 'toxic' waste had been dumped at Arturo's sheep farm outside Pazzoli, exactly according to plan.

Beppe let out a sigh of relief, but slumber had deserted him. He got up at six o'clock and wandered round the neighbourhood, looking for an early morning bar. He found a bar a few hundred metres away from the presbytery and was greeted by the bar owner with frenetic enthusiasm. He wondered if anybody in Naples ever spoke quietly or moved about slowly. He was presented with a coffee and a *brioche* with a flourish and a beaming smile before he had even opened his mouth.

Ah, Napoli! There's no place quite like it on the face of the planet, was the thought that ran through Beppe's mind.

25: Commissario Coppola misreads the signs...

"OK, *ragazzi!* This is it!" called out Gennaro Coppola to his men – which included Gino Martelli and Danilo Simone. "Don Alfieri and his two bodyguards left his mansion about thirty-five minutes ago. That should give them time to put themselves into a compromising situation by the time we arrive. We don't want to scare them off too soon."

"But our *commissario* isn't here yet!" Gino protested.

"Where is he, for heaven's sake?"

"He went back to the church to pick up Father Alfonso – at the priest's insistence that he should be present too."

"Priests! I ask you – they get everywhere these days! Phone your Beppe and tell him to get a move on, Gino. We've got to leave without delay. The priest will know where to go!"

And so, quite against their natural instincts, Officers Gino and Danilo travelled with the Naples team – Gino clutching his phone and selecting Beppe's number as he was running towards the police van whose engine was already being revved up by the driver."

After a tense minute, Gino spoke urgently into the phone. Then he nodded in relief at Danilo to indicate that their *capo* would be only minutes behind them.

"He told me he it didn't matter if we got split up," said Gino. "We were all headed in the same direction anyway."

After a day of inactivity and waiting, the frenetic departure into unknown territory was underway.

* * *

Don Emanuele, Gianluca Alfieri and his wife, Isobella, were by contrast, sitting round the kitchen table having a perfunctory supper. They had discussed and finalised their plans to the last detail – whilst admitting that whatever they had planned might well be overtaken by events. Don Emanuele's quiet authority brought them together. He had declined their offer of simply walking out of the house and finding safety in the forest.

Looking at his watch, Don Emanuele saw it was already past nine o'clock. Outside, the moonlight and a few feeble garden lights round the edge of the parking area provided scant illumination.

Don Emanuele looked serene. His companions were on edge.

"You must be careful, Don Emanuele. My nephew will not hesitate to let his thugs loose on you, if he is in the mood to do so."

Isobella nodded in agreement.

Don Emanuele grinned at them both disarmingly.

"Have faith, my friends," he said simply.

At that moment, the shaky peace was shattered.

"They're here, Don Emanuele," said Gianluca Alfieri, turning pale. "I would recognise the sound of that engine anywhere!"

"Stay calm. Don't stand up when they come in," ordered the Archbishop. "We must not show our fear!"

"Ah, so you *are* afraid, Don Emanuele!" whispered Isobella – not looking reassured by this discovery.

"Fear is not necessarily a sign of weakness, *mia cara!*" he replied in a stage whisper as the door was flung open by the two hoodlums, brandishing revolvers. Don Emanuele frowned at Gianluca who, he felt, was about to raise his arms into the air in a gesture of surrender.

The two goons had obviously been watching too many police raid films on television. Their knee-joints were bent in anticipation and they were clutching their weapons with both hands, performing a sweeping gesture from one side of the vast kitchen to the other.

Don Emanuele was laughing at their antics.

"There isn't anybody else here, *ragazzi*," he called out in heavy dialect. "Stop waving those ridiculous things around and relax."

The reaction of both of Salvatore's henchmen was to swing their revolvers round to point them at the Archbishop.

He raised his hands in the air in mock surrender.

"OK, lads, we'll come quietly!" he said. "I don't think your boss will be too happy if you shoot me before I've signed off the rest of the money. So, for heaven's sake, stop acting like a couple of teenage gangsters and relax."

To Gianluca and Isobella's alarm, Don Emanuele was standing up and walking round to the opposite side of the table. He was heading casually for the open door.

"It's quite safe to come in, Don Alfieri-the-second," he called out mockingly to the figure of the mafioso lurking outside in the courtyard, clutching Don Emanuele's computer in its carrying case. "We are completely unarmed and alone."

"What do you mean, *Signor*-whatever-your-real-name is?" snarled *Totò u curtu* as he stepped over the threshold. *"I'm* the number one here!"

"Fine! Whatever you say, *signore*," said Don Emanuele, keenly aware that the mafioso boss seemed to be implying that he, Don Emanuele, was not whom he had claimed to be.

The computer was taken out of its case and placed on the table in front of the now seated Archbishop.

"Now, let's get on with this business, *signore*," growled the mafia boss. When the money's gone through, you've got some explaining to do. And if this turns out to have been a scam, your time on this planet is over – and that goes for you too, *zio*," he added with relish, looking at Gianluca Alfieri.

Salvatore did not even deign to include Isobella in his glance. She had turned very pale.

"I don't know what you are talking about, Salvatore," said the Archbishop. "But our transaction will not be completed while your two goons are pointing those guns at our heads. You can act the big tough boss later on if you so desire."

Salvatore was looking nonplussed. He could not understand why this tall, distinguished-looking, bald-headed man was not scared of him. He therefore became more aggressive to cover up the nagging doubts that were passing through his mind. He had been set up in some way. But by whom? There was some aspect of this whole scenario which he had not yet grasped.

"The price has just gone up, *signore*. You're gonna pay another 20 000 euros – or I shall order my lads to take you out into the forest and shoot you in the back of your head."

He was even more disconcerted to find that the man in front of him was smiling insolently at him.

"Well, it will be the last time we do business with you, Salvatore Alfieri. You can't even keep to the terms of our agreement. Now, you owe me some kind of explanation for your treachery," Don Emanuele shouted at him – in perfect dialect.

Inside, he was beginning to wonder how long he could continue with this act. His faith was indeed being put to the test. The inner temptation to despair was growing. *"Wherefore hast though deserted me, oh Lord?"*

Don Salvatore made up his mind.

"I want you to tell me, *signore*, why the rubbish we dumped on that sheep farmer's land was not really toxic waste."

Don Emanuele found his courage again. He laughed out loud in the mafioso's face. He was, he knew, taking a gamble.

"What on earth made you come up with that ridiculous notion, Don Salvatore?"

"Because one of my men broke open one of the bags with a skull and crossbones sticker on it – and all he could see was a tube of toothpaste."

Don Emanuele was thinking fast. He managed a disdainful look at the mafia boss.

"You are ignorant, *signore*. You think the toothpaste we use at our clinics is ordinary toothpaste? Have you never heard of nano-toothpaste? We are obliged by the authorities to dispose of it in the proper manner because it may become radioactive after a few months. For which they make us pay far more money than you were demanding. I thought I was making a wise move enlisting your aid, Don Salvatore. It seems I was mistaken. Now I suggest we complete this transaction – on the terms we already agreed. Then you will let me go."

Salvatore Alfieri was deflated. But he still had the nagging suspicion that this was some kind of trap.

Don Emanuele could see how his adversary's mind was working. Time for a bit of a distraction.

He had opened up his laptop computer as if ready to proceed with the payment.

He appeared to be prodding the keys angrily.

"You are a fool, Don Salvatore. You have allowed my computer battery to discharge. I shall have to recharge it now before we finish the deal. *Che stronzo sei!*"[131]

This man's use of the familiar 'you' form plus the insult of calling him a *stronzo,* was the last straw.

"Take him outside into the forest, *ragazzi.* You know what to do with him. I don't give a damn about the money."

That was the signal for Don Alfieri and Isobella to play their last card.

"You can't murder him," they shouted in unison.

"You'll have to shoot your own family too," snarled Gianluca Alfieri at his nephew, with the last iota of courage that he would need to muster during his remaining days on planet Earth.

"This man is the Archbishop of Pescara," said Isobella quietly. "You're the victim of a police trap, Salvatore – and it bloody well serves you right!"

Totò u curtu was filled with a silent, disbelieving rage.

Outside, they heard the sound of a car arriving, being driven very fast. It braked and the tyres skidded on the loose gravel. The cavalry had arrived at last, thought Don Emanuele, making the sign of the cross in thanksgiving – somewhat prematurely, as destiny would have it.

***

---

[131] Che stronzo sei – What a bloody fool you are

Beppe and his navigator, Father Alfonso, had arrived on their own at a junction in the wooded countryside. There were two sign posts – one pointing to the left and the other pointing to the right. One said Civitella della Torre – but so, misleadingly, did the other sign.

"This is just so Naples!" thought Beppe.

"It's the one to the left that leads to Don Alfieri's house," stated the parish priest. "I visited this place once to administer the last rites to some family member, when I was just a young priest. The road to the right leads to the hamlet of Civitella itself."

What Beppe could not know was that, a mere five minutes prior to their arrival, the police vehicle had been faced with this same dilemma.

"Which way should I take, *capo?*" the officer in the driving seat of the police minibus had asked.

"The right fork," stated *Commissario* Gennaro Coppola with confidence. He had learnt that, as a man in authority, it was unwise to admit you weren't sure of the answer, or display indecisiveness. Thus, unknown to Beppe, his escort, including his own two officers, had gone off in the wrong direction.

Their error quickly became apparent to Beppe as he drove noisily into a gravelly courtyard. The house was brightly lit. There was one car parked in the drive, a grey Lancia Delta, which it was safe to assume belonged to *Totò u curtu*. He was about to break his solemn promise to Sonia that he would never act alone. He had to assume that the mistake by the other officers would be rectified immediately – if indeed that was where they had landed up. Beppe felt confident that they must be near at hand. He had seen the tail lights of the two police cars about a kilometre ahead of him on the same road only minutes beforehand.

He sighed heavily as he got out of the car.

"You had better stay where you are for now, Father. It may well be unsafe for you out there. If anything goes wrong, I shall need you to witness what happens. You can drive, I assume?" Beppe asked the priest. I mean..."

"Go, *commissario*. I can drive – I just don't have a driving license, that's all. That will hardly matter if I have to get out in a hurry. I'll be your witness. God be with you!"

Beppe grunted in response and headed on foot towards the house. Two men had appeared in the doorway. They must be Salvatore Alfieri's sidekicks. They were armed – that much he could make out.

He silently begged Sonia to forgive his rashness. He would try to bluff his way into the house without using the gun he was carrying.

He was drawing level with the two men who were approaching him fast.

"Who the hell are you?" asked gangster number one.

"My name is *Commissario* Stancato," he said waving his identity badge in their faces. "I wish to talk to Salvatore Alfieri – and the three people he is holding prisoner in the house."

Gangster number two leered at him in disbelief.

"You come here trespassing on private property – without back-up? You must be insane – or suicidal."

"I just want to talk," replied Beppe as calmly as he could. Inside himself, he was cursing his own rashness. This time he had played his final trump card – and lost.

"So, talk to *us, commissario*. They will be the last words you ever speak."

Despite being addressed in their unfamiliar dialect, there was no escaping the tone of sadistic anticipation of these two killers. He had fatally miscalculated this time. He could see four people standing silhouetted in the doorway of the house – one of them the unmistakable figure of Don Emanuele.

The two hoodlums had drawn their automatic pistols and were pointing them at him.

"Where would you prefer to be shot, *commissaaario?*" said the leader. "In the head or in the heart?"

The other gunman sniggered.

"Addio commissaaario!"

Beppe even saw their fingers tightening on the triggers.

"GIÙ PER TERRA, BEPPE!"

The words had been shouted from behind him by two voices in unison – a man and a woman.

He dropped onto the ground as two simultaneous shots were fired above him.

When he opened his eyes, he saw two dead bodies lying on the ground. The figure of Don Emanuele was running towards him with great athletic strides.

Beppe looked up at the star-laden skies and wept with undiluted joy.

Don Emanuele was helping Beppe to his feet, overwhelmed by a sense of wordless relief for his friend.

* * *

Less than one kilometre away, eight police officers and one embarrassed *commissario* had come to the conclusion that they were in the wrong place.

"*Dio ci aiuti*"!¹³² muttered Gennaro Coppola as two loud gunshots could be heard echoing through the trees.

"Come on, *ragazzi*. Let's go! You can pillory me later on."

In under three minutes, the police minibus arrived at breakneck speed in the now crowded courtyard in front of Salvatore Alfieri's house. They might have made it even sooner had not the police van driver been forced to brake suddenly to avoid a yellow sports car driving in the opposite direction at breakneck speed.

Gennaro Coppola was looking mortified and guilty. He could see their local parish priest kneeling beside two dead men, giving the victims their final blessing. He had even thought to bring his purple stole with him for the occasion, thought the *commissario* in wonder. One look at the bodies filled him with a sense of inner peace. Neither of them was his colleague from Pescara.

"That's *Totò u curtu's* car, *ragazzi*," said Gennaro Coppola. Two of you – go and sit in it to make sure Don Salvatore Alfieri can't drive off in it. He probably has a remote ignition system for just such an escape. I've made one error of judgement tonight. I don't intend to make another one so soon afterwards."

He headed for the house, accompanied by Gina and Danilo.

"You'll probably want to tell your *capo* what a blunderer I am - and to find out how come he's still alive!" declared *Commissario* Coppola.

"We shall say no such thing, *commissario*. Without you, none of this would have been possible," Danilo told him.

---

[132] Dio ci aiuti – may God help us

"*Tutto bene ciò che finisce bene,*"[133] added Gino.

"*Grazie, ragazzi!*" said Gennaro Coppola, putting an arm round each of their shoulders as he led them into the kitchen.

The various officers posted outside were making themselves busy. One lady officer was holding an excessively lively black Labrador on a short leash, its tail wagging in delight. The animal was full of canine curiosity about the two dead mafiosi lying on the ground. The second lady officer had found a blanket in the boot of the minibus and thrown it roughly over the corpses.

"Amen," she said. "And good riddance."

She had once nearly been raped by one of these forms of low-life.

Inside the house, there was an air of rejoicing. The centre of attention was the Archbishop of Pescara, who was being praised to the skies for his courage by Isobella.

Beppe Stancato was spotted sheltering in the broad recess of the fireplace. He was phoning Sonia and reassuring her that the mission had been a total success. He omitted to mention to her that he had been one hair-trigger's distance away from annihilation. That would have to wait until they were once again in a state of intimate togetherness.

Gino and Danilo approached him and apologised for not being there when they were needed.

"We always seem to mess things up, *capo*," said Gino sadly. "But it really was out of our hands this time."

"You are both forgiven. In fact, there is nothing to forgive."

---

[133] All's well that ends well

"Thank God you are safe, *capo*. When we heard the two shots, we were convinced that you must be…"

Beppe described his near-death experience.

"But do you know who it was who saved your life, *capo?*" asked Danilo.

"Well, I have an idea – but it is so outlandish that I can give no credence to it at all. But I felt there was something familiar about the two voices that shouted at me to throw myself to the ground. It sounded like…but no, it can't have been."

Gino was looking at Danilo. Danilo was looking at Gino. They nodded in accord.

"*Capo,*" began Danilo, "when our police van was being driven towards this place, after it became obvious that we had taken the wrong road, we nearly collided with a yellow Alpha Romeo Spider…"

"I saw the passenger clearly in the split second that the car shot past us. It was our very own Luigi Rocco, *capo*. He is instantly recognisable."

"Ah!" said Beppe. "I was right then. Subject closed for now. In fact, subject closed, full-stop! Thank you both, *ragazzi*. I don't want to talk about my rescue right now."

Outside, the forensics 'clean-up' team had arrived and were loading the corpses into their unmarked ambulance.

Beppe sighed. The three of them re-joined the main group. *Commissario* Coppola was eyeing Beppe meaningfully and tapping the side of his nose in a conspiratorial manner, as if to say: 'Your secret is safe with me, Beppe.'

On the table, a bottle of wine, snacks and glasses had appeared. Beppe nodded in approval. What the hell! They deserved it.

Totò u curtu, hemmed in unfettered between two policemen, was looking strangely vigilant. In the festive atmosphere which prevailed, nobody had bothered to handcuff their prisoner.

Suddenly, Isobella, glancing out of curiosity at her wristwatch, called out a warning which meant nothing to most of the people present in the room at that time.

"*O mio Dio!* We forgot all about the timer! It's half past ten!" she shouted.

The house was plunged into total and unexpected darkness.

26: A 'normal' dog called Bella...

It was nobody's fault, Beppe tried to convince himself as soon as candles had been found and police torches had been fetched from the minibus.

But the simple truth was that *Totò u curtu* had slipped away in the confusion. No wonder he had looked so expectant, thought Beppe. He must have been waiting for that moment to make good his escape.

Commissario Gennaro Coppola was trying to laugh it off. He had not covered himself with glory since the arrival of his colleague from Pescara. But when did he *ever* appear organised? Normally speaking, it did not matter because being disorganised was his sort of non-conformist trademark.

"He won't get very far," he said confidently to those in the kitchen.

"Did anyone confiscate his car keys?" asked Beppe.

His question was greeted with an uncomfortable silence.

"No, but I've got two officers sitting in his car, just in case he was thinking of making a run for it," Gennaro Coppola explained.

"Does anybody know where the electrics are?" asked Danilo. "If the lights are on a timer, then we should be able to override it."

"In the stable next door," said Isobella. "At least, that's where the fuse boxes are."

Danilo set off with a borrowed torch in the company of Isobella, who held the torch steady whilst Danilo fiddled with various gadgets. It was obviously a trial and error job, but he felt he had to contribute something positive to the day's proceedings.

Back in the kitchen, Beppe wanted to get organised. Inactivity irritated him at the best of times.

"We must start searching for our man at once," insisted Beppe. "He might slip into the woods and we would never find him until daylight."

"Ah, *commissario*," said an ebullient Gennaro Coppola, "we have a secret weapon. She is outside with Officer Davide. She never lets us down!"

This, Gennaro Coppola admitted to himself was several degrees removed from the truth, but the situation needed to be talked up, he felt.

"One of you go and get Bella – and Officer Davide," ordered the local *commissario* with a serenely optimistic smile.

Beppe, of course, was not expecting a dog to arrive, least of all an over-friendly Labrador which had to sniff every single person in the kitchen before it considered that canine regulations had been observed.

"Is she a police dog?" asked Beppe with an acerbic edge to his voice.

"Not exactly, *commissario*. More like a policewoman's dog," said someone. "But she's pretty smart all the same."

"Is there anything here that Salvatore Alfiera was wearing before he disappeared?" asked Officer Davide.

Once again, there was an uncomfortable silence in response to his question.

"He arrived by car, didn't he?" said Beppe in the same tone of voice as before. "I presume he did not travel here in the boot of that Lancia Delta in the drive?"

"Bravo, Beppe," said Gennaro Coppola looking gratefully at his colleague.

Beppe had little faith in this amicable domestic pet. It was just too happy-go-lucky to be plausible – just like the whole of the Naples team.

The dog accompanied her owner outside and was encouraged to sniff the back seat thoroughly.

Still on the lead, Bella bounded back enthusiastically into the kitchen, with Officer Davide being tugged along behind her. She sniffed around the chair where the mafioso had been sitting. That was an encouraging sign! Officer Davide made an assumption and dragged her pet dog by force out into the grounds. All her efforts failed. Bella simply wanted to return to the kitchen each time Officer Davide relaxed her pull on the leash.

It was, once again, Beppe who intervened, having had one of his intuitive thoughts.

"I think maybe we shall find that our quarry might have a hiding place inside the house. Every mafia boss I've ever tracked down in Calabria has made himself a hidey-hole *inside* his house."

That was the accent he hadn't quite detected, thought *Commissario* Coppla enlightened. He's an artful old *Calabrese!*

"*Bravo, commissario* Beppe!" Gennaro exclaimed. "Let the dog off the lead in the house, *Agente* Davide - but all of you, keep on Bella's heels – tail, I suppose I mean."

It took this remarkable animal all of forty-five seconds to sniff out her quarry behind a secret panel in the main bathroom. Bella wanted to celebrate her feat of retrieval skills by licking the mafioso's hands. She was rebuffed by a vicious kick on her rump from Salvatore Alfieri which caused her to cry out in pain. Officer Davide had to be restrained from punching their prisoner on the nose.

"Come on, Annamaria! He's not worth it," said her fellow officer.

Don Salvatore Alfieri was led – humiliated and handcuffed – into the kitchen amid cheers and applause from everybody – especially, Beppe noticed, from his own uncle, Gianluca Alfieri.

Commissario Coppola was all for arresting Gianluca Alfieri too. Beppe intervened.

"But he's a *lattitante,* Beppe!"

Beppe spoke earnestly with his Neapolitan colleague for several minutes. At one point, Beppe lowered his voice to an inaudible whisper. Gennaro was looking alarmed at his new colleague – and distinctly crestfallen. Beppe maintained his well-known stare until his *commissario* colleague from Naples broke into a wry smile.

"You would really go that far, Beppe?" he asked with grudging admiration.

"I hope it won't be necessary, Gennaro."

Beppe spoke again into his colleague's ear. This time, Gennaro smiled and nodded in whole-hearted agreement.

This was the moment which Beppe had been waiting for.

The house lights came on with perfect timing as a triumphant Officer Danilo Simone returned in time for the ritual moment.

"Salvatore Alfieri, I declare you under arrest for the illegal dumping of toxic radio-active waste on four separate occasions in the countryside of Abruzzo. I am also arresting you for the culpable homicide of a seven-year-old girl named Ginevra Ianni – an innocent victim of your murderous greed.

You will, I am certain, be tried in a law court in the city of Pescara – well away from your cronies."

The audience's applause was prolonged and enthusiastic. *Commissario* Coppola clapped the longest and loudest of them all.

"*Bravo, Commissario!* That was truly masterful! My warmest congratulations for bringing this despicable form of low-life to justice."

Another round of applause – led by a very weary looking Archbishop of Pescara.

Commissario Coppola spoke quietly to Gianluca Alfieri and his wife.

"You may stay here for now, *signori. Commissario* Stancato has persuaded me that you deserve this privilege. We shall take care of your transfer back to your safe house in Abruzzo within the next few days. We shall take no further legal action against you."

"*Grazie,* commissario," said the former mafioso boss.

Only after much hand-shaking and hugging, was it possible to leave the farmhouse. Beppe drove Father Alfonso and Don Emanuele back to the presbytery.

Danilo and Gino returned in the police minibus with an enthusiastic bunch of Neapolitan police officers and one self-satisfied-looking Labrador. It was well after midnight before the two officers from Pescara returned to their lowly B and B after being fêted Neapolitan style in a local pizzeria.

They were to meet Beppe at the Secondigliano police station early the following morning for their return journey to Abruzzo.

Beppe did not attempt to phone Mariastella Martellini. He assumed that she would already have guessed the likely outcome of that tumultuous day. She was undoubtedly still heading back at speed towards Pescara at that moment in time, in the company of *Agente* Luigi Rocco.

How drastically he had misjudged the nature of their secret assignations! *Che vergogna,*[134] *Commissario* Stancato, he accused himself roundly. "How could I have jumped to such an absurd conclusion?"

---

[134] Many meanings. Here – What a blunder! How shameful!

27:   First stop, Pazzoli...

Commissario Gennaro Coppola had persuaded Beppe to let him buy him one final cup of coffee at seven o'clock the next morning. Danilo, Gino and the Archbishop of Pescara had, out of courtesy, gone and sat at a table in the bar when it became obvious Gennaro wished to speak in private to his opposite number from Pescara.

"I apologise for my performance whilst you have been with us, Beppe. I must appear like a bumbling amateur to you. But life is so different down here. We are literally working on a daily basis in the mafia's back yard, so to speak. You can have little idea how frustrating it is. I have just had to adapt my approach to life to suit the circumstances. And my officers are all good men and women..."

Beppe held up a hand to stop his colleague from continuing.

"I know what it's like working in the mafia's back yard, Gennaro – from my days in Catanzaro, where my parents and sister still live. We simply could not have achieved what we did yesterday without your unique and effective brand of leadership. I simply thank you for being such an endearing colleague. I shall never forget you – and I am sure we shall always keep in touch."

"But would you *really* have told my superiors about my blunders yesterday, Beppe, if I had arrested Gianluca Alfieri?" he asked with a wicked smile on his face.

"I think it highly improbable, *commissario*," replied Beppe.

They shook hands warmly as Beppe and his team got into the car. Don Emanuele looked very solemn and thoughtful as the four of them headed back towards Abruzzo. It was difficult to judge what was passing through the Archbishop's mind. Had anyone asked him, Don Emanuele would probably have replied that he was not at all sure himself.

***

Their first stop was at Arturo Annunzio's sheep farm, since that was where they had finally decided to park Gino's car. He and Danilo would travel directly back to Pescara.

Beppe was surprised to see that Officer Claudio Montano's tent was still there. He emerged from the house with a genial smile on his face, pleased to see the three of them safely back.

"Arturo has become somewhat dependent on me to help him with the animals and keep him company," he explained. "And then, my boss said I could stay a bit longer to make sure Arturo and Maria Pia didn't have any trouble with the mob coming back. That mini digger must belong to the clan. We were afraid they would return and reclaim it by force."

Beppe had a ready reply – even if he could not pretend to have foreseen this eventuality.

"That machine will count as evidence against Salvatore Alfieri, Claudio. You could spend your last days here hiding it somewhere where it cannot be found."

"Already done, *commissario*," replied *Agente* Montano a shade too smugly, thought Beppe, who was growing ever more conscious that other people in his life were pre-empting his every move.

"Well done, Officer Montano!" replied Beppe, gritting his teeth. "Might I know why you are so sure that the mob won't find it?"

He wanted to add: 'And no smart answers please!' But it was too late.

"Because it is no longer on his land, *commissario*. It is locked up in a garage belonging to the neighbours. If the mob returned, I instructed Arturo to say it had been stolen."

"Claudio Montano, you are too smart to remain a substitute sheep-minder for much longer. Your talents are being wasted," Beppe grudgingly informed his junior colleague. "And no smart answer to that, please!"

"I was merely going to say that the mayoress, who has been up to visit the farm with your wife and adorable kids, is looking out for someone that Arturo can employ as a help-mate," said Officer Montano. He gave Beppe an ingratiating smile.

"You're a good lad, Claudio."

"How did the operation in Naples go, *capo?*" asked Claudio.

"Let's say it was touch and go – but we got the bastard in the end. I'll regale you and your team with that story when we are next together. Meanwhile, could you reassure Arturo that we shall clear up the buried waste material as soon as possible. We shall have to have the forensic department record and photograph everything for the trial. So, impress upon him that it will have to remain where it is for a bit longer. But I will make sure the area is cordoned off immediately."

Beppe was anxious to be back with his family. He shook Claudio warmly by the hand and waved at Gino and Danilo as they drove off on their way to Pescara.

"*A domani, ragazzi,*" he called out as they drove off.

Beppe got back into his car and drove down the road leading to the little town of Pazzoli – which already held its own distinct set of memories.

Don Emanuele smiled wanly at Beppe.

"I have never been so close to death as I was in that farmhouse back in Naples, Beppe."

"Neither have I, Don Emanuele. It changes one's outlook on life, doesn't it?"

"Much more than you can imagine," replied Don Emanuele, as if the comment was addressed to himself – or, more likely, to his invisible God.

Beppe gave Don Emanuele a sidelong glance to see if he could read some greater significance into his companion's final words.

* * *

Finally, Beppe could hug Sonia long and hard, rocking her from side to side as if they had been absent from each other for months. Then it was his children's turn. He had never felt so grateful to see them. He remembered the words Don Emanuele and he had exchanged so recently in the car.

The near-death experience of the night before tripled the joy of being alive and sharing the feeling with his family.

Then he had a fleeting glimpse into the significance of the final words Don Emanuele had spoken in the car only a few minutes ago. Don Emanuele had nobody with whom he could share that feeling of being alive and loved.

As usual, it was Eugenia who unwittingly restored a sense of the emotional bonds which united the whole group.

"We waited for you to arrive before we had lunch, of course, Beppe," announced Eugenia, but she was, Beppe noticed, looking at Don Emanuele while she spoke. Sonia noticed the fleeting gesture and looked at Beppe with a certain light in her eyes.

"But it's nearly four o'clock!" exclaimed Beppe. "You must all be starving by now."

"*A tavola, ragazzi!*"[135] announced Eugenia. "Fetch the wine from the fridge please, Alice," she said as, with a single flourish, a huge bowl of pasta appeared on the table.

"Only if I can have a small glass too, *mamma!*" declared the mayoress's daughter.

"You see?" said Eugenia, "my daughter knows exactly what she can get away with – even though she's only nine years old. What a handful she is!"

"*Grazie mamma,*" said Alice, looking lovingly at her mother. Don Emanuele smiled approvingly at both mother and daughter.

"*Buon appetito,* everybody!" said Don Emanuele, who seemed to have forgotten to say grace on this occasion.

* * *

"I expect you would like to go and change into a comfortable cassock, Don Emanuele, before we girls who had to stay here at home get to hear about what happened to you two boys?" said Eugenia light-heartedly.

The meal had been devoured and the table cleared to make room for coffee and desserts and – the moment Beppe was dreading – when his near-death experience would

---

[135] A tavola – lit: To the table.

inevitably come to light. He had been hoping to postpone the inevitable revelation that he had acted alone until he had Sonia by herself in the intimacy of their bed.

Don Emanuele came to his rescue. He had understood perfectly how Sonia would react if the account of Salvatore Alfieri's capture was related the way it really happened.

"Just wait until I get a change of clothing on," he said. "You're right, Eugenia, I feel very uncomfortable in this business suit – which I have been wearing for an eternity, or so it seems."

When Don Emanuele came downstairs, he was dressed in a burgundy-coloured track suit.

Only Eugenia pretended to be shocked.

"That doesn't look very ecclesiastical!" she said as if reprimanding him. "Despite the semi-ecclesiastical colour of the material!"

"Well, to tell you the truth, I don't feel very ecclesiastical at the moment, Eugenia. I hope you are not too shocked?"

"O *mamma's* not at all shocked. She's secretly pleased, aren't you, *mamma!*" said Alice.

Beppe and Sonia were both covertly amused by Alice's unfailing insight into her mother's true feelings *vis-à-vis* their Archbishop.

Eugenia was looking flustered and was fanning her face with her hands again.

"Alice, I shall send you to bed if you're not careful. You look very relaxed and *homely,* Don Emanuele. That's all I was trying to say."

Don Emanuele was smiling broadly at their hostess.

"That's because I do truly feel at home here with you – and Alice," he added without embarrassment.

The nine-year-old looked smugly pleased that she was included.

"*YOU* tell us what happened, Don Emanuele," said Alice. *Zio* Beppe is looking very tired."

So, he had been promoted to 'uncle' in this lively girl's eyes, he thought. How engaging!

Don Emanuele related the story of *Totò u curtu's* arrest – completely omitting the part when the Naples police team had shot off in the wrong direction. He managed not to touch on the unusual manner in which Beppe's life had been spared.

Beppe looked at him almost lovingly. The Archbishop had understood Beppe's dilemma and had saved his face. His account set great store by the disappearance of their prisoner and his subsequent recapture by a Labrador called Bella. Beppe shot a look of covert gratitude in Don Emanuele's direction when his narrative came to an end.

It was Beppe who suggested that they should retire to bed early. He was exhausted.

"We shall have to return early to Pescara tomorrow – sadly," he said.

Don Emanuele turned to Eugenia and shocked the whole room by saying:

"If it is alright with you, Eugenia, I would like to stay on in Pazzoli for a couple more days. I have a week's holiday, you see. I don't feel ready to go back to hearing confessions and having to face my housekeeper's cooking just yet."

There was an embarrassed silence in the kitchen before Eugenia, blushing even more than on previous occasions, managed to articulate the words:

"Of course, you are welcome to stay on, Don Emanuele. As long as you wish – as is anyone else," she added pointedly.

Alice caught Beppe and Sonia's eye as she accompanied them out of the kitchen, holding Veronica by the hand as she and Sonia left to put Veronica and Lorenzo to bed.

"I told you *mamma's* in love!" her expression clearly stated.

In the intimacy of their own bed, Sonia and Beppe were finally reunited in a long embrace.

Then Sonia whispered in his ear:

"Now, perhaps you would like to tell me what really happened in Naples, *amore*. I've heard the version suitable for children, now I would like to hear the adult version."

Beppe sighed.

"I love you, Sonia. You know me too well for my own good."

He told her exactly what had happened – omitting nothing.

"It would appear, *amore,* that you owe your life to Mariastella Martellini – and it looks as if I should thank her for the survival of our beautiful family..."

There was nothing relevant for Beppe to add – so he didn't.

He was wondering if it were possible that Mariastella and Luigi Rocco were unaware that their presence had been detected. He would have to wait until he arrived at Via Pesaro the next day before deciding what he would say to his *capo*.

He drew Sonia to him and held her tight. They both commented sleepily that the voices of Don Emanuele and

Eugenia Mancini could be heard drifting up from down below. Eugenia and her house guest talked late into the evening before they could be heard retiring to their separate rooms.

Beppe and Sonia were too tired to even attempt to interpret what had passed between their hostess and Don Emanuele. Beppe would be very wary in the future before he jumped to any conclusions about the private lives of those around him.

L'apparenza inganna,[136] he said to himself. How true that saying was!

---

[136] Appearances are deceptive

28: *Beppe's reassessment of women bosses...*

He had worked out how he would approach Mariastella whilst driving down from Atri towards Pescara early the following morning.

The only flaw with his plan was that Officers Martelli and Simone might have arrived before him and been unable to restrain their desire to go into the details of their covert operation outside Naples.

He found them having a coffee in the room reserved for official meetings. Nothing unusual about that. This room was where most of the team would go either to discuss strategy, exchange gossip or sit down and drink a coffee, when they didn't have time to go to the local bar.

"No, *capo!* We were waiting for you to arrive," began Danilo in answer to Beppe's question. "We haven't discussed Naples with anyone. We assumed you might want to play a cool hand with...her upstairs. She hasn't arrived yet. Neither has Luigi – but they must have arrived back very late in Pescara. And as we know, Luigi sleeps like a..."

"... mountain bear?" suggested Gino.

"Do we actually *know* how mountain bears sleep?" asked Beppe.

"Like Luigi, I imagine," said Danilo.

"Just keep everything to yourselves for now, *ragazzi* – until I have spoken to Mariastella. I am sure she intended her intervention to be covert. It was purely by chance that she ran into you and the Naples officers – almost literally!"

"Acqua in bocca, commissario!" they said simultaneously. "Not a word to anyone!"

"It all worked out brilliantly in the end, *vero capo?*" said Gino.

"Despite the fact that they were all *Napolitani!*" added Danilo. "But they were a good bunch, really. And they treated us like old friends from the outset."

Gino was looking embarrassed – as if he was not sure whether he had the right to ask the direct question which he had been bottling up since they left Naples.

"Go on, Gino," said Beppe. "I know what you want to ask. So, I'll tell you: Mariastella and Luigi saved my life – with less than a second to spare. It was my usual impetuousness that got me into trouble. It was not *my* finest hour either!"

"That's what we gathered," said Gino. "But we weren't sure."

"Trust us, *capo* – we'll keep what happened two nights ago to ourselves," added Danilo.

"*Grazie, ragazzi!*" said Beppe, placing a hand on each of his colleagues' shoulders. "It's best that way for now. Save it up to tell your grandchildren."

* * *

Beppe ran nimbly upstairs as soon as he noticed that his chief's unwashed Alfa Romeo had arrived. The impetus, he hoped, would propel him right up to Mariastella's office door. His fingers were already poised to knock on the door. It was already wide open and the *Questore* was smiling at him and beckoning him in. Somehow, she had the knack of catching him unawares each time he entered the hallowed precincts of her office.

"Welcome home, Beppe!" she said. "Do come in and sit down. I was hoping you would come up and see me soon. Tell me all about it. I know the outcome was successful because I've been in touch with the *Vice-Questore* who is responsible for the Secondigliano police station. Salvatore Alfieri is safely locked up in an out-of-town prison – along with his lawyer."

"Ah, with his lawyer already, is he?" asked Beppe, just for something to say. Mariastella's words had taken the wind out of his sails.

"Yes," laughed Mariastella. "I understand the lawyer is one of the residents of the prison at the moment."

"How convenient for him!" said Beppe. "I was hoping the trial would take place here in Pescara, Mariastella. Is there any possibility…?"

"Oh, it will be here, Beppe. Rest assured! The crimes with which he is accused took place on our soil. Don't worry, I am working on it with the authorities in Naples."

There was a protracted silence.

"Well, Beppe? Aren't you going to tell me the details of your side of things? I'm dying to know!"

Was it possible that his *capo* really believed her presence outside the mobster's house in Civitella della Torre was still a secret?

"Beppe repeated almost word for word the version of events which Don Emanuele had related to the gathering in Eugenia Mancini's home the evening before. He went into great detail about the exploits of a dog called Bella and his relationship with an unconventional *commissario* named Gennaro Coppola. Mariastella's eyes were aglow with curiosity during his narrative,

Of course, thought Beppe, she would be completely unaware of what had transpired after her hasty escape from the forest surrounding the mafioso's country house.

But her fascination with the story was so compelling that Beppe was wondering if there really had been a duplicate yellow Alfa Romeo Spider and a cloned version of Luigi Rocco in existence which had been present to save his life – like an earthly *deus ex machina*. But he was obliged to reject such a notion purely on the grounds of common sense. This charming woman had the ability to feign innocence more than any other woman he had ever known. He had never had to cope with this kind of situation during the years that Dante Di Pasquale had occupied her chair.

Or was this just a game of who will blink first, Beppe wondered?

"Thank you, Beppe – for taking the time to go into the details of this fascinating arrest. Your ability to create complex situations which appear doomed to failure and making a success of them all remain unchallenged in the annals of Italian crime solving. I am deeply impressed. Now, since you are technically on leave, I beg of you to go home for a few days and be with your family. I somehow overlooked the detail of cancelling your salary – so you can relax on that score. I am just so pleased that you are safely back in one piece."

"Ah," thought Beppe, interpreting the subtlety of her choice of words. "She *does* know that I know!"

He debated whether she was willing him to stand up and leave the building without another word. He came to the simple conclusion that she was, in point of fact, wishing to be told the truth.

He could exact a few seconds' worth of revenge, he considered. He stood up solemnly as if to take his leave. He looked at her directly with his unblinking stare – which was returned unblinkingly.

"Mariastella," he said after fifteen seconds had elapsed, "I wish to thank you both with words which are quite inadequate for the occasion, for saving my life. You were running a huge risk yourself – and so was Luigi. You have gone well beyond the duty of protecting your staff. I shall never forget what you did for me for as long as I live."

"How did you know, Beppe?"

"I was sure I recognised your voices when you shouted *Giù per terra,* a split second before it was too late. And then, I have to say, Gino and Danilo spotted your car with Luigi inside when the police minivan narrowly avoided colliding with you."

"Ah yes. I was afraid that little encounter might have given the game away," she confessed as she stood up to walk round to Beppe's side of the desk – her hand already held out.

Beppe was never sure how their handshake unpremeditatedly became a warm and protracted hug of affection. Beppe was sure that the spontaneity of the gesture had taken Mariastella equally by surprise.

"I am sure we shall make an excellent team in the future, Beppe," she said simply before she retreated behind her desk and sat down with her composure intact.

Beppe smiled at her.

"I am sure you are right, *signora Questore.*"

"However, I may be less tempted to help you out to the same extent in future, *commissario.*"

Beppe bowed in acknowledgement of the clarity of her message and left her office with a degree of respect for his new boss that he would never have dreamt possible even minutes beforehand.

It's not, he thought to himself as he went downstairs, anything to do with her being a woman. But just because she happens to be Mariastella Mancini.

＊＊

The lady in question sat at her desk, feeling she was in a good place – perhaps for the first time since her arrival in Pescara. But she hoped and prayed that Sonia would never reveal to Beppe that she and Sonia had discussed the visit to Naples well before Beppe and his team had left for that city.

"Don't be concerned, Sonia. I promise you I shall be close at hand - just in case Beppe gets himself into a tight situation again by acting alone," she had rashly promised. "Luigi Rocco is convinced that your Beppe has a predilection for exposing himself to risks."

"It seems that way on occasions," Sonia had replied. "When he knows he's near his goal, he just cannot abide any delay."

29: *The story of a baby and an archbishop...*

Oriana Salvati took advantage of her baby girl being asleep to phone the presbytery in Pescara. She was not impressed by the middle-aged woman who took the call. It was, she assumed, the house-keeper, who sounded as if she believed it was her role in life to protect the Archbishop from unwanted approaches – especially when it involved young female callers.

"I would like to speak to Don Emanuele, please, *signora*."

"May I ask who is calling, *signorina?*"

"Not really, no! This is a personal matter between myself and Don Emanuele," said Oriana sharply.
"The archbishop knows me very well, *signora*. I can assure you he will want to speak to me – I need spiritual guidance which only he can give me."

Oriana, whose patience was barely contained at the best of times, could almost 'hear' the housekeeper struggling to sift her conflicting thoughts into a negative response.

"Well, *signora?*" Oriana asked after a five-second-long pause.

"The Archbishop isn't here, *signorina...*"

"It's *signora*," corrected Oriana sharply – although she was usually reluctant to admit to this status unless it became absolutely essential.

"So, do you know how I can contact him? My name is *Agente* Oriana Salvati from the police station in L'Aquila, although I should not have to give you my status or my name to talk to Don Emanuele on personal spiritual matters. You are not the Income Tax Office, after all!" Oriana ended sharply.

The housekeeper relented under the verbal onslaught of this forceful young woman.

"Is the Archbishop in trouble?" she asked, concerned that this young woman was from the police.

"Not as far as I know, but you will be if you continue to be unhelpful."

"I'm sorry, *Agente* Salvati. I don't know where the Archbishop is. He should have returned yesterday."

"Do you know where he went, *signora*? It is really important that I speak to him, you see."

The obvious urgency in this young woman's voice persuaded the housekeeper that she would be in trouble with Don Emanuele if she continued to be obstructive.

"He had to go to Naples with that *commissario* from Pescara. I've forgotten his name – something like Stingato."

All the housekeeper heard was the line going dead.

* * *

"I would like to speak to anyone who can tell me where to find the Archbishop, Don Emanuele."

"Oriana? Is that you?" asked Danilo Simone, on desk duty in Via Pesaro. He instantly recognised the crystal-clear tones of their much-missed and somewhat daunting colleague. "Would you like to speak to the *commissario*? He's standing right here."

"Oriana?" said Beppe. "What a pleasure! How can we help you?"

"I need to speak to Don Emanuele, *capo*. Do *you* happen to know where he's disappeared to?"

"Are you going to give me a hint as to why you should want to talk an archbishop? It doesn't seem quite in character."

"That is true, *commissario*. I am definitely not acting in character at the moment. It's about him baptising my little girl."

"I was so pleased to hear your news, Oriana. *Congratulazioni!*"

"So... *commissario?*" continued Oriana sharply. "Are you going to tell me where I can get hold of him, or shall we go all around the houses in L'Aquila before you tell me?"

Beppe laughed softly at Oriana's fearsome directness.

"I am happy to be able to tell you that Don Emanuele is staying in one specific house - in Pazzoli, however. Try the mayoress's house, Oriana."

"Really?" said Oriana, quite taken aback by this unexpected revelation.

"Yes, and if you can shed some light on what is going on, then I shall be very happy to benefit from your considerable powers of deduction – or your feminine instincts."

"I shall drive over there now. *Mille grazie,* Beppe."

If Beppe had wished to remonstrate with Oriana over the use of his first name, he would have been too late. Oriana had brought the call to an abrupt halt, only realising too late that she had just committed a minor gaffe.

"He won't mind," she said loyally. "He always understands me so well."

* * *

Oriana loved the times – often measured in hours – where she was alone with her daughter. She could drop her defiant public stance about motherhood; stop pretending to all and sundry that having a child was a burden and a chore that she had to endure. Only the child's father, Giovanni Palena, saw the real Oriana. The sole bone of contention between them concerned the naming of their daughter. Oriana seemed to have hatched up some secret scheme which she refused to divulge – even to Giovanni.

Oriana talked constantly to the baby girl – while she was breast-feeding her, changing her nappies, bathing her minute body and comforting her when distressed.

"Yes, *tesoro mio*, it must be such a shock to suddenly find yourself in this topsy-turvy world. But don't you worry yourself, I'm here for you."

She was reacting instinctively – as she reacted instinctively to most things in her life. In her experience, this approach had always worked in her favour. So why should it not work when bringing up her child?

Now Oriana was preparing to shoot off in the direction of Pazzoli and accost the Archbishop. She had even called Eugenia Manicini up and asked her to warn Don Emanuele that she was on her way.

"May I tell him why you want to…?" ventured Eugenia.

"No, it's too personal to say over the phone. But you can stay with us while we talk. I'm just about to set off."

"Don Emanuele has gone to the presbytery. I'm not sure…"

Eugenia Mancini was by no means the first person that day to find that their interlocutor had cut short the call.

"Well, I wish her luck," said Eugenia out loud to nobody but herself. "I don't suppose she realises that my archbishop is going through a bit of a spiritual transformation at the moment!"

* * *

Eugenia Mancini had referred to Don Emanuele's troubles as a 'transformation'. Don Emanuele, pouring out his inner anxieties to Don Francesco, the parish priest of Pazzoli, made it sound more like a crisis.

"I volunteered to help Beppe – the *commissario* – because I thought it would give me a break from ecclesiastical life, Francesco. But my encounter with the underworld in Naples was like being hit with a club in the dark. Meeting someone like Salvatore Alfieri made me realise just what evil means. And being a priest, whether a parish priest or an archbishop, allows one to live in a make-believe world of candles and incense while the rest of the world outside is falling apart..."

Don Francesco sighed deeply, in total sympathy with what his spiritual 'superior' was telling him.

"I am too old to fight that level of evil, Don Emanuele. I just carry on from one Sunday to the next, hoping I'm giving a bit of reassurance to the faithful few – who, I am happy to say, outnumber the bad guys here in Pazzoli. But I understand exactly what you are saying."

"This is beginning to sound as if I am confessing my sins to you, Francesco – and I am sorry. But I need to be honest – with myself above all else. Because I have, for the first time in decades, developed 'feelings' for someone else."

"So has *she* for *you*, Don Emanuele. And I can't say how I know. But the change in that woman is so noticeable. It's as if she has put aside the desertion by her unfaithful husband and embraced a new world of hope. Eugenia – I presume that is who we are talking about – is breathing fresh air into her body and exuding a kind of veiled happiness in every step she takes. She brings you into the conversation with almost every other breath she takes.

Don Emanuele fell silent – a secret inner joy was in conflict with his episcopal conscience.

"I have to say that I am in a quandary, Francesco. Did you know that the notion of celibacy in the Church is only a few hundred years old? It has nothing to do with the teachings of Jesus. I am happy to believe that Jesus was married to Mary Magdalene and I would not be disturbed by the discovery that they had children together. Why should Jesus have been so different to all other men? I am so against celibacy in the priesthood. It has nothing to do with Christianity..."

Francesco was looking troubled.

"There – I've gone and upset you, Francesco. I am so sorry..."

"No, I am not upset. I will tell you – and only you – that when I was a young priest in Pescara, I fell in love with a beautiful woman called Cristina. And yes, we did make love – on many occasions! There, that's my confession for today. You are the first – and the last person I have ever told."

They both looked at each other in amazement that they had been so alarmingly open with one another. Such words could never be undone. Further discussion was rendered impossible when Don Emanuele's phone rang. It was Eugenia.

"PLEASE come back home, Costanzo. I have Oriana Salvati with me – and her baby girl. She is desperate to speak to you and won't tell me what is on her mind until you are here."

Don Francesco was smiling broadly at the Archbishop.

"Costanzo?"[137] he said. "I wouldn't have put you down as a 'Costanzo' – but it does have a dependable ring to it!"

"*Noi andiamo d'amore e d'accordo.*[138] I can't have her calling me Don Emanuele all the time - it's too formal.

"I simply hope you can resolve your dilemma, my friend. I am only relieved that I am too old to suffer from those torments now. But I'll tell you something – when it happened to me, I consider I took the cowardly way out."

* * *

The Archbishop took great strides up the hill – to meet this double challenge: his feelings for the lady mayor of Pazzoli and the challenge he was sure he was going to be set by that engaging and sparky young police officer. He had more than an inkling that Oriana was going to compound his problems – however delightfully.

He held Eugenia by cupping her elbow in his hand and giving it an affectionate squeeze. He made a half playful sign of the cross as he walked into the kitchen where Oriana was sitting, cradling her child in her arms. The gesture did not escape Oriana's notice.

"You don't need to ward off the evil spirits, Don Emanuele. "I'm not going to embarrass you."

---

[137] Costanzo – Constance. It can be a man's name too. Cf 'Costanza'
[138] We get on like a house on fire

"Do you want me to leave you two alone?" offered Eugenia, out of politeness rather than discretion.

"No, I want you to stay, Eugenia, as I already told you," replied Oriana.

Don Emanuele was not expecting anything predictable or mundane to issue from the mouth of Oriana. Indeed, Oriana was silent for a long time.

She was not the kind of person, Don Emanuele suspected, to come out with a formula of words prepared in advance.

"You want me to baptise your baby girl, don't you, Oriana?" he said in the expectation that this would get her started.

"Yes, of course I do, Don Emanuele," she said brusquely. "But I want to tell you why, and that is far more complicated. I'm not used to talking about this kind of thing. I have new feelings, you see, which I have never had before."

"You mean about your daughter, don't you? I bet you have had difficulty deciding what to call her – am I right, Oriana?"

She smiled thankfully at Don Emanuele.

"Yes, Don Emanuele, I knew you would understand. I never realised that the choice of names was so vitally important. But it's more than that. I never knew what a wonderful, complex and mysterious gift life is until I gave birth. I want to do everything that is right for my child – even have her baptised, if necessary. And it has to be you who carries out that ritual. You are the only man I know who is actually stronger because he believes in God. And to be honest, father, I would not trust any normal priest to hold my baby in his arms, because they all seem to be at least eighty years old and I would be afraid they would drop her into the font."

Both Don Emanuele and Eugenia had to suppress their laughter, before they both grew solemn again.

"There is just one snag, Oriana," said Don Emanuele. "I have been to Hell and back in the last few days. I'm sure you knew I was involved in helping the police capture the mafia boss responsible for dumping toxic waste in our beautiful part of Italy. I nearly met my end because of what I did. And now, I am in the strange position of growing fond of this beautiful lady here. But the church won't allow me to…"

"No, Don Emanuele!" cried out Oriana. "Please don't do anything rash. Not until you've baptised my baby girl. It has to be you! Even if it is the last thing you do in church. Here in Pazzoli. It needn't take very long! It would mean everything to me," she pleaded with such an earnest expression on her face that the Archbishop looked at Eugenia. She looked at him and shrugged as if to say: "Why not? We are still unsure where we two are going."

"Alright, Oriana. How can I refuse to do this for you? But you will need to have witnesses, godparents – and a name for your baby."

"Oh, I have a name for her, alright. Can't you guess what it will be?"

"I know," said a third voice from behind them. "You want to call her Ginevra."

Eugenia's head swivelled round in shock. Her daughter, Alice, was standing there, looking very adult for her age and sure of herself. Oriana simply nodded.

"And I want to ask Diego Ianni and his wife, Adele, to be her godparents. And ask their permission to call my daughter Ginevra".

Don Emanuele thought about it for all of five seconds.

"You are a passionate and persuasive woman, Oriana. And you are a brilliant mother. I love the way you constantly talk to your little girl."

It was Oriana's turn to look shocked.

"You can't possibly know that, Don Emanuele! What makes you think...?"

"I don't know how I knew. The words just came out."

"Please baptise my little girl. I can't call her by her name until she is baptised."

"Alright, Oriana, I will. Did you mean today, by any chance?" he asked.

"We shall need to go down and see the family first and I shall have to see if Giovanni can come over from Pescara. Can we say this evening, if you, Eugenia, are willing to be a witness?"

"Come on, Oriana. We had better go and see what the Ianni family have to say."

* * *

The Ianni parents were receptive to the idea of sharing the name of their daughter with Oriana's newborn child. Adele needed no persuading to being named as the godmother. But Diego baulked at the task of being a godfather. Oriana looked crestfallen.

"I'll be the godfather! I would love to do that!"

It was Sandro, the nine-year-old son who had made the offer. He was beaming with pleasure. "I'll do it for the sake of *our* Ginevra."

"Does anybody know if there's an age limit for godparents?" asked Eugenia.

Nobody knew the answer to that question.

"I shall have to ask Don Emanuele," said Eugenia. "I'll phone him now."

"May I go and feed my baby, please?" asked Oriana. "She's waking up and she'll start crying. You don't want to hear that, I promise you!"

Adele went upstairs with Oriana and child.

Alessandro wanted to accompany them but was restrained by Eugenia.

"Let you and me talk to Don Emanuele, Sandro. He'll know whether you can become a godfather. We'll ask him now over the phone."

Don Emanuele's voice could be heard but Sandro could not make out his exact words.

After the call was over, Eugenia turned to an expectant Sandro.

"You have to be sixteen and confirmed to be a godfather, I'm sorry to tell you, Sandro."

He looked as if he might burst into tears of frustrated disappointment.

"Oriana won't wait that long, will she?" he asked desperately.

"But," continued Eugenia, "you can be a witness even at nine years old and become the godfather when you are sixteen and have had your first communion. You need a sponsor, but Don Emanuele will step in there until you are old enough. Are you happy with that?"

Lorenzo looked content with that arrangement.

"I'll tell *our* Ginevra next time I talk to her," he said.

"Don Emanuele asked me to say that he saw your Ginevra just for a brief second in a house in Naples, Sandro, while he was a prisoner of the mafia. He thought you'd be happy to know that," said Eugenia.

* * *

In the end, the baptism was fixed for the following Sunday to allow time for the ceremony to be organised properly. Giovanni was out on some investigation and would not be free until much later that evening. Oriana accepted the delay with good grace.

Her baby girl was duly baptised Ginevra Isabella - protesting loudly - by Don Emanuele in the church that once again was filled with flowers. It was Eugenia who had paid the florist this time out of her own pocket.

"Tell nobody it was me, Diletta!" Eugenia commanded the florist.

Beppe and Sonia were present with their children and – a sight never witnessed before since he had arrived in Abruzzo – Oriana had dragged her parents and a younger brother and sister along from distant Pescara.

Beppe noted with amusement that Ginevra-number-two had ended up with the initials G.I.P. – the same initials as an Examining Magistrate, he pointed out to Sonia.[139]

Oriana looked radiant throughout the ceremony. Her colleagues from L'Aquila hardly recognised her. She was full of gratitude for their presence and never snapped at them once.

---

[139] G.I.P – Giudice per le Indagini Preliminari – an examining justice. The 'P' comes from Palena, Giovanni's surname.

"Now when I want to return to active police work, I can farm out Ginevra to her godparents!" she announced at some point during the *festa*,[140] held afterwards at Eugenia's house. Nobody believed Oriana was being serious.

Some months after Ginevra's baptism, Costanzo Sepe, alias Don Emanuele, and Eugenia Mancini came to a momentous decision.

"I was right all along!" announced a young lady called Alice triumphantly. She had succeeded in finding herself a *real* father at long last.

---

[140] Festa - party

30:   The trial of Salvatore Alfieri...

The main courtroom was a hive of legal activity on that morning of the 15th of October. The local *pescarese* newspaper, *Il Centro,* had been running articles on a daily basis ever since the news of the death of a seven-year-old girl called Ginevra had broken a few weeks previously.

Abruzzo was up in arms over the invasion of their largely pristine land by some Neapolitan underworld gang. The news had shocked the three-and-a-half million inhabitants far more than any previous self-inflicted instances of pollution in their region.

The story had quickly been taken up by the national newspapers and the state television company, Rai Uno. The eyes of Italy were focussed on the town of Pescara – and its police force. A somewhat watered
down account of the cooperation between the Pescara police force, led by one *Commissario* Stancato, with the aid of his counterpart in the mafia stronghold of Secondigliano, had been avidly devoured all over the Italian peninsular.

'Outrage' was the most bandied-about word used to describe this scourge of Italian life – hitherto confined mainly to Campania, Calbria and to a lesser extent Puglia, where great efforts had been made to stamp out the illegal dumping of toxic waste.

Commissario and *Questore* worked for weeks in perfect harmony making sure that every piece of evidence they possessed would hold up in the face of the onslaught they could expect from Salvatore Alfieri's defence lawyer.

By the 15th of October, they were as ready as they ever could be for what they imagined would be a legal ordeal.

"I would say," their lawyer for the prosecution had pointed out, "that your weakest point is the fact that you used a form of entrapment to entice Don Salvatore Alfieri to dump that last lot of waste. Especially as he somehow got wind of the fact that it was only innocent non-medical waste that he was dealing with. His lawyer should make great play of that."

Beppe had nearly gone into revolt mode when he had first set eyes on their own prosecution lawyer – chosen by Mariastella herself. He had been persuaded to relocate for the duration of the trial from his native Bologna. He was short in stature, bespectacled, frail looking – apart from a pair of steely grey eyes, which appeared to be able to remain unblinking for double the length of time that Beppe himself could manage when doing his notoriously disconcerting stare.

By the time the trial began, Beppe had tentatively begun to revise his opinion about the Bolognese lawyer.

Beppe had spent hours in the company of Don Emanuele, prior to the trial. He had got wind of Don Emanuele's spiritual dilemma whilst he was in Pazzoli, attending baby Ginevra's baptism. Was Don Emanuele seriously thinking of abandoning his religious life, throwing away the awesome status and respect with which he was held throughout Pescara?

Beppe took *Agente* Pippo Cafarelli with him on his next visit to the presbytery only days before the trial was due to begin. He needed moral support in tackling the Archbishop on this occasion.

"Don Emanuele, you know how much we depend on you and your unshaken belief in the existence of another dimension...alright, God and The Holy Spirit. But I beg of you to hold off making a decision about your personal life until this trial is over."

Pippo Cafarelli contented himself with nodding fiercely in the Archbishop's direction.

"You are absolutely our key witness in all this. What you went through and what you witnessed during your captivity in that house are absolutely crucial to bringing that man to justice. Wasn't it all done for the sake of an innocent life lost needlessly that you offered to risk your own life to help us? Can you imagine the effect on this trial if you are involved in the public revelation that you are intending to abandon the institution which you have upheld so valiantly for all these years? It could prove to be a fatal blow to our joint venture. Please, Don Emanuele, I beg of you."

More enthusiastic nodding from Pippo, who added:

"I can share what you must be going through, Don Emanuele. I have been through that wilderness myself – the feeling you need an intimate partner to tread life's often lonely path. We would never condemn you for following that road. But, if you follow your instincts before the trial is over, we could lose this chance to deal a fatal blow to this mafioso. Just think of the lives of all the people he has ruined or the families he has deprived of loved ones – not just Ginevra's family..."

Beppe looked at Don Emanuele and smiled mischievously.

"I promise I didn't brief Pippo to say all that, Don Emanuele."

The Archbishop was silent for what seemed like an eternity to the two detectives, before he said, quite out of the blue:

"I would ask the pair of you to follow me into the cathedral. I need to clarify things with the Holy Spirit. I need you two there for me – as friends."

Don Emanuele knelt on the altar steps. Beppe and Pippo sat side by side in the main body of the church. It was a very long vigil, which ran on well past Pippo's lunchtime.

After an eternity, Don Emanuele rose up and turned round to face his 'congregation' of two. He seemed, not for the first time, to have grown in stature. He was smiling with a light in his eyes which Beppe thought had been singularly absent since their return from Naples.

"It's all so clear to me now. I can't imagine why I have been torturing my soul over nothing."

Beppe and Pippo could not begin to fathom what this man had decided – or rather what explosion of clarity had been imparted to him during that strange silence.

"I shall come with you now to the *Questura.* I gather that Mariastella and your lawyer would like to talk to me."

The two detectives did not even bother to ask the Archbishop how he knew he was expected at the police headquarters. He would merely have replied that he wasn't sure himself.

* * *

"All rise," declared the usher, as the three robed high court judges entered the main court and sat down solemnly on their three high-backed thrones. Two of the judges were from Pescara, but the third, darker skinned and shrewder-looking, was from Naples – appointed, 'officially' to counteract any accusation of unfair prejudice against the accused.

Salvatore Alfieri was escorted into the court room, dressed in a suit and tie, which he wore as if he had been forced into a straitjacket. There were titters from the gallery – mainly filled with men and women from the media – when the mafioso's own lawyer, Federico Liguori was ushered in between two policemen. He was a swarthy man in his forties who looked across at the counsel for the prosecution, Mariastella's lawyer, with feigned aggressivity – a wrestler who wanted to unnerve his opponent prior to the conflict.

Beppe's heart sank.

The senior judge commanded silence by scowling at the chattering court.

"Read out the charges," he ordered the clerk of the court.

- Salvatore Alfieri, you are charged on four accounts. Firstly, on the illegal dumping of toxic waste on five separate occasions. Once on the banks of the River Aterno, just outside the township of Pazzoli and on four subsequent occasions on the property of one Arturo Annunzio.

Secondly, you are charged with manslaughter. Your actions directly caused the death of a seven-year-old girl called Ginevra Ianni, who died from toxic poisoning as a result of your illegal act of dumping toxic and radio-active waste by the river.

Thirdly, you are accused of the abduction of your uncle Gianluca Alfieri from a house in Cimabianca in Abruzzo where the said Gianluca Alfieri was serving a sentence for murder and mafioso activities. The virtual imprisonment of Gianluca Alfieri and his wife against their will took place in a property owned by you outside Naples.

Fourthly, you are accused of the attempted murder, while present at the said property, of Commissario Stancato of the Pescara police force.
How do you plead? Guilty or not guilty.

Don Salvatore Alfieri was attempting to look scornfully at the judges as he stood in the dock.

"My client pleads 'not guilty' on all four counts, Your Honours," stated his lawyer.

"Avvocato Liguori," intervened the main judge, "your time spent in the institution where you are currently residing appears to have blunted your memory as to correct courtroom procedure. Kindly encourage your client to answer the charges."

"Not guilty!" snarled Salvatore Alfieri, sounding as if his tie was choking him.

* * *

Officer Giacomo D'Amico, the longest-serving member of the Via Pesaro police team, was eternally grateful to their new *Questore* for allowing him time off regular police duties to be present at the trial of Salvatore Alfieri to chronicle the whole event. He had often displayed enthusiasm for attending the convoluted legal toing-and-froing involved in cross-questioning witnesses and criminals during the course of a trial. This one, he particularly did not want to miss. He was charged with reporting back to the Pescara team the ins and outs of each day's proceedings.

The part of the trial which went easily in favour of the prosecution lawyers, led by *Avvocato* Cosimo Modugno was the sequence of events which had taken place at the country house at Civitella della Torre. The principle witness was the Archbishop himself, dressed in his whitest and newest alb.

Avvocato Modugno had deliberately concentrated on the events at the mafioso's house at the outset of the trial because he knew that he could incriminate Salvatore Alfieri with the greatest of ease. The Archbishop, the *Questore* and Officer Luigi Rocco were all directly involved in the incident which only just failed to eliminate their *Commissario* for ever.

Winning that victory would make it much easier to cast severe doubts on the mafioso's inevitable denials of his involvement in the earlier events, considered the lawyer.

"Don Emanuele, may I ask what impression you had when the accused dispatched his two, armed henchmen outside into the garden to confront the arrival of *Commissario* Stancato?"

"*Objection!*" shouted *Avvocato* Liguori. "Leading question!"

It was the Neapolitan judge who called out the word 'Overruled'.

"Please do not interrupt proceedings again, *Avvocato* Liguori – at least until you have learnt the proper meaning of the terms you are using."

The senior judge, taken aback by the initiative of his colleague, merely nodded his head in reinforcement of the Neapolitan judge's admonishment.

"Don Emanuele?" said the lawyer.

"Salvatore Alfieri clearly implied they had a free hand to deal with the intruder as they wished. Obviously, none of them knew the identity of the person who had just driven into the drive. This underlines the merciless manner in which the order was given."

"In what language was this order given, might I ask?"

The lawyer had asked the question on purpose, to pre-empt the self-same question being asked by Counsel for the defence.

"The instruction, for want of a better word, was issued by Salvatore Alfieri in Neapolitan dialect."

"So how come *you* claim to have understood the subtle implication behind Alfieri's words, Don Emanuele?" the prosecution lawyer snapped at him – as if he was acting for the defence.

This lawyer is brilliant, thought Beppe. Mariastella was right – again!

"Because, *Avvocato* Modugno, I was born in a back street of Naples. Their dialect is my first language. If you like, I can give the court a demonstration!"

For the first time, the lawyer for the prosecution gave a wry smile.

"I don't think that will be necessary, Your Eminence," he added.

Mariastella Martellini and Officer Luigi Rocco backed up the sequence of events which led them to shoot at the two gangsters – with *Totò u curtu* watching from the farmhouse doorway.

"May the court know why you were present at the scene, *Signora Questore* – obviously incognito?" asked the main judge – merely out of curiosity, it seemed.

"To protect an invaluable team member, your honour," was all Mariastella said.

The judge did not consider it necessary to delve any more deeply into the circumstances of the lady's presence at the scene of the crime. He could satisfy his curiosity at a later stage – in person.

Don Emanuele was asked to repeat the subsequent events of that frenetic night in the country house belonging to Salvatore Alfieri.

"It seems a shame, *Avvocato* Modugno," said the judge, "that you are not able to interview the dog, *Bella!* She would have been able to make a valuable contribution to this trial."

The lawyer for the defence had not interrupted once during the Archbishop's account. Even when asked if he wished to cross examine any of the witnesses, he declined the invitation.

"How strange!" thought *Avvocato* Modugno.

The judge decided that was enough for day one and closed the session at two in the afternoon.

"Tomorrow morning, *alle 10 spaccate!*"[141] he announced, as the trio of judges rose to their feet.

* * *

"Today should prove to be interesting, *commissario*" said the counsel for the prosecution with the hint of a smile in Beppe's direction.

What Beppe had initially read as repressed nerves now appeared to be quiet confidence.

"Do you have any doubts as to the successful outcome of this trial, *Avvocato* Modugno?" asked Beppe with some trepidation.

---

[141] Ten o'clock, on the dot.

"Not for today's hearing, no, *commissario*. Slightly less confident about the next stage – attaching direct blame on *Signor* Alfieri for the death of Ginevra might prove to be a bit trickier."

"Ah, interestingly enough, some new evidence has come to light – something that might help us…"

On hearing Beppe's explanation, Cosimo Modugno looked much more relaxed.

At that moment, they were summoned into the main court room. The counsel for the defence was marched in with his police escort flanking him. He gave a broad smile in the direction of *Avvocato* Modugno.

"*C'è qualcosa che non mi quadra con lui!*"[142] muttered the Counsel for the Prosecution as if to himself. To Beppe, he added: "If I'm right, then we're home and dry, *commissario*."

Beppe only heard the lawyer with half an ear. Officer Claudio Montano accompanied by *Ispettore* De Sanctis, from L'Aquila had just entered the vestibule outside the court room. They entered with a very nervous-looking sheep farmer, whom the lawyer had never met in person. Cosimo Modugno went up to the group and shook the farmer by the hand, uttering reassuring words to the man who was to be one of his witnesses.

* * *

Beppe was in the witness box for only seventy-five minutes. Cosimo Madugno fired a non-stop barrage of questions at him taking the courtroom through the complex events which had led up to the final visit of the gangsters who had arrived to dump the 'fake' rubbish. The lawyer and he had rehearsed this interrogation beforehand over two

---

[142] There's something that doesn't add up with him.

three-hour periods until the lawyer had been able to reduce the number of questions to the minimum whilst conveying the sense of all that had transpired in the lead up to the finale on Arturo Annunzio's farm.

"Now, I want to ask you, *commissario* Stancato, a question which I am sure my learned friend for the defence is dying to ask you. He will raise the question of entrapment with you. I understand you were at great pains to create a situation where Salvatore Alfieri would be tempted to make another delivery of waste – hoping thereby to make something in the region of 25 000 euros. May I ask if the ploy you devised was in any way carried out in the hope of identifying the mafia gang responsible for the previous midnight deliveries?"

"No, *avvocato*," Beppe replied in a clear voice. "We had already established the identity of the clan involved. The Archbishop has an old friend, Don Alfonso, who is the parish priest of the local church near to where the accused has a large house. It is common knowledge that our mafioso friend has been regularly involved in the shipping of toxic and radioactive waste to various parts of our peninsular."

"Objection!" shouted *Avvocato* Liguori. He had been suspiciously quiet all morning, but this he could not let go.

"This is pure hearsay!"

The judge looked upset by the interruption. He had been entirely engrossed in the narrative of events. But he could not ignore this interruption.

"I am inclined to agree with the counsel for the defence, *Avvocato* Modugno. Can you offer us anything more concrete in support of your argument?"

Avvocato Modugno allowed himself a self-satisfied smile. He had been leading up to this crucial moment.

"We have here a document taken from the mechanical digger on loan to the sheep farmer so that he could excavate holes large enough and rapidly enough to bury the toxic waste when the consignment arrived. It was on hire from a company called *MeccaDig* only one hundred metres from Salvatore Alfieri's residence…"

"Objection, your honour!"

The judge merely flapped his hand for the lawyer to sit down.

"Let your colleague finish speaking."

"The owner of the digger, a lady called Sabrina Molè, is waiting outside this courtroom to confirm that the hiring of the digger was negotiated by Don Salvatore Alfieri's chief secretary, in her boss's name. *Signora* Molè is quite upset that she has so far received only one deposit payment for the hiring out of her brand-new machine."

The judge looked triumphant. His two colleagues remained impassive. *Totò u curtu* was looking daggers at his lawyer.

"Please carry on, *Avvocato* Modugno, unless you wish to stop there?"

"I would like to repeat my question to the *Commissario*. Just for clarity. Do you believe that there is an element of entrapment in your deliberate setting-up of a fake load of waste?"

In the gallery, a worried-looking Mariastella was praying silently that Beppe's reply would carry weight. It was the weak link of their prosecution case.

Beppe had been waiting for this crucial question and had a ready answer which would require a bold, unequivocal reply.

The judge from Naples, Beppe saw out of the corner of his eye, had leant over to his colleague from Pescara. The judge nodded, gesturing with a hand to go ahead.

"I apologise for interrupting the court at this juncture, but I hope I might save the court some considerable time if I speak now..."

Avvocato Modugno caught the eye of the *Questore* sitting in the gallery. He shrugged a mystified shoulder but he was smiling openly for a brief second. He had read the situation correctly. There *was* some undercurrent at work which he had not yet been able to define.

"The matter of entrapment in the legal sense of the word is very clearly defined in Italian law. It has a very precise application. Any action carried out by the police in the pursual of their duties – that of convicting criminals – can only be considered entrapment if the aim is to make the accused person perform an illegal act that he would not otherwise have contemplated. Such a subterfuge is patently absent in the present case."

The judge fell silent. A few people in the gallery had tentatively begun to applaud, but stopped when the response was minimal.

"Well, *commissario?*" said Modugno. "Have you any comment to make? And no, *Avvocato* Liguori, that is NOT a leading question."

"I thank the Judge for the clarity of his explanation. I can confidently say that there was no entrapment intended. We simply wanted to precipitate an event that was bound to happen sooner or later," said Beppe.

"Then I think we may proceed. I would like to call my next witness to the stand: *Signor* Arturo Annunzio.

Avvocato Modugno led the sheep farmer through a series of questions, concentrating particularly on the killing of the sheep and the details of the final visit of the gangsters who dumped the waste.

"Why did you allow the repeated dumping of toxic waste on your land, *Signor* Annunzio?"

"I was afraid for our lives," replied the farmer.

"And yet you threatened the leader of the gang with a shotgun?"

"I knew I had police back-up. I was told to make my performance as convincing as possible, *avvocato*. I thought it wasn't loaded."

"A couple of final questions, Arturo. Do you recognise the accused gentleman?"

"No, I have never met him before. But I recognise his voice. He's the man who phoned me up each time to tell me to dig a hole in the ground for the next consignment of waste."

"Objection!" shouted *Avvocato* Liguori. "The caller could have been anyone with a Naples accent."

"No," stated Arturo Annunzio. "Don Alfieri has a habit on the phone of catching his breath if he says more than six or seven words at a time. You can even hear it plainly in this court when he speaks."

Avvocato Liguori felt he had made an effort and sat down again.

"My final question to you, Arturo," continued Modugno, "is quite simple. Do you see any of the individuals who arrived at your farm to unload toxic waste sitting in the court room now?"

"Yes, I do."

He pointed to the four men sitting in a row – now wearing suits.

"They weren't always the same four. But the boss is the man on the right. His body is covered with tattoos."

"Would you be so kind as to stand up, *signore,* and display your chest for the benefit of those present?"

Amidst titters from the courtroom, the thug did as he had been bidden – with misplaced pride – as if he had been showing off the football shirt of his favourite team.

"I think that concludes my argument for now, your Honours," stated *Avvocato* Modugno.

On invitation, the lawyer for the defence made great play of the trial being conducted in such a way as to disadvantage his client.

"In view of what your client is accused of, *Avvocato* Liguori, I hardly think that is a matter for surprise. You will have your chance to retaliate very soon."

The judge looked at his watch. By the time he and his fellow judges had swapped notes, it would be lunchtime. He had been politely asked by *Avvocato* Modugno for a free afternoon to await the arrival from Naples of a couple of further witnesses.

"I shall have to notify *Avvocato* Liguori of their names and status. Otherwise, we shall have no peace.

"*Agente* Annamaria Davide and…Bella."

"Who is Bella?" asked the judge. "Another police woman?"

"No, she's the dog, if you recall, Your Honour, who sniffed out Don Alfieri from his hidey-hole."

"I see, *Avvocato,* does this mean my trial is about to turn into a comedy show?"

The judge did not seem too upset at the idea.

"I trust not, Your Honour."

* * *

The four men were still in their suits but looking shiftily at each other. They were aware of their *capo* – known as *Totò u curtu* – looking menacingly at all of them. If these low-ranking skivvies admitted to dumping the first load of toxic waste by the river near that town called Pazzoli, he might be in real trouble.

It was the lawyer for the prosecution who suggested to the judges that the accused mafioso should be removed from the court.

The three judges consulted each other.

"In fairness to the accused, he should be allowed to witness the interrogation of these men, *Avvocato*. But we will keep an open mind as the morning proceeds. Their obvious fear of the accused – take comfort from this, *Avvocato* Modugno - dispels any doubts in our minds that they were indeed employed by the accused, despite their earlier denials."

The lawyer for the prosecution nodded in assent. He had merely wanted to hear the judge stating this obvious truth.

"Besides which, *Avvocato,* I understand there is a witness which places them at the scene of the crime. Don't worry, the counsel for the defence was notified yesterday.

The consternation on the face of Salvatore Alfieri was intense. He looked wildly round the courtroom, the first hint of anxiety darkening his features.

The mafioso's lawyer, Federico Liguori, was studiously avoiding eye contact with the man whom he was supposed to be defending.

"*Che sarà, sarà,*" the lawyer muttered to himself.

The judge nodded at *Avvocato* Modugno. He was displaying obvious signs of enjoyment as the lawyer for the prosecution began speaking.

"Gentlemen, you have been most cooperative so far. Your acceptance of the fact that you were responsible for dumping waste on the farm of Arturo Annunzio has been most helpful. Not that you were in a position to deny your participation on that last occasion; the presence of the police and the photographs of your van number plates would have made denial simply ridiculous. And of course, the young officer responsible for taking those photos succeeded somehow in taking a fairly good picture of you and your tattoos," he said, looking at the gang leader.

"Now, gentlemen, I will ask you this question once only. Were you – any of you or all of you – present when the toxic waste, which subsequentially killed a seven-year-old girl from Pazzoli, was dumped by the river?"

Four petrified heads made a silent gesture of negation.

"Out loud!" said the judge, raising his voice in terrifying God-like authority. Indeed, two of the mobsters instinctively made the sign of the cross before declaring each one in his turn: *"Nossignorgiudice"*[143] as if it had been one single word. The quicker one uttered a lie, the more convincing it sounded, they had learnt from past experience.

Avvocato Modugno was, as if by sleight of hand, holding up a pair of what looked like heavy-duty gardening gloves enclosed in a sealed plastic bag.

---

[143] Nossignorgiudice! - Lit: 'No, Mr, Judge!'

"This pair of gloves was found by the forensic team responsible for the removal of the toxic waste by the River Aterno. Fortunately, they had the presence of mind to realise that the gloves, not concealed in a plastic bag, but thrown away separately at the time must belong to one of the mobsters who had dumped the waste. They have subsequently taken DNA data from the gloves, which, if you are all innocent as you claim, will not match your DNA."

The silence in the court room was absolute. The fear on the faces of the four men in the dock was obvious. *Totò u curtu* had lost his expression of disdain and turned very pale. Close observers – like Beppe from the upstairs gallery – could see the mafioso mouthing a silent curse.

"This is exhibit number... I cannot remember," said *Avvocato* Modugno. With your honours' permission, I would like to carry out an interesting experiment. I ask the court for its indulgence."

The three judges, already *au fait* with the planned subterfuge, looked intrigued for the very first time. The ushers were asked to position the four suspects in a straight line in front of the judges' bench. A space of three metres was left between the quaking mobsters, totally unaware of what experience they were about to be subjected to.

"With your honours' permission," said *Avvocato* Modugno. "And that of my learned colleague, *Avvocato* Federico Liguori, I would like to proceed."

The lawyer for the defence looked inexplicably more intrigued than worried.

"That figures!" thought Cosimo Modugno, as he signalled for the usher to admit one police woman and one slightly subdued Labrador into the court room. Beppe was delighted to be joined in the gallery by his colleague, *Commissario* Gennaro Coppola, smiling broadly.

"No way I was going to miss this, Beppe!" he stated, sitting down.

The lawyer for the prosecution had broken the seal on the bag containing the gloves.

Officer Annamaria Davide led Bella down to where Cosimo Modugno was standing. For the first time during the trial, the lawyer was feeling anxious. Relying on children or dogs at such a crucial moment of a trial had been far too risky a venture in his opinion.

Officer Davide was stroking the dog and uttering coaxing words to put her pet at its ease.

As soon as the gloves were held up to its nose, Bella's tail began wagging. Life was looking up again after being cooped up in a car for hours on end.

Agente Davide let Bella off her lead. For a few tense moments, she ran round in small circles sniffing the floor. Hearts began to sink. The dog hadn't picked up *any* scent. It was as if the Labrador suddenly noticed the row of men standing tensed up against the magistrates' bench. She did one run along the line of men. On the way back she stopped in front of one of them. As on the previous occasion, she seemed delighted to have found what she was looking for and treated her 'victim' to a display of canine amity, which was not reciprocated. It was the mobster who had slaughtered the sheep on Arturo Annunzio's farm.

The guilty man aimed a kick at the dog which Bella, learning from her former gesture of misplaced trust towards the mafia in general, managed to dodge. *Agente* Annamaria Davide looked menacingly at the mafia thug, but restrained herself from retaliating on behalf of the Labrador. She reattached Bella's lead and led her away, rubbing her head affectionately and whispering words of praise into her ear.

Beppe ran downstairs from the gallery to the main body of the court, closely followed by his Neapolitan counterpart.

Beppe caught the eye of *Totò u curtu* and mouthed the words *Omicidio colposo*,[144] in the mafioso's direction, accompanied by a triumphant grin all over his face. He held up ten fingers to indicate the minimum number of years the mafioso could expect to be spending behind bars.

---

[144] Omicidio colposo - manslaughter

Epilogo

The main witnesses, including Beppe, Mariastella Martellini – and even *Agente* Luigi Rocco, were obliged to attend another day in the courtroom, to ensure the proper legal procedures were observed. The judges succeeded in keeping the cross-examination of the main witnesses to a minimum. The fate of *Totò u curtu* had already been decided on the previous day.

Beppe and his counterpart from Naples, Gennaro Coppola had talked at length before Gennaro returned to his native town.

"Thank you so much for rounding up those thugs who turned up at the Annunzio farm. The collapse of their credibility won the day."

"It was nothing, Beppe. Having the photographs of the number plates in itself was enough for us to identify who they were. They are a notorious gang of trouble-makers in Secondigliano, as you can imagine. They specialise in intimidation."

The detectives shook hands warmly as they took leave of each other outside the courtroom. The farewell turned into a fraternal embrace.

"If ever you and your family want to see the *real* Naples, just let me know," *Commissario* Coppola called out as he shot off as if he was already driving through the streets of Naples.

* * *

Beppe was sitting in Mariastella's office the morning after the trial.

"We shall have to wait a few weeks for the judges to pass their sentence. But Salvatore is behind bars – here in Pescara, with no chance of house arrest, as his lawyer requested."

"There was something which didn't quite add up with the defence lawyer, Mariastella. He didn't seem to be concerned about defending Salvatore Alfieri. And why did he always arrive with a police escort? Did you glean anything about him?"

"Oh yes," said Mariastella. "I spoke to the judges after we had finished. I'm sure you noticed they pushed *Avvocato* Liguori through his paces at lightning speed..."

"*Appunto,*[145] Mariastella. That's what made me suspicious."

"He was being held in custody. He is in prison for giving false evidence in defence of a client. He knows Salvatore Alfieri and has defended him on occasions too. I understand the Naples DIA had a hand in appointing him as counsellor for the defence – as well as the appointment of that judge from Naples. It seems they were determined not to let *Totò u curtu* off the hook at any cost," explained Mariastella.

"That makes sense of a lot of things," admitted an enlightened Beppe.

"The lawyer, Federico Liguori, was 'persuaded' into accepting the role of defending Alfieri on the understanding that he would ensure that the trial went against his client. He was promised that he would be let off his prison sentence and offered police protection as long as the outcome of the trial was successful," concluded Mariastella.

---

[145] Appunto – exactly : precisely

"That's fascinating. I am sure your lawyer, who was brilliant by the way, suspected there was something like that going on behind the scenes. So, *capo,* what's next?" Beppe asked.

"We should celebrate our first successful investigation, Beppe. The whole team, I mean. You did brilliantly – even though it *was* nearly your last case."

"The least said about that the better," said Beppe contritely. "I am so…"

"Don't thank *me*, please, Beppe. However, you can thank Officer Rocco. He personally volunteered to accompany me. He reckoned *I* needed protecting too. He's a real sweetie underneath the gruff exterior."

Beppe smiled and nodded. He would rather not dwell on that aspect of his salvation.

"Are you suggesting we all go out for a meal, Mariastella?"

"No, I am suggesting we hold the celebrations here in Via Pesaro. We should get a catering company in to provide the food. That way, none of the team get left out. What do you say, Beppe?"

"That it's an excellent idea, Mariastella. But we should not exclude the L'Aquila team – who played a vital part in the operation. Not to mention the Archbishop and the mayoress of Pazzoli," he added.

"I agree. Leave the logistics of that to me, Beppe."

* * *

On a sheep farm outside Pazzoli, Eugenia Mancini led a very wary Dario Tondo up to the farmhouse and introduced the now twelve-year-old boy to Arturo and his wife Maria Pia.

"This is the lad I was telling you about, Arturo. He would do anything on earth not to go back to school again. He would love to learn about sheep – and cheese making, because he loves food, don't you Dario? Can we give him a trial run for a couple of weeks?"

Arturo Annunzio looked very reluctant but he had talked himself into a corner when he had asked the mayoress to find him a helpmate.

"I can't pay him much," he protested.

"Dario will work for free for the first two weeks. Just give him lunch. Now, you do your best, Dario, and don't let me down. Promise?"

"*Giurin giurella*[146] muttered Dario Tondo.

After the two-week period, Arturo was begging Eugenia to allow this unlikely and reserved boy to stay.

"You wouldn't believe it, *Signora* Eugenia," declared Arturo Annunzio. "He's given most of the sheep names – he can tell them apart better than even I can. He picked up how to use the milking machines so quickly. He can even milk them by hand. We want him to stay."

"There, Dario. How much better for you to be outdoors while your classmates are all stuck in a classroom, don't you agree? But you come to me at the end of every working day and I'll teach you how to read and write – and count sheep of course!"

Dario was beaming with pleasure for the first time in his life.

---

[146] Giurin giurella – Cross my heart and hope to die. An expression used by young children.

"Voilà!"[147] exclaimed Eugenia to herself as she rode off on her motorbike. "There's always a simple solution to problems when you put your mind to it, isn't there!"

She was thinking she should apply the same logic to her own particular domestic situation. It was easier to solve other people's problems than one's own, she concluded.

* * *

Mariastella made a point of reading the local Pescara newspaper on a daily basis. She often found out about minor crimes or local disputes from the pages of *Il Centro* well before a reluctant public turned to the police for help. It was so different to Bologna, where crimes committed were often several degrees more violent. Here, in Pescara, it was sometimes necessary to delve beneath the surface to discover where trouble spots might be lurking.

Her daily study of reports in *Il Centro* alerted her to host of minor misdemeanours that might otherwise have gone unchallenged:

A Chinese restaurant where a number of people had reported having to go to hospital with food poisoning. A kick-boxing champion of local fame causing injury to an intruder in his garden. The local water company failing to properly treat sewage over a period of two days. A man on the outskirts of Pescara who was reported by his neighbours for starting to build an eyesore of an annexe onto his house without asking planning permission from the local council. The list was endless. There should never be a lull in their

---

[147] Voilà – the French expression is also used by Italians.

activities on behalf of the good people of Pescara, whom they were there to serve and protect.

Mariastella Martellini was gratified to gather from the feedback she got from her team and even members of the public how the involvement of the local police – often unasked for – gave them a sense of security.

It was, similarly, via the front page of *Il Centro* that she learnt, two days after the trial of Salvatore Alfieri, that a certain Inspector Fabrizio De Sanctis from L'Aquila had discovered the existence of a painting by Antonio Vivarini, stolen a month previously from an art gallery in Venice. The painting had been hidden in the attic of a house in Monticchio – immediately opposite an *Agriturismo* called *La Bella Addormentata*.

Ispettore De Sanctis had, it was reported, following diligent research by his team of all the local CCTV cameras – including the one outside the *agriturrismo* - identified the number plate of a dark blue van which had arrived mysteriously at the house some two weeks previously.

"It was an anonymous tip-off which started it all off," the Inspector had modestly informed the paper.

The lady *Questore* thought it was time that *she* was informed too. She summoned Beppe upstairs. She simply laid the paper out in front of him on her desk.

"It seems that our inspector from L'Aquila has been making a name for himself, Beppe."

The surprise on her second-in-charge's face told her what she wanted to know.

"He did mention it before we got involved with the Alfieri arrest," Beppe told Mariastella. "To be honest, I had completely forgotten about it."

"I was wondering if you could make a tactful phone call to Fabrizio, Beppe. You might suggest that it was a sin of admission on his part not to tell us about his achievements before the press was notified. Incidentally, I actually want to talk to him about his promotion. But it wouldn't be too unkind if I were to remind him of what his responsibilities will entail before I break the good news to him. What do you think Beppe?"

"I think that would be quite in order, *Signora Questore*," replied Beppe, smiling. "These recalcitrant males need bringing to heel from time to time."

In point of fact, Fabrizio De Sanctis was as shocked as his superior, it turned out.

"I told the local editor in L'Aquila not to broadcast the details until I had made it official. She obviously took no notice, *Signora Questore*. I apologise unreservedly. She won't do it again, I promise."

"You are forgiven, *Ispettore*. What can you tell me about the affair?"

"Well, I went to the house in question with Officer Simona Gambino – and a local woman who is Chinese by birth but entirely Italian in outlook. We discovered the painting hidden under the eaves wrapped in a piece of material. The Chinese couple – and their two kids – claimed they did not speak a word of Italian.

"They're lying, *Ispettore*," my Chinese lady told me. "The Chinese are even bigger liars than the Italians!" was her judgement of the situation.

Mariastella Martellini laughed at this.

"She has obviously lived here for some time, Fabrizio," she said.

"The painting we recovered looks very unremarkable. We have an expert coming from the art gallery in Murano to authenticate it. He sounded overjoyed at the discovery..."

"And the dark blue van?" asked Mariastella.

"It belongs to the owner of the house in Monticchio. He's Chinese too – quite well-off, I understand. But he lives in your area – Montesilvano. He owns at least six of those new apartments up there. I was going to phone you later today, *Signora Questore*..."

"Text me this man's details. We'll take over from here, *Ispettore*. In fact, that is what I wanted to talk to you about, Fabrizio."

"What exactly?" asked Fabrizio de Sanctis, puzzled.

"You are no longer an *Ispettore*. As of this morning, you are a *Vice Commissario* – congratulations!"

* * *

"Please go home and have a well-deserved break, Beppe. You still have ten days' leave. Go and be with your family, I beg of you," said Mariastella.

"If you're sure..." said the *commissario*.

"You, Sonia and the kids come down to Pescara next Wednesday when we have our lunch. But apart from that, be with your family. I didn't save your life just for you to be in the *Questura* every day for the rest of your life."

"*Grazie, Mariastella.*" he said simply.

* * *

The fate of Don Emanuele had faded somewhat as the weeks went by. Beppe gave the Archbishop's 'spiritual crisis' very little thought. He continued to preach every other Sunday to half the population of Pescara. He went on saying mass regularly and visiting his subjects in hospital – or in jail.

Beppe's church-going acquaintances noted in the Catholic press that a contributor to the columns of the Catholic newspaper *Avvenire,* Costanzo Sepe, wrote a weekly article decrying the rigid notion of celibacy in the priesthood.

"No wonder there are fewer and fewer postulates in Italy," was the overriding theme. "Times have changed – celibacy is no longer considered a virtue, rather an aberration."

The articles were widely discussed and disputed in the Catholic world. But only a tiny minority of people in the Italian peninsula would know that Costanzo Sepe was the Archbishop of Pescara. It was as if the Archbishop had succeeded in dividing himself into two separate people.

There were, many people noticed, longer periods when Don Emanuele was inexplicably absent from the presbytery in Pescara. Even the local parish priest was unsure how the Archbishop spent his time or where he was situated geographically speaking.

The people of the town of Pazzoli were aware of the frequent presence of the man who had given them an uplifting sermon that day when they had attended the funeral of a little girl called Ginevra. But being members of a small rural community, they never gossiped outside the confines of their town.

There was a slow change in the lady mayor of Pazzoli. Apart from being visibly cheerful – which she had always appeared to be – it was progressively obvious that she was expecting a child.

"Just a casual brush with some stranger," Eugenia insisted. "Nothing serious at all, you understand."

"My *mamma?*" said Alice, when her school friends asked her about having a new brother or sister. "You've heard of the immaculate conception, I suppose?" she asked her nosey friends.

None of them, it seemed, knew what on Earth she was talking about.

"Nine-year-old girls just don't talk like that, *tesoro mio,*" her mother chided her daughter affectionately, after one of the teachers at Alice's school had confided to Eugenia what was being said behind her back.

"Maybe that's because I'm nearly ten, *mamma.* Or had you forgotten it is my birthday next week?"

FINE

© COPYRIGHT Richard Walmsley 2020

This book is copyright. Subject to statutory exception and to provisions of relevant collective licensing agreements, no part of this publication may be reproduced or transmitted in any form or by any means without the prior consent of the author.

In this work of fiction, the characters, places and events are either a product of the author's imagination or they have been used entirely fictitiously.
The moral rights of the author have been asserted. Any resemblance to actual people or places is entirely coincidental – or is without intended malice.

About the author…

Richard Walmsley spent his professional life teaching French, Italian and English as a Foreign Language in various schools and colleges near London until early retirement set him free at the age of fifty-six.

He has two sons and four grandchildren – in England and Australia.

Armed with a qualification to teach English as a Foreign Language, he lived, loved and taught English at the University of Salento, Lecce, in Puglia, until he was reluctantly obliged to retire officially at the tender age of sixty-five. At this point, he began to write. His love of Italy, its language and people are the inspiration for all eight novels and one travelogue about Puglia.

Still an ardent Remainer and a convinced European, the author is appalled at the political chaos into which this country has been led by a handful of misguided and self-indulgent politicians.

Che Dio ci aiuti! (May God help us!) The author hopes that this story will give all who read it an opportunity to smile – at least once – at the idiosyncratic nature of the delightfully Italian cast.

November 2020

Printed in Poland
by Amazon Fulfillment
Poland Sp. z o.o., Wrocław